TEMPT MY DESIRES LACHLAN & HALEY PART I

STEELE INTERNATIONAL, INC. - JACKSON CORPORATION A BILLIONAIRES ROMANCE SERIES CROSSOVER BOOK 1

CHARMAINE LOUISE SHELTON

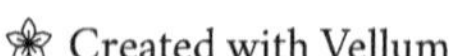 Created with Vellum

CONTENTS

FREE BOOK

Get the start of the STEELE International, Inc. A Billionaires Romance Series with *Discover My Desires Sebastian & Lola Prequel* FREE!

Click Cover Below or visit **bit.ly/CLBooksNewsletter** to subscribe to my newsletter for latest news and launches, books from my author friends, and sizzling reads in book promotions. Plus, start reading the steamy billionaire romance *Series Prequel* of Sebastian Steele and Lola Lewis.

Their stories. Their discovery of unknown desires...

FREE BOOK!

EXCLUSIVE FOR SUBSCRIBERS!

STEELE INTERNATIONAL, INC. - JACKSON CORPORATION
A BILLIONAIRES ROMANCE SERIES CROSSOVER

ABOUT STEELE INTERNATIONAL, INC. - JACKSON CORPORATION A BILLIONAIRES ROMANCE SERIES CROSSOVER

Welcome to the titillating world of the multibillion-dollar global companies and the love affairs of the families that controls them.

STEELE International, Inc.- Jackson Corporation is a series of interconnecting Billionaire romance. Follow the Steele and Jackson families as they fly around the world chasing the women they love and their happily ever afters. Get ready for glitz, glamour, and steamy romance books. What's better than that? The Jet-set Lifestyle has never been hotter...

The Desires Series is not for the tea set; it's for the top-shelf vodka straight up in a pretty crystal glass coterie!

Don't miss any of the sizzling romance books in the STEELE International, Inc. - Jackson Corporation A Billionaires Romance Series Crossover:

Tempt My Desires Lachlan & Haley Part I

Tease My Desires Lachlan & Haley Part II

Grant My Desires Lachlan & Haley Part III

Intrigue My Desires Harris & Kat Part I

Decode My Desires Harris & Kat Part II

Honor My Desires Harris & Kat Patt III

A Trilogy of Desires Lachlan & Haley Parts I-III

A Trilogy of Desires Harris & Kat Parts I-III

Series Extras

Series Playlist

Visit CharmaineLouiseBooks.com for the complete list.

ABOUT TEMPT MY DESIRES
LACHLAN & HALEY PART I

First comes love.

Then comes marriage.

Then comes Haley with a baby carriage!

Well, at least that's how Haley Steele—shy, tech wiz—romanticizes her life with Lachlan Jackson, sexy as all sin.

Lachlan... Not so much. Haley is temptation personified.

His best friend's kid sister.

His best friend's *untouched* kid sister.

Their families are so close they consider themselves cousins...

Can their off-limits romance take flight, or will circumstances prove too much for the taboo pair?

Journey with Lachlan and Haley from Southampton Village to New York City to Paris to London as their love affair grows in this steamy romance story.

Their love story is a standalone romance trilogy in the series. Get a glimpse of their dynamism in other books.

Anthem: "Let's Wait a While" Janet Jackson
https://www.youtube.com/watch?v=q67WffU9t48&
list=PLXwYvn0e218Ak-4oI6AHV7tBXs2yQA2vG&
index=9

Playlist:
https://www.youtube.com/playlist?list=
PLXwYvn0e218DvWekZcaf_aKkxdH4UJtPp

Visit CharmaineLouiseBooks.com

PROLOGUE

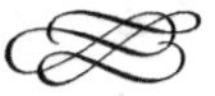

1 3 Years Ago — Southampton Village, NY

HALEY — 16

"HI, SEBASTIAN!"
  "Oh hi, Malcolm!"
  "Hi, Roger!"
  "Hey there, Harris!"
  "*Hello* to you guys, too!!"

SHALL I hurl now or later?
  Cue the biggest eye roll in history!
  If I'd known my friends would go gaga over my older

brothers and my cousins, I would've told the girls we'd hang out at one of their beach houses instead of at mine. Give me a freaking break already…

Eyes batting; duck lips in full effect; cheeks flushed; bouncing on their blankets with uncontainable excitement.

Is this what I have to look forward to all summer???

Gag. Gag. Gag some more. Did I say… gag (all caps)?!

"Uh, hi, girls," Sebastian says followed by similarly surprised greetings from the rest of the boys as they stride past in various board shorts, fit physiques on blast.

My eldest brother tosses the football to Roger—my third older brother after Malcolm—then ruffles my jet black, mid-back-length hair that matches the rest of my siblings. Our signature gray eyes—in me are soulful, set in my heart-shaped face with cheeks that display dimples when I smile or laugh—shine with brotherly affection.

"Hey, little sis. Where's your one-piece?" Sebastian asks with a frown at my new hot pink, triangle string bikini. "What's with theses bits of material, huh?"

Before I can respond, my fraternal twin chimes in.

"Oh, she went *shopping* the other day, Baz," Harris says with a smirk. "Who are you trying to impress, little Haley?"

I scowl in consternation at both of them. But once again, I'm cut off before I can even open my mouth.

"Leave her alone, Harris. I think you look nice, Haley. Who says you have to follow the rules?" Malcolm demands, glaring at Baz.

I smile at my rebel brother Malcolm, also known as *The Enforcer.*

He and Baz used to go at it all the time. Malcolm hated they resembled one another from their muscular six-feet-four-inch frames to the stubble on their chins and their dominant personalities. Plus Malcolm felt he had to follow in our eldest brother's footsteps, being a year younger and the second son. At twenty-three and twenty-two, many people confuse them or assume they're twins. Not good at all.

I know how Malcolm feels since I'm the youngest of the Steele clan at sixteen. The *baby* of the family, as Harris likes to point out since he was born a few minutes before me. We are the double surprise for our parents, who had not planned on having more children. Then a twofer to boot. Roger is three years older and had been the baby of the family until Harris and I popped up.

"Shall we play football or bug Haley?" Roger asks, tossing the ball back to Baz as he winks at me.

Roger *The Responsible* takes his role as the middle child seriously. We can always depend on him to keep peace and order under his intense gaze.

I wink back at my savior, but swallow my words around the nervous butterflies that fill my belly suddenly.

"Yeah, leave Baby Girl alone, Baz, and get ready to have your ass handed to you, cuz!"

Lachlan.

O... M... G! Lachlan!

The second oldest of the Jackson clan at twenty—he's two years younger than their eldest sibling Lydie—and Baz's best friend.

My heart skips a beat when he flashes his movie-star smile at me. Everyone says he resembles Cary Grant with his rugged masculinity and gorgeous looks.

His fit, six-foot-four-inch well-formed frame topped by a face so incredible it takes your breath away. Blazing green eyes lock in on you as your gaze takes in his thick, dark brown hair slicked back from his chiseled cheekbones and strong jawline. The cleft chin adds to his heartthrob persona.

"Screw you, Lach! *You* are going down, man!" Malcolm jeers.

Can Lachlan go down on me?

Oops, what??? Where the heck did that thought come from, Haley Steele! I admonish myself as a hot, crimson flush spreads from my hairline to the tops of my newly developed breasts. I duck my head to avoid my brothers noticing my reaction to Lachlan—especially Baz.

"Yeah, right, Malcolm! We'll see about that, *cuz!*" Lucien retorts as he snatches the ball from Baz and tosses it to his younger brother Laurent, who laughs and shoulders past Harris.

They're the third and fourth of the Jackson siblings at nineteen and sixteen and best friends with Malcolm and Harris, respectively. And just like Lachlan, they share the Jackson family traits of emerald green eyes, dark brown hair, and six-plus feet in height.

I hear the girls whispering about his hint of a Scottish accent—*He's so James Bond, OMG!!!*—and cover up a gag with a cough. An unstoppable eye roll happens behind my glasses, though. I push them up the bridge of my nose.

Yeah, our cousins spend most of the year—and their lives—in Scotland where their family's company is based in Aberdeen at the Jackson Town House. Like the Steeles, they have a multigenerational, multibillion-dollar company. Jackson Corporation's repertoire is fine dining, distilleries, and vineyards worldwide. Their Irish and Scottish family created the finest single malt Scotch Whiskey and became billionaires years ago.

STEELE International, Inc. is my family's luxury real estate development and management corporation based in New York City in The STEELE Tower with offices and properties around the globe. The Tower is also our family's residence on the top three floors of the fifty-seven-story building. Morgan, our father, is the CEO and Chairman of the Board. In time, each of us will take on a leadership role within the company. For now, we intern during our school breaks to learn our family's business from the ground up.

Our mother Michelle—known by friends as Shelley— insists we do more than as she calls it "lounge around the pool working on our tans" in Southampton Village during the summers. As the head of STEELE Foundation, she contributes through our philanthropic arm that builds and manages attractive, affordable housing for urban, lower-income families. My siblings and I help to construct some properties, too.

She and her best friend Lucinda—aka Lucie and the Jackson Matriarch—spent most of their adult lives together, forming a closer bond than they have with their blood siblings and relatives. Incredibly, our mothers met our fathers while working as a shopgirl in a STEELE retail space and as a bartender in one of the Jackson pubs. Both families became super close even without sharing DNA. Hence our cousin relationship and Aunt Lucie and Uncle Connor.

Not that I desire for Lachlan to be my *cuz* or for him to consider me a *Baby Girl*...

While my brothers and I are at our family's private beachfront compound in the Hamptons, our cousins came over from Aberdeen for the last half of the summer. They'll intern at Jackson Corporation's New York City offices while we're at STEELE International. Aunt Lucie uses the same playbook as our mother.

Baz and Malcolm and Roger are on break from Harvard University Business School and Harvard University, respectively. Harris and I are still in high school at Collegiate School and its sister school, The Brearley School. They're all the Steele family's legacy schools.

Lydie starts her first year at Saïd Business School at the University of Oxford in the fall. Lachlan is in his third year and Lucien in his second at Pembroke College at the University of Oxford. Laurent attends Gordonstoun School. All are the Jackson family's legacy schools.

Tradition ranks high for our families.

"Haley, who is that fine specimen of a man?!"

My best friend Natasha Bond's question and nudge draws me from my musings.

I sigh inwardly and plaster on a smile before I glance over at her.

She's all gorgeous face, long blonde hair, big blue eyes, and willowy figure compared to my only now forming curves and gawky self. She's tall like me, more so since she's two years older at eighteen and not from my genetics. At first it shocked me the most popular girl at school wanted to be friends with me this past year. Oddly enough, others started asking me to hang out for lunch or sleepovers. I'd always been a bit of a loner, so it took me a moment to get used to their constant attention.

"Which one?" I ask with a hint of sarcasm.

My tone goes over Natasha's head.

Did I mention she's not the brightest lightbulb in the box…?

She elbows me with a giggle, and her big boobs almost pop out of her minuscule bikini top—I went with her shopping for my new bathing suits.

"The movie star one with the sexy Scottish accent, that's who!" She giggles as she tilts her chin towards the boys playing near the surf.

I scowl.

My Lachlan.

Could this situation get any worse?!

I choose to ignore her question—rude, yes, but oh well —and rise to get a bottled water from the cooler.

Is Natasha serious with me right now?!

I uncap the bottle and let my gaze drift from my brothers and cousins—including my man Lachlan—to my friends, who whisper amongst themselves as they point at the sweaty boys and giggle.

With a harrumph, I gulp down half of the bottle.

It's just not fair Lachlan only sees me as a baby girl and not someone he's attracted to, like he's eyeballing Natasha. She's grinning at him all coy like as she adjusts her breasts in her bikini top.

Why can't she back up off of him?!

Since I was little, I used to follow Baz and Lachlan around like a little stray puppy, just wanting to be around my eldest brother, who I've always admired. Until recently when I realized I wasn't just following them to see what they were up to, rather to be near to Lachlan as much as possible. When he returned this summer, something just clicked inside of me. Suddenly, I wanted him to pay attention to me as more than his little cousin or *Baby Girl*.

I even picked out this bikini in hopes he'd see my new curves and want me.

Is it too much to ask for???

Lachlan — 20

EVEN WHILE WE PLAY FOOTBALL, my gaze keeps going to the sexy as fuck blonde who all but drops her top for me. Baz sacked me good a minute ago when her feminine wiles distracted me, and I ended up on my ass in the sand.

It's not like I don't get laid whenever I want. Hell, girls

—and women I might add—throw themselves at me. A Jackson male with billions in the bank and a more than willing ten-inch cock. Not that I'm interested in settling down with one female at the moment. No, ma'am!

Like my father Connor tells us, "Live life to the fullest, boys. But do not bring home any unexpected bundles…"

Yeah, not something he says to our eldest sibling, Lydie. He's never hidden his intention to marry her off to improve Jackson Corporation's business with some type of alliance. Can you say old-fashioned?

Even though Lydie is older than me and should be the heir to the family's business, our father wants me to take over when he retires. My loyalty lies with my sister. So, we'll see…

But this bird here.

No question. I would shag her in a heartbeat.

But she's Haley's friend, so she can't be of age despite her banging body.

"Pay attention, Lach You dolt!!"

Laurent's fierce growl and shove to my chest returns me to the football game at hand. Right.

"Okay, damn!" I retort, wiping the sand from my hands.

We play some more, and I remain focused despite the wolf whistles from our impromptu cheerleading squad. The Jackson clan wins, and we do a victory dance before both teams dive into the cool Atlantic Ocean.

When I come up for air, the blonde appears and wraps her arms and legs around me like a starfish.

"I knew you'd win!" She exclaims as she covers my

mouth with her full lips in a passionate, no-holds-barred kiss.

Well, damn.

I cup her ass and kiss her silly. Not once do I hide the burgeoning erection of my thick cock from her eager, hot snatch. Nor does she try to deny me access to her greedy core. Her hips pump to their own beat.

It's good being a Jackson.

I tangle my tongue with hers as my hands caress her willing body.

"Damn, Lach. Is she even legal?"

Roger's question pulls my mouth from devouring the blonde's.

Damn, is she? I wonder.

She giggles and nips at my ear.

"I'm eighteen. No need to worry," she pants, breathless from my domineering kiss.

When she whispers she's on the pill, my cock twitches beneath the water.

She giggles.

"Um, Natasha. We need to go to the deck. It's time for lunch."

The sound of Haley's soft voice makes me wince. I release the blonde and move away from her guiltily.

What is it about my youngest cousin that makes me feel like I'm doing something wrong or hurting her in some way?

. . .

Haley

To see Lachlan kiss Natasha makes me physically ill. I have to do something to stop them from going further. Or I really will hurl all over the sand.

"Um, Natasha. We need to go to the deck. It's time for lunch," I say lamely from a distance, praying he'll let her go.

So unfair.

As though she's a live wire, Lachlan releases Natasha quickly. She tries to cling to him. But he swims away without a backwards glance at either of us.

The butterflies in my stomach sink.

"What, Haley?!" Natasha demands angrily as she storms towards me.

I stare at her with my mouth agape.

"Just because you can't have them doesn't mean *we* don't want a chance to be with them!" Natasha exclaims in a loud whisper as she approaches me. "Did you really think we were hanging out with *you* to be friends?! You're some tech nerd who's boring AF! We knew you have the hottest brothers. And now cousins too? Give us a break for wanting access to them!"

Now my mouth drops to the sand, and my eyes fill with tears behind my glasses.

I should have known it was too good to be true.

Why would the It girls of Brearley want to hang out with me—the geek—all of a sudden?

I've been friendly with girls at school, but not really

friends. I had hoped to have a real best friend at last. I mean, Lydie is nice to me and all, treats me like her little sister since we're united by the abundance of testosterone around us. But she's so much older and always focused on acing her exams and work at Jackson. We don't spend a lot of time together.

But I guess she's better than this bunch of pseudo-friends…

"Well, you can't cock block us!" Natasha shrills when she stands before me, and the other girls echo her sentiment.

I take a breath to calm myself before I lose all cool points.

"Well, then go!" I retort. "I don't need *friends* like you, anyway!"

The girls glare at me, then gather their things and leave in a huff.

Natasha's icy blue stare sends chills down my spine. But I glare gray shards of molten platinum at her until she grabs her things and stomps away.

My stomach lurches, and I rush from the beach to my bedroom suite. I've had enough for one day.

LACHLAN

"OKAY, let's go now before Malcolm and Roger notice and want to tag along. I need a drink and to get laid pronto."

Baz says before we creep out of his bedroom suite to go to a party.

We make it out of his rooms and down the dimly lit hallway past his parent's wing.

CRASH!

"Oh! Ow!!"

Baz and I whirl around to find Haley sprawled out on the floor. A crystal vase shattered beside her.

Unbeknownst to us, Haley—who is forever tagging along with us since she was a kid—must have heard us when we passed her set of rooms. This time, it appears she tripped on the rug right outside of their parents' bedroom and knocked the vase down when she reached for the table to catch herself.

"Haley? What the hell?!" Baz whisper shouts.

"Are you all right?" I ask, concerned.

When she turns her heart-shaped face up to me, tears shimmer in her platinum gray eyes behind her glasses. Her cute dimples disappear on her flushed cheeks.

As her chin wobbles, I crouch in front of her and cup her face. My hand tingles from the contact.

"Hey, Baby Girl, don't cry," I murmur as I stroke her cheek with my thumb. "It's okay."

Baz nudges me out of the way and reaches for her. His shocked anger replaced by his big brother concern.

"Haley, are you hurt? Did the glass cut you?" He asks as he checks her out.

"What's going on?"

We jolt at the commanding voice of Uncle Morgan and turn to face the Steele Patriarch.

Aunt Shelley hurries past him and shoos Baz and me away.

Haley's cries must have woken them.

As Uncle Morgan reprimands Baz and me, my eyes flick to Haley, who's being led to her rooms by Aunt Shelley. As they walk away, Haley peeks at me over her shoulder.

My heart skips a beat, and I have a sudden urge to care for her, to protect her.

I shake my head, and I glance away, confused by my reaction.

BAZ and I decide to forgo the party. Instead, we hang out at the bar and play pool on their mansion's entertainment level.

"Ha! You lost, again, Lach," Baz guffaws as he takes a sip of his Jackson Special Blend Scotch.

Yeah, my head isn't in the game. It's still churning over the emotions Haley brought out in me earlier. I shake it again and sigh as I take a drink from my crystal snifter.

"What the fuck's eating you, cuz?" Baz asks.

I shrug, then plow ahead despite a niggling not to draw attention to my predicament.

"Doesn't it bother you Haley could've cut herself?" I ask in return.

Baz's eyebrows lift, and his eyes narrow on me. They

turn a stormy gray. Carefully, he places his snifter on the ledge of the pool table.

"What do you mean, Lachlan?" He asks, still eyeing me.

I give zero fucks he's going all Alpha male on me. I'm one too.

"You did not appear overly concerned for Haley, Sebastian," I reply as I place my snifter down.

"Oh, so you think you can take care of Haley better than me?! She's *my* little sister. *I* know what's best for her, Lachlan, not *you*!" He retorts, as his face flushes in anger.

I don't back down. Something urges me to defend Haley even over her eldest brother who I know truly loves her as he does all of his siblings. Hell, he prides himself on being their third parent.

But again, my mind is in a confused state.

"Yes, I can! She's my—"

She's my what? Not my little sister. And from the way my heart stuttered as her soulful gray eyes stared up at me —touching something deep inside of me—she's not just my cousin anymore, either.

As I think more on it, she's been acting differently towards me all summer, not like her usual self over the holidays and last summer. More shy; averts her eyes when our gazes meet; lingers near me with a faraway look on her face. It makes me wonder.

Haley cannot feel the same. Can she?

But she is Baz's little sister—*my best friend's* little sister. And I cannot have her. No matter what deep part of me she's tapped into all of a sudden. No matter what I sense from her. Besides, she's only a sixteen-year-old girl, and I'm twenty-year-old man.

Fuck. Me.

I lift my face towards the ceiling and blow out a frustrated breath.

"Haley is your *what*, Lachlan?"

Baz's menacing tone draws me from my errant musings.

"My youngest cousin who needs to be more careful, cuz," I answer, schooling my face into a stoic expression.

Baz scans my face for any sign of deceit. None found, he nods and racks the balls.

"Ready to lose again, cuz?" He taunts with a smirk.

I return his smirk with one of my own and take a grateful sip of my Scotch.

Crisis averted.

LACHLAN

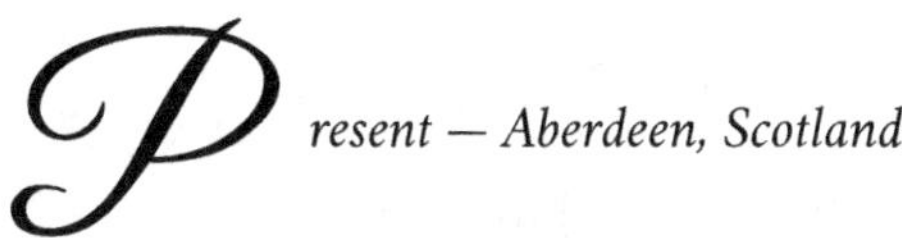

Present — Aberdeen, Scotland

"OH... MY... GOD... LACHLAN... FUUUCK!!!"

I continue to pound my rigid ten inches into the woman's tight, soaking wet pussy, forcing an orgasm on the tail of the last one. Beads of sweat drop onto her back from my forehead as my torso hovers over her equally damp body. My grip increases on her narrow hips as I flex my fingers to hold her in position—ass up, head down.

Best to keep her faceless like the countless ones before her.

One hand raises to spank her ass.

Left. Right. Right. Left.

The toned flesh blooms a rosy pink. Not good enough.

Left. Left. Right. Right. Left. Left.

Now crimson and hot to the touch. Perfect.

Her gasps urge me on. Her mewls make my dick harder than a diamond-point drill.

Her pussy walls clamp on my cock like a vice, and I grunt from the erotic pain.

My hips snap as I command her body to cum for me again.

The sounds of skin on skin as my groin meets her heated ass and my balls slapping her engorged clit mingle with the woman's breathless cries and my growls. The musky scent of our fucking wafts around us. It's a heady carnal environment.

And I want more.

I reach around her hip to pinch her swollen clit between my thumb and index finger. Then I tug the sensitive bud once, twice, thrice, and she explodes.

"AAAAAHHHH… FUUUCK!!!"

Her body convulses beneath me as her elbows slide outward on the red silk sheets, unable to support her limp frame.

I palm her throat and grip her hip to secure the woman in place.

"We have not finished, yet, little toy," I growl with my full lips pressed to the delicate shell of her ear. Then I nip the lobe, and she squeals.

With ease, I pull out with a slick pop, flip her onto her back, and drape her thighs over my broad shoulders. As I plank over her, she bends her knees to draw me closer to her tits The spreader bar taps the tops of my shoulders. I smirk.

Then slam inside of her in one brutal thrust. My condom-covered tip hits her cervix, and she squeals as her hips buck up to meet my stroke.

I drop my head and latch onto her puckered nipple. Strong suckling elicits a carnal cry and the walls of her pussy to flutter along the length of my turgid cock.

Damn, she feels good.

My cheeks hollow out as my wicked tongue pulls on her other nipple. Another set of flutters, and her back arcs from the bed as her thighs try to squeeze the sides of my head despite the spreader bar keeping them wide apart.

"YEEESSSS… Oh. My. God!!!"

The woman screams as I wring a final orgasm from her before I release my own.

My heavy balls draw up as a zing makes its way down my spine. Muscles flex in my back, ass, and thighs with pistoning strokes. When stars dance before my eyes and my hearing fades, I throw my head back and roar through my toe-curling release. My hips continue to jerk with the need to empty my balls in her depths completely. Every. Single. Drop.

I collapse on top of the woman, bracing myself on my elbows, and bury my face in her neck. Warm puffs of air blow her sweat-dampened tendrils around my face.

Fuck. Me.

A final shudder wracks her body, and she sighs in erotic bliss.

"Oh, Lachlan, baby. So good… So good," she murmurs, with her lips against my damp hair clinging to my temple.

The sensation of her fingernails trailing along my flanks and the way she settles in for a cuddle remind me it's time to make myself scarce.

No interest in forging a bond with her or with any of the women I fuck regularly. Nope.

I extricate myself from her clutches and remove the full condom as I sit on the edge of the bed. A shudder goes through me when she caresses my shoulder.

Deftly, I jump from the bed and stride to the bathroom for a quick shower. I'll release her from the spreader bar once I'm dressed and ready to go out the door. The BDSM piece serves more than one purpose, I chuckle to myself wickedly.

In less than ten minutes, I'm headed through the lobby of STEELE Aberdeen. I told the woman—no need for her name or her number—to spend the night at the hotel and have breakfast on me. She doesn't have to rush out. She might as well enjoy the luxurious suite I keep reserved for my trysts. This is just another of my usual fuck-and-go rendezvous.

I nod at the concierge and tip the valet as he opens the back door of my Rolls-Royce Phantom Extended.

"Where to, Mr. Jackson?" Theodore Doyle, my driver, asks.

"Home, thanks," I respond as I slip onto the sumptuous leather seat and let it envelop me. I'd rather cuddle with the seat than with a random little toy any day.

My gaze takes in the scenery as we drive through the streets of the Granite City headed towards my penthouse off Union Street near Jackson Town House, our corporate headquarters.

The images blur as my thoughts go back to the conversation I had with my father Connor the other day.

"Lachlan, you are thirty-three years old. It is time for you to settle down and to have heirs. As my eldest son, you have a responsibility to our family and our company to step up when I retire in a few years," my father says as we have lunch at our gentleman's club, The Royal Northern & University Club Aberdeen. "The time of living your life to the fullest ended with your twenties. There are some appropriate young women who would make a suitable wife for you. I arranged for them to attend our Jackson Foundation fundraising gala next week. Do you understand, son?"

I nearly choke on the piece of filet mignon and take a sip of my Jackson Special Blend Scotch to wash the beef down.

Inwardly I cringe, knowing how much Lydie wants the role of successor to Jackson Corporation. And she deserves it as hard as she's worked over the years from the moment our father gave us a tour of Jackson's first distillery at eight and seven, respectively.

I won't go against my sister. My loyalty to her runs deeper than my father realizes. The past few years, I've stalled him. But obviously I cannot deter him any longer.

Not to mention the fact I'm not interested in getting married now. At least, not to any of the women he has in mind. There's only one woman for me. And I can't have her.

I shake my head to clear that depressing thought and refocus on my father, who's still prattling on. Blah. Blah. Blah.

"—your age, I had your sister and you, and I was being groomed to succeed my father as CEO. I spoke with your mother after she met the young women at some function, and she agrees any one of them could be an excellent match for you. They come from old families and have the proper pedigree. And family businesses, of course," my father adds with a satisfied nod. His dark-brown hair shifts with the movement while his green eyes glitter.

He's a distinguished older man in his mid-sixties—and still very fit—from whom my siblings and I inherited the Jackson family traits of emerald green eyes and sable brown hair. And for Lucien and me, we gained his Alpha Dom inclination for submissives. Laurent is an Alpha male but doesn't go the D/s route. Lydie, she's an Alpha female—as she has to be to put up with our father's old-fashioned mindset.

Our mother, Lucie, plays the buffer as is her personality. Originally from New Orleans, Louisiana, she moved to New York City to get away from her family with whom she rarely speaks of or to. With her independent streak and fun-loving ways, she counterbalances our father. Plus, being ten years younger than him, she's not into his stodgy ways. Talk about opposites...

I'll have a conversation with her separately about this new scheme my father has in play. For now, I give a noncommittal grunt and finish my lunch before a forgotten meeting forces me to leave early. Thank fuck!

My thoughts return to the present when Theodore opens the sedan's door. I give him a nod of thanks and ask him to be ready in the morning to take me to Jackson Town House. Then I stride into the lobby of my residence. More greetings to the doorman and concierge, and I'm on my private elevator, undoing the Full Windsor knot of my silk Hermès tie.

The doors open to my entry foyer, and I place my palm on the plate by the front door to unlock it. Thanks to Harris and his technology, I have no need for keys.

He and Haley co-found STEELE Technology and Cyber Security. They share a similar love of technology with Haley being a hacker and Harris a coder. We tease them for being nerds, but they're wizzes at what they do. As co-heads, they're responsible for all of STEELE and external clients from around the globe, including Jackson Corporation. They're smart as fuck and we've grown to depend upon them.

I groan at the thought of Haley and the beautiful woman she's grown into over the years. My cock twitches at the memory of our last encounter a few months ago when she hugged me hello. She tempts me like no other.

Down, big boy.

I try to keep her out of my mind. Hence the nameless women I fuck who are the direct opposite of Haley with their blonde hair, slim figures, and not stellar brains. No one can compare to her, so I keep my trysts on the other end of the spectrum.

All these years, I've waited for her to exhibit a concrete sign of wanting to be more than my little cousin since that day at the beach with her friends. But nothing. Sometimes

I wonder if I imagined the tingle in my fingers when I touched her face or the way she stared at me with eyes pleading to convey her need for me.

I chalk it up to mistaken emotions, nothing more. Besides, I'm out of time. Duty calls.

As I pass through my living room heading towards the bar, I toss my tie and bespoke suit jacket onto the leather tufted sofa. Then I roll back the sleeves of my custom dress shirt after I pocket the gold knot cuff links. A glass of my new blend of Jackson Scotch I'm testing will do me right before I go to my empty king-size bed.

I carry my Waterford Crystal snifter to the windows and stare out into the night. As I swirl the amber liquid in the glass, my mind drifts.

Each sibling works at Jackson Corporation: Lydie, Overall Vice President and Vice President of the Board; me, President of Liquor and Second Vice President of the Board; Lucien, President of Jackson Corporation Restaurants/Bars/Lounges and Third Vice President of the Board; Laurent, Director of Jackson Corporation Cigars Division and member of the Board.

The Steele Matriarch and our mother being best friends carry beyond us being cousins into our family businesses. STEELE serves and sells Jackson products in STEELE properties around the world as well as in our restaurants, pubs, stores, and businesses.

I love my job and want to make a lasting impact on our family business, but not at the expense of my sister. I also do not want to marry for a merger. Call *me* old-fashioned, I want to marry for love. And there's only one woman who can fill that role for me.

I tip the snifter rim to my lips and finish my drink with a disappointed sigh. One last glance at the stars above, and I make a wish. When we were little, I would tease Haley for wishing upon a star. Now, I wonder if dreams can come true.

Doubtful, if Baz has any say in the matter…

Between the pressure from my father and pissing off my best friend, I'm screwed. And not in a good way.

Fuck me for real.

"Oh, Haley, come on! It'll be fun. My husband says David is really nice. He might surprise you."

Maribelle Hayes' pleas with her hands clasped under her chin make me laugh as we stretch on mats after our indoor cycling class. My gym buddy has been trying to get me to go on a double date with her and her husband Calvin for months. Unsuccessfully...

I rarely go on dates since it's been nonstop with graduating from Harvard undergrad followed by B-School then co-founding STEELE Technology and Cyber Security with Harris. I've thrown myself into doing well in school and advancing my hacking skills and understanding of code. Harris' excellence in developing tech gadgets and his knowledge of code combined with my mind for manipulating the system could make our impact on STEELE a positive one.

Even after all of our years of internships through the

company, neither of us wanted to lead a division that existed. We wanted to put our love of all things tech to the benefit of our family's company. Fortunately, our father and Baz saw the lucrative potential of adding a tech division to our internal processes and for high-net-worth individuals and our external business partners. Both our father and Baz focus on the net net: will it add to STEELE International's bottom line or subtract from it?

After our initial trial runs, Harris and I proved we could generate revenue for STEELE in ways no one ever thought of in the past. Especially since we use innovative technology. When Jackson Corporation along with two other key STEELE partners signed on with us, no one could deny our contribution. Our father and Baz granted Harris and me our subsidiary within STEELE a few months ago. Talk about success!

Recently, we thwarted an attempt to hack a Fortune 100 company. The word spread about our services and landed us multiple, eight-figure contracts. Harris and I had to expand our initial teams and office space within The STEELE Tower. They don't call us the Dynamic Duo for nothing!

Our family celebrated with a surprise dinner at the three Michelin star Lecture Room and Library at Sketch in London's Mayfair hotel. It's my favorite restaurant in the world with its Special Treat menu that features eight courses of magnificent dishes paired with eight esteemed wines. Yum.

Work excites me, and I love what I do. With my laptop

and tech gadgets, I can manage my business anywhere, at any time. Since our client base spans the globe, I travel frequently. Each day differs and brings new challenges to keep me on my toes. Who can beat doing what you love wherever in the world it takes you?

Sure, it's not as satisfying as having a man in my life. But staying busy helps me to keep my thoughts of a certain someone at bay. He Who Shall Not Be Named remains locked in an impenetrable box buried deep within the outer recesses of my brain.

However, I can't always avoid HWSNBN. Especially since our families are such a close-knit group. Birthdays, holidays, just because… Even with him based all the way across the Pond in Aberdeen, it's just impossible to ignore him. A quick hug hello, and I preoccupy myself with catching up with Lydie or spending time with my mother and Aunt Lucie.

After that summer fiasco, I learned two things.

One: never ever trust these gold diggers who befriend me for access to my brothers and my cousins.

Two: Lachlan really doesn't want me. At. All.

Despite the connection I thought we made when he caressed my cheek after my fall, and his touch sent a tingling sensation through my body. Not once has he mentioned that afternoon or behaved any differently towards me—still *Baby Girl*. If I were back in junior high school, I'd make the hugest eye roll in recorded history…

For friends, I have a couple I hang out with occasionally. Like Maribelle, who I met during gym classes. Since she has a dedicated, loving husband, there's less of a chance she's after the men in my life.

And trust me, from Baz to Harris to Laurent, they've had their more than fair share of run-ins with women who are after their near-limitless wealth with hopes of a wedding ring or compensation. Fake pregnancies, pretend slip and falls, you name it.

The media dubbed my brothers the STEELE Quaternity and my cousins as the Jackson Trio—the most sought-after of the world's eligible billionaires.

Now I *will* eye roll until they almost fall out of their sockets.

Me and men?

Well, other than the fact I have pit bulls mixed with Rottweilers for guard dog brothers who block any man from me as unworthy, I'm not interested in a relationship with anyone. Unless of course a certain HWSNBN has an epiphany…

However, I am a red-blooded woman with carnal needs. I've made out with guys over the years—no penetrative sex. Call me a romantic, but I want to wait for the man I'll marry. Okay, let me be honest completely… for HWSNBN. There! I admit it!

Aaargh!!!

When my needs get too much, I turn to my trusty wand and fantasize about a certain someone taking me. Sometimes nice and sweet. Other times wild and rough. But one constant is my need to submit to his dominance. Give the control to him: to care for me and to satisfy my every erotic desire.

Sigh…

Unlike my brothers and cousins, who run off to a LEVELS club to get their freak on.

Malcolm and Lucien opened the flagship LEVELS New York five years ago that provides just what they need. They —along with the male siblings—are Global All Access Members. Me? Nope. My brothers forbid a membership for their little sister.

While completing his hospitality and culinary training at the prestigious Le Cordon Bleu in Paris, Lucien thought of a BDSM/dance club with a restaurant. He figured the club would fill the void for safe, uninhibited sexual activities amongst the world's wealthiest and most influential people. They convinced Sebastian a global, luxury, members-only entertainment venue focused on hedonism would add to STEELE's bottom line. Baz, again the net-net guy, saw the potential and gave them the green light.

Their venture with a high profit margin proved it's bigger than "a titty bar," as Baz originally called LEVELS. Malcolm and Lucien opened additional locations in Paris and London. An idea Lucien, who's now referred to as *The Sexy Chef*—as legions of his female followers dubbed him— literally cooked up is worth millions.

And I can't partake. At least I haven't had the guts to go, not even during Masquerade Night when I can shield my identity with an ornate mask.

Okay, I'll give in to one final major eye roll.

I've been in a drought lately, so maybe Maribelle's idea of a double date could assuage the emptiness in my pseudo-sex life. Plus, I just bought a cute little number the other day and will take any excuse to wear it.

"Okay. Okay," I giggle at Maribelle's puppy-dog eyes. "I'll go. Text the restaurant name to me."

I CHECK the contents of my crocodile Hermès clutch while I wait in my penthouse's entry foyer for our family's private elevator to arrive on my floor. My full-floor residence spans the fiftieth floor of The STEELE Tower. Above me in order are Harris, Roger, and Malcolm with floors of their own, then Baz and our parents with duplexes.

As graduation presents from Harvard B-School, our parents gave each sibling a penthouse. Some may think it's odd to live in the same building as your parents and siblings. But then those people never experienced the luxury of The STEELE Tower on Fifth Avenue and Fifty-Seventh Street aka Billionaires' Row. Or the joy of a loving family—pit bull Rottweilers and all. Why would we want to live anyplace else?

Don't hate the player, hate the game, as Harris says. I giggle to myself and snap the cabochon closure of my clutch closed.

The elevator doors ping open, and I come face-to-face with Roger.

He's dressed immaculately as ever in a navy pinstriped

bespoke Saville Row double-breasted vest suit that emphasizes his fit physique a white custom dress shirt with silk tie, and black A. Testoni Oxfords.

When his eyes meet mine, they widen in surprise. Then he slips his hands in the pockets of his trousers as his intense gaze takes me in from head to toe.

Normally, I don't wear a figure-fitting outfit. But I feel a bit sassy tonight. My new number is a sky blue ribbed knit midi dress with a tank top bodice. It hugs my curves to my knees where it flares to mid-calf slightly. The matching long-sleeved sweater allows my cleavage to peep between its hem and the top of the dress. I paired it with crocodile strappy sandals to lengthen my toned five-feet-eight-inch legs. Minimal makeup with sheer pink lip gloss and my hair sweeping down my back in waves finish my look.

I push my glasses up the bridge of my nose and step onto the elevator.

"Hi, Roger, I didn't know you were in town," I say as I reach up on tiptoe to kiss his stubbled cheek. Like the rest of my brothers, he towers over me even in four-inch heels.

Roger spends only twenty percent of his time in New York City since he's based out of STEELE Paris. So it's always good to see my middle brother in person, not via FaceTime.

"I flew in a couple of hours ago. I have a last-minute meeting tomorrow morning with a developer for a new property in FiDi," Roger responds, then raises his eyebrow and checks his Vacheron Constantin Patrimony

Traditionnelle. "Where are you headed to at this time of night?"

Here we go…

"To dinner at Scarpetta on a double date with my friend Maribelle, her husband, and a friend of his from work named David," I spew the full details with no animosity.

I've learned there's no point hedging with my brothers. They'll ask until they get everything, anyway. Then they'll have their guy run an extensive background check on my said date.

As expected, Roger doesn't miss a beat.

"What's David's last name?" He asks as he removes his mobile from his jacket's breast pocket, fingers at the ready above the screen.

I suppress a giggle.

"I don't know. Maribelle only mentioned his first name. How about I text it to you while I sit next to him at the table, hmmm?" I ask.

Intense platinum gray eyes snap to mine. The eyebrow raises higher.

"Sarcasm, Haley? How cute," Roger replies. "You know it's for your own good. Trust me."

I reach up again and kiss his cheek as the elevator doors open at the lobby. With a smile, I loop my arm through his and steer him towards the Tower's entrance.

"I know, I know. And where are you headed to, Big Brother?" I ask, not quite ready to cut out on my taunting *The Responsible* one.

Roger stiffens and coughs.

"Um… Out for a bit," he responds, hedging.

I stop before our cars at the curb and glance up at him with my eyebrow arched expectantly. Oh, if I have to give it up, so does he.

Roger tugs at the collar of his shirt and clears his throat.

Without looking at me he says, "LEVELS New York. Here, let me get your car door."

I giggle and tell him to have fun as I slip onto the back seat of my Bentley Bentayga.

Roger's eyes narrow and he smirks, "I will. And you damn well better not!"

He shuts the door with a firm click and raps on the roof for Gary Jones, my driver, to pull away.

I lean back and laugh out loud.

Gotta love my protective brothers!

"Steele? As in STEELE International, Inc.?"

Oh, boy. Not what I needed: a fanatic…

David Ross: thirty-one; works at a Wall Street hedge fund; single; Yale University undergrad and B-School; oldest of three boys; from Wichita, Kansas.

All of this he told me within five minutes of our introduction. Well, eight if you include the pause he had to take as the hostess led the four of us from the bar to our table, where he finished his monologue.

Now that Maribelle could get a word in and gave him my name, he's gobsmacked.

David's bulging eyes bounce between Maribelle and

Calvin. Both avert their gazes, embarrassed by his blatant fanaticism over meeting a Steele—the only female of the multibillion-dollar family. I'm sure the peals of wedding bells ring between his ears.

We're saved from the pregnant pause by the server who asks for our drink orders.

Instead of a double shot of Gran Patrón Burdeos, I request a glass of Barolo. Maribelle suggests we get a bottle, and I couldn't agree more.

David cuts in to ask for a bottle of Jackson Cabernet Sauvignon instead, and my heart stutters in my chest.

"It's from the best vineyard. You'll enjoy Jackson's full-bodied red wine with dark fruit flavors and savory taste of black pepper. It has a smooth finish," David says to impress me.

Little does he realize I'm more than impressed by Jackson's President of Liquor and would more than enjoy his smooth finish in my mouth…

The thought brings a smile to my full lips.

David smirks, thinking he's got me hooked.

Can I get one more eye roll? Pretty please???

"So, Haley, you're a member of the Steele family?" David asks like a starved dog with a bone.

Too bad. He's a nice-looking guy, fit, well dressed, smart. He could have been a pleasant distraction. Ah well.

"Yes," I respond. "Do tell me more about your work, David. It sounds fascinating."

The best way to deflect with a guy like David is to keep him talking about himself. Make him the focus, not me.

Happily, he takes the bait with gusto.

Our meal goes well enough despite Fan David. Maribelle and Calvin are so cute together. They finish each other's sentences, and he stares at her with undisguised love. By the time we're done with dessert, I wish I had a Calvin in my life.

"Haley, let's go to dinner. How's Friday night at 4 Charles Prime Rib? I know it's hard to get a reservation, but I can get one easily," David says as we leave Scarpetta, chest puffed up.

Again with impressing me…

Inwardly, I sigh. Outwardly, I plaster a smile on my face and shake my head with an air of dismay.

"I fly out to Hong Kong tomorrow for business. But thank you for the offer," I respond, then turn to give Maribelle a hug and Calvin a pat on his forearm. "Thank you for dinner. It was lovely. Next time, it's my treat. Mari, I'll see you at the gym when I return."

Out of the corner of my eye, I see David part his lips.

I pivot and give a wave over my shoulder as Gary opens the door to my SUV. I settle behind the cover of its tinted windows and throw my head back with a robust laugh.

No need for Roger to investigate this guy! No, sir!

I'll end my evening with a pretty crystal glass of Jackson Reserve Scotch, my oh so magical wand, and the man himself making love to me in my mind.

HALEY

"**W**hat do you think of this?"

Lola Lewis asks as we stand in one of Positano's fine watches shops perusing a selection of vintage Rolex, Patek Phillipe, Audemars Piguet, and Vacheron Constantin.

Along with my family, a few of Baz's friends, and of course the Jacksons, including Lachlan, we're on the Italian Riviera to celebrate Baz's birthday.

So much has happened in the last few weeks.

Baz formally introduced us to Lola, his girlfriend—his first one ever, not one of his sexual encounters.

Our family went to his penthouse for an Italian alfresco dining extravaganza on the large terrace off of the living room. They had it decorated with strings of fairy lights and bright pillows on the furniture while soft music played over the surround sound system.

Lola prepared her famous saltimbocca dish with a tasty antipasto of mushroom and mozzarella arancini, then a tomato and burrata salad with basil oil and homemade garlic sticks. She explained away the undertaking as her love of cooking. And it was *delizioso!*

Our family took an immediate liking to the petite spitfire who claimed Baz's heart. Morgan even proposed a toast with his Limoncello Gin Collins. *"To the first and the last woman our eldest son Sebastian has ever introduced to his family. We welcome you, Lola!"* We agreed wholeheartedly.

Even more so when Lola and I had dinner at La Goulue.

I sensed how serious Baz was about his relationship with Lola, so I invited her as a chance for us to get to know each other better. When I asked her about their plans for Baz's upcoming birthday, she admitted she didn't know about it as it slipped her mind with all they'd been through.

When I explained my mother and I always organize his birthday since he never takes time to do something for himself, Lola asked us to help her. So we were grateful she encouraged our participation and didn't isolate Baz from his family. Another score for Team Lola!

As we awaited Shelley's arrival, Lola and I shared things about ourselves. Lola just turned thirty, so we're a year apart. Both speak fluent French. Where she lost her parents in a tragic car accident before her eighteenth birthday and is a single child with no other relatives. I'm fiercely loyal to my large family. We share a lot in common from food to movies, even favorite color.

She founded her luxury lingerie company Lola's Coterie based in Paris at the age of twenty-five, as I did with STEELE Technology and Cyber Security. With her company as a new STEELE retail partner, I told her my subsidiary is available to assist her tech needs.

It'll be good to have a female friend who doesn't have ulterior motives. Also, I feel I can be free with her since she's so normal. I can see Lola and I forming a great friendship. Even having a sister at last!

Our dinner at La Goulue led to everyone being in Positano a few weeks later. It's also apropos since Lola had an Italian-themed dinner for us. Kismet at its best!

We're staying at my parents' Villa Sogno since we haven't been there all together in a while. The weather is perfect this time of year. Swim at the beach, go out on *Serendipity*—the megayacht my father gave to our mother for their thirtieth wedding anniversary—and of course dine alfresco.

I smile at Lola as I inspect at the watches displayed.

Baz collects vintage timepieces, so any of them would be perfect for her birthday present to him. I point to an Audemars Piguet that looks as powerful and dominant as Baz, and just as complex.

"That's it!" Lola proclaims triumphantly. "Thanks, Haley!"

"Sebastian will love it!" I clap gleefully before pulling Lola into a tight hug.

While they wrap the watch up, we stroll through the

shop. So many beautiful pieces. We pause at the collection of diamond rings.

"Your mother's ring is far superior to these trinkets," Lola teases. "I wonder why she's not wearing it now. I would wear it every day for the rest of my life if it were mine!"

I duck my head, causing my hair to fall across my profile like a curtain. I refuse to glance Lola's way. Instead, I walk at a clipped pace to the other end of the store. I vowed to Baz I wouldn't spill the beans, and my face is an open book…

"Haley," Lola touches my arm as I stand in front of the cuff links' display case. "Please forgive my lack of tact—"

I cut Lola off with a wave of my hand, "No, no. You did nothing wrong or distasteful—"

"Madame, your gift is ready."

The salesperson hands the discrete package to Lola with a flourish. Thank goodness for a distraction, I sigh to myself in relief.

We thank the salesperson, and Lola links arms with me to walk a few streets over. We promised my mother we would pick up Baz's cake from her favorite bakery in town. She stayed at Villa Sogno to manage the party decorators and caterers and the villa's staff for the influx of guests, some of whom will stay at the property.

We chat about what we're wearing tonight for the party and who's coming.

As always, we invited our extended family of the Jacksons and some of Baz's closest friends. Aunt Lucie and

Uncle Connor drove over from their nearby villa. Lachlan flew in from Aberdeen and is staying at his parents' place. Baz sent the helicopter for Lucien, who's at his villa in Monte Carlo and will join his parents and brother. Laurent sent Baz a vintage lacquer humidor filled with Jackson Cuban Cigars since he's unable to make it. Lydie—who caused a bit of a kerfuffle between Baz and Lola—declined because of a business conflict.

Baz's Harvard roommate Scott and his wife Lauren arrive later today. Some of Baz's friends from Dubai and London flew in this morning for a few days. They round out the list to twenty.

"I've not met the Jackson parents nor Lachlan. What are they like?" Lola asks.

At the mention of Lachlan's name, I stumble, caught off guard. I've been doing well avoiding Lachlan and squashing amorous thoughts of him. Damn!

"Are you all right? Did you trip on something?" Lola asks, glancing over her shoulder at the ground.

I push my glasses back up the bridge of my nose as my eyes dart away.

"My foot caught on a crack," I shrug. "Anyway, here's the bakery."

Again, thank goodness for a distraction, I think as I avoid Lola's questioning hazel eyes and waltz ahead of her through the door. I just have to get through tonight and tomorrow. I move my lips in a silent prayer.

. . .

"Hey, Baby Girl. Where have you been hiding?"

Lachlan! Fuck!

I was so busy admiring my mother's handiwork for Baz's party, I didn't notice Lachlan materialize beside me.

Baz's party begins on a terrace one level below the villa. The view at night just as spectacular with the lights of the villas and hotels along the cliffside, the waterfront restaurants and shops, and the boats moored at sea or docked at the marina. The breeze is warm with the ever-present fragrance of flowers and lemons wafting through the air.

Our mother did a fantastic job with the transformation of the terrace from a lush verdant space where you can unwind to a festive party spot. The decorations, musical quartet, and bar service keep the guest in lively spirits. One of Lucien's two Positano restaurants catered the dinner and provided the servers. The cocktail hour gives guests time to arrive, Lachlan being one of them...

"Uh... Lachlan... Um... Nowhere special. Just right here all along... Taking in the view and all that—"

"Haley! There you are. Mom's looking for you."

I close my eyes for a moment to offer a true prayer of thanks for Harris interrupting my embarrassing babbling!

"Okay! Thanks. Um... Excuse me, Lachlan," I say, overly bright, as I make my way between the two men.

Crisis averted!

THE REST of the evening is a blur of tears, congratulations, and hugs after Baz surprises Lola with a romantic wedding proposal—and my mother's ring Lola so admires. When she pulled me into her embrace, she whispered she now understood my hesitancy in answering her question at the watch shop. I giggled and squeezed her tightly.

A few times, I had the sensation of being watched and glanced up to find Lachlan's emerald green eyes glittering in the torchlight as he stared at me. My cheeks flamed crimson, and I dodged him all night.

My mind, however, wondered if he were watching me simply because we haven't seen each other in a while and he missed me or because the underlying hunger in his gaze was for much more. I shuddered then, and I shudder now as I lie in bed tossing and turning, unable to sleep.

The thought of Lachlan wanting me heats my body to epic proportions more than any fantasy I created. An ache grows in my lower belly as the silk of my Lola's Coterie negligee brushes against my pebbled nipples with each turn.

I flop onto my back and stare at the ceiling, willing my body to calm down. After a few minutes, I give up and reach into the drawer of my nightstand for my trusty magical wand. With a frustrated sigh, I fluff up the pillows and toss my negligee to the side.

Completely bare to the warm breeze of the Tyrrhenian Sea floating through the double doors of my balcony, I lie back and let my mind run uninhibited. Right away a vision of Lachlan dressed as he was tonight in a buttery yellow linen suit with a cream-colored shirt open at the collar and brown Gucci loafers appears before my closed eyes.

His handsome face—clear of stubble accentuates his strong jawline and cleft chin—turns to face me. Emerald green eyes blaze with forbidden lust, denied no longer. He strides across the terrace and scoops me into his arms like a new bride. All others—my father, Baz, Malcolm, Roger, Harris—fade into the background as Lachlan carries me to my suite of rooms.

Once inside, he stands me before the bed and bares my quivering body to his eyes that ravish me. When I cross my arms over my heaving breasts, he shakes his head and clasps my wrists to pull them apart. His head dips to my pebbled nipple and laves it with the flat of his tongue.

A shudder wracks my body from head to toe as my back arches. My D-cup breasts jiggle.

He takes advantage of my move and dips me into a deeper arc with my hands held in one of his sizable ones at the base of my spine. His full lips and teeth feast on my nipples. His long, thick erection presses against my lower belly, and I mewl as I grind my hips up to meet him.

I need Lachlan inside of me.

Pounding inside of my greedy virgin pussy.

Making me his and his alone.

"Lachlan…"

I pant through a slack mouth as the first flutter of my pussy walls signals my orgasm. The head of my magical wand vibrates against my swollen clit as my fingers press my wet folds apart. I gasp as the wand touches a particularly sensitive area on my bundle of nerves.

"Oh My God... please," I whine, tossing my head from side to side, wanting the carnal crest to break.

Bolts of lightning zip along my spine as my fantasy shifts to reveal a naked Lachlan in all his masculine glory, with his head between my thighs. My pussy juices coat his nose, mouth, and chin as he devours me.

"Mmmmmm..." I cry out, toes curl, back bows from the bed.

Emerald eyes dazzle, locked on my hooded grays as he prowls up my body, fists his ginormous cock, and glides the angry purple tip between my weeping pussy lips. A prod at my puckered bottom hole elicits a throaty moan from my upper lips.

"Oh, Lachlan... Please... Please take me..." I cry out as I writhe beneath his powerful, muscular frame.

Once again, he dips his head, this time to my mouth. As he did with my breasts and pussy, he consumes me. Tongues entwine in a display of dominance. The sub in me gives in happily with a contented sigh as I melt into him.

My fingers tangle in his hair, only to have him capture my wrists and press them above my head in one hand. The other grips his cock that thumps against my quivering inner thighs. He aligns it with my pussy entrance and snaps his hips forward in one savage thrust.

"MINE!" Lachlan growls possessively.

I scream as he breaches my maidenhead and claims me as his at long last.

Fantasy and reality merge as I buck my hips and pinch

my fully aroused nipple through my spine-tingling climax. Lachlan's name a groan on my lips.

Pants subside to deep breaths. Clenched thighs fall open at the knees. The magical wand slips from my fingers. My sated body collapses into the damp Egyptian cotton sheets.

I rest in a state of sheer euphoria.

Oh, Lachlan.

"Hi, sweetheart! I'm so happy to see you. How was your flight?"

I stoop down to my mother's welcoming embrace; her hazel eyes shine with love. At five foot seven in her Chanel ballet flats, I tower over her by eight inches. We double kiss as her jet black wavy bob brushes my cheek. I give her a tight squeeze before I release her.

"It's great to see you, too, Mom," I respond with a grin. "It was smooth, thanks. All good with you and Dad?"

Our family spends a lot of time together, even though we're scattered around the globe now that we're older.

My parents split their time between Jackson Castle—our family seat in Banff, Aberdeenshire—and their maisonette on Fifth Avenue and Sixty-Sixth Street in New York City. Lydie and Laurent maintain the City as their base since they work out of Jackson New York with our father. While Lucien and I live overseas in Paris and

Aberdeen, working out of Jackson Paris and our headquarters, respectively.

But we make the effort to meet up somewhere in the world at least twice a month for dinner or a weekend getaway. Often our gatherings coincide with the Steeles' activities. Baz's birthday proves the perfect example. Even though Lydie and Laurent can't make it, they sent gifts. Quite honestly, Lydie didn't need to come after the headache she caused Baz and his girlfriend, Lola…

Which is the reason I want to tread lightly around Haley while here. It's been a while since I last saw her, and I don't want to put Baz on edge so soon after the Lydie fiasco. And especially since it's his birthday weekend with him proposing to Lola. Lucky wanker.

At least he's marrying a woman he loves, and with whom he chooses to live the rest of his life. He's older than me by two years, and Uncle Morgan and Aunt Shelley didn't badger him about "family duty."

The fundraising gala slash match game came up short. Sure the three women my father introduced to me are beautiful and "have the right pedigree and family business." But one was a complete ditz and another self-absorbed.

However, under different circumstances, the third woman could make a doable match. Fiona Ridel—the twenty-eight-year-old daughter of an oil magnate from one of the oldest Sottish families—intrigued me. She's a stunning young woman with waist-length ash blonde hair, striking violet eyes, and a willowy figure at five feet, nine inches.

Laurent remembers her from their school days at Gordonstoun School. He says she was popular and smart. When I asked if he dated her, he grinned wolfishly and said she's too traditional for his taste. In other words, she wasn't putting out for him. Interesting.

Unlike the other two women, Fiona doesn't sit around idly. After she graduated from St. Andrew's University with a degree in art history, she opened a gallery in Aberdeen. I remember attending a few events there, not knowing her at the time. It impressed me. As does the woman herself.

But again, different circumstances.

As though sensing my inner turmoil, my mother loops her arm through mine and leads me to Villa Whisky Collina's stone terrace overlooking the sparkling turquoise waters of the Tyrrhenian Sea. A table set for afternoon tea awaits us.

"Come sit with your mother before your father returns and Lucien arrives," Lucie says with a bright smile.

Once we're settled, she pours our tea while I place cucumber-rye and deviled-ham salad on marbled rye bread sandwiches and double-lemon scones made from Sorrento lemons on our plates.

We chat about new Scotch blends I'm creating, and she brings me up to date on the foundation's latest research. Our easy conversation flows to the personal side seamlessly.

"I had lunch the other day with Fiona Ridel's mother. Such a charming young woman. Would you agree, sweetheart?" My mother asks nonchalantly as she sips her tea. Hazel eyes watch for a reaction.

Instead of an immediate response, I nibble on a scone and glance at the panoramic view. I would appreciate the fragrant aroma of the Sorrentine lemons in the tasty quick bread, but her question makes it dull as lead in my mouth.

A light touch to my forearm draws my attention back to my mother. I glance at her and notice the concern on her face. My head bows to avoid her seeing the angst in my eyes.

"Lachlan, honey, you know I am here for you. Talk to me," she says, softly patting my arm.

Fuck it. Mother knows best and all that…

"Fiona is a lovely young woman. Perhaps if things were different. But she's not the one for me," I respond.

Lucie arches an elegant eyebrow, a signal for me to continue.

Yeah, mothers know.

"Haley," I breathe.

When my admission meets silence, I swing my gaze to Lucie.

She stares at me with eyes that penetrate the deepest parts of my mind. I remain open to her, not blocking any thoughts. After a moment, she nods in satisfaction.

"Shelley and I had an inkling for a few years now"—she raises her hand to stop my questions—"But you nor Haley mentioned a word to either of us. We won't pry, you know. Nor will we judge if that's your concern. They're your lives to do as you will."

She pauses for my reaction, and I nod in relief. At least our mothers side with us. If there is an *us*.

"Well, what are you going to do about it, Lachlan Jackson?" Lucie asks.

Once again, my gaze turns to the Sea as though seeking the answer in its majestic beauty of endless shades of blue. Or perhaps it's Haley's Siren Song I hear floating on the wind as it beckons for me to claim her as mine.

A comfortable silence envelops my mother and me as we continue to enjoy the sweet and savory morsels. I appreciate how she allows me time to collect my thoughts and to plan my course of action.

"Do you and Aunt Shelley think Haley wants more from me?" I ask, still enraptured by the Sea.

Without hesitation, my mother responds, "Absolutely. Otherwise, I wouldn't encourage you to do something about it and would advise you to leave Haley alone."

Lucie adds the last part with pursed lips on top of the arched eyebrow. She's feisty and does not play. Even Connor—Alpha Dom and all—knows how far to push her limits.

Speaking of…

"Dad wants me married and producing heirs like yesterday. I'm not sure where Haley stands—"

"Leave your father to me. You focus on Haley and you. Understand?" Lucie says.

I chuckle. Is she the sub or the Dom? Hell, or even a switch? Not that I care to know anything about my parents' sexual lives. Nope.

Instead, I heed her advice and focus on my own.

"This gathering is about Baz, and Haley being shy, I want to broach her carefully. No need to upset our time with an air of discomfort in the atmosphere. I'll keep my interactions with Haley the same as normal," I decide.

My mother agrees.

When the memory of Baz about to lose his shit with me after Haley's fall all those years ago resurfaces, another roadblock appears.

"But the big issue—rather The Big Four—are her brothers, particularly Baz and to an extent Malcolm. I can guarantee my best friend and *The Enforcer* will not appreciate me being with their little sister," I add.

Lucie nods and shifts her gaze to the Sea, deep in thought.

I give her time too and finish my tea.

"Well, I can understand their protectiveness of the youngest sibling and a girl, to boot. But... But... They know you and respect you. You're not some schmo who's after her fortune. Besides, when did you let a challenge stop you from what you want? And you do want Haley, don't you, Lachlan?" My mother says the last part with both eyebrows raised, and a I-didn't-raise-a-wimp expression on her beautiful face.

I chuckle and shake my head vigorously.

"No, ma'am, you absolutely did not!" I respond.

"Huh! I didn't think so," she huffs and takes the last bite of her scone with a wink at me.

* * *

HALEY TAKES my breath away in a strapless frothy tulle playsuit that showcases her mile-long legs ending in fuck-me strappy sandals. Legs I want wrapped around my hips as I take her against the stone wall. The sexiness of the ensemble tamed by the baby pink color. Her long hair cascades down her back in a ponytail I'd like to wrap around my fist as I mount her from behind. Oversized diamond hoop earrings sparkle as bright as the smile on her face when she swats at her twin playfully.

But a frown replaces her laughter when she notices me staring at her.

Well damn…

All yesterday and today she's avoided me. So I didn't need to act normal. We never interacted at all. But tonight I can't help myself. Haley captivates me—My Baby Girl.

At least I think so if what Aunt Shelley confirmed for me earlier when I asked her opinion on Haley's interest in me.

"Oh, most definitely, Lachlan, darling! You know Haley was a shy girl and now a young woman who's coming into her own. Lucie and I sense an undercurrent between the two of you. Give it time," Shelley said.

Well, we'll see, I think, sipping my Limoncello Gin Collins as I watch Haley from afar.

. . .

"Hey, Baby Girl. Where have you been hiding?" I ask Haley as she stands observing Baz's birthday party cocktail hour on the terrace of Villa Sogno. Not all the guests arrived yet, so I take advantage of the quiet moment to approach her.

She jumps, and a gasp escapes her full lips as she whirls to face me. Her platinum gray eyes widen behind her glasses and her mouth forms a perfect O. It's obvious she didn't notice I came up beside her.

"Uh… Lachlan… Um… Nowhere special. Just right here all along… Taking in the view and all that—"

"Haley! There you are. Mom's looking for you."

Haley closes her eyes for a moment when Harris interrupts her. She takes a deep breath and avoids both of our faces as she scoots between Harris and me.

"Okay! Thanks. Um… Excuse me, Lachlan," she says, overly bright, as she makes her way to Aunt Shelley.

Harris chuckles as he watches Haley's fleeting figure. Then he turns to me.

"What's happening with you, Lach?" He asks. "All well in the esteemed liquor world?"

We shoot the shit until it's time for dinner alfresco. Not surprisingly, Haley is my dinner partner. I give a nod of thanks to Aunt Shelley as she smiles at me knowingly from across the terrace.

I help Haley into her chair and take mine beside her. Our thighs brush together; she jolts; my cock twitches. Another thanks for the table linens as I adjust my bulge unseen.

"You look lovely, Haley," I tell her.

She gulps audibly, then whispers a thank you. Preoccupied with arranging her napkin on her lap, she doesn't notice me inhale the delicate yet intense floral scent of her elegant perfume. Jasmine, orange flower, and musk blend harmoniously. The contrast again, like Haley—sensuous yet untouched.

The way she's so shy around me and her lack of boyfriends—thanks to The Big Four—makes me wonder if she's ever been with a man. The thought hardens my cock to the point of pain, and my inner caveman roars to the surface. I close my eyes and let the sensations wash over me.

"Lachlan?"

Haley's soft voice wakes me from the spell she cast on me unknowingly.

I blink in her direction and shake my head to clear it.

"Pardon?" I respond.

Her eyebrows knit together as she bites her plump lower lip.

At the sight, a low growl escapes my mouth unbidden. She hears it, and her eyes widen. Mine narrow when I notice her pupils dilate and a rosy flush colors her cheeks to the tops of her ample tits that heave with her breaths.

I open my mouth to speak, but Lola's laughter rings through the air. The intimate moment between Haley and I passes when she turns towards Lola and Baz. He's whispering in her ear while she giggles. A wistful expression clouds Haley's face before she averts her gaze.

I can make you laugh, My Baby Girl, if you'd just let me, I think to myself.

The rest of the dinner she's polite to me but keeps her attention on Porter Huntington—a friend of Baz's from Dubai, who sits to her left. Fortunately for him, he's here with his date.

Sadly, the woman next to me is more than eager to chat me up, even ghosting her palm along my muscular thigh. When I jolt from her unexpected touch, she giggles. I bump into Haley accidentally. She looks around me to the giggling woman and frowns. Then turns her back on me.

Great.

After dinner and Baz's proposal, I retire to my parents' villa. Tomorrow I'll get a chance to test Haley's interest in me—us.

* * *

"You are doing well, son. STEELE exceeding revenue projections for three consecutive quarters. Your impressive leadership of your division, the company, and of your younger siblings. Now, a lovely fiancée to settle you down —start on heirs to continue our legacy," Uncle Morgan looks at him pointedly with a cocked eyebrow. "You make your mother and me proud, Sebastian."

I chuckle, realizing Baz has it just as bad with family duty.

My gaze flicks to Haley, who's floating in the Tyrrhenian with Lola, Lauren, and Huntington's date. It's our last day in Positano. Our favorite spot to soak up the sun and to swim in the crystalline waters is at beautiful Fornillo Beach.

It's a little hidden secret in Positano on the Amalfi Coast. Unlike tourists, those in the know spend time here. The overcrowded hot spots hold less appeal. The small, pebble stone beach sits at the bottom of the plunging cliff face below the town with an unobstructed view of the sea. Two ancient stone watchtowers flank the ends of the beach. A bathhouse with lounge chairs and a restaurant provides amenities for beachgoers.

My mother and Aunt Shelley shopped with their friends. While Malcolm and Lucien drove to a potential site for some new venture they plan. Roger, Harris, and Scott eat at the restaurant. My father, Morgan, Baz, Porter, and I sit on lounge chairs near the shoreline.

"I had urged a more permanent alliance between the Jackson and Steele families. Sebastian and Lydie would have made an excellent strategic match," my father harrumphs.

Oh, fuck no…

Baz's Limoncello Gin Collins chokes him as I glance apologetically. Uncle Morgan releases a barely audible sigh.

"Our combined businesses would increase revenue and monopolize the markets," Connor continues, blatantly unaware of our reactions and silence. "I told Lydie a marriage would be conducive to both company's bottom lines."

It's unbelievable he would voice such inane thoughts on

the heels of Baz's proposal to Lola. I cannot let his boorish behavior slide.

"Father," I start before Morgan or Baz can speak. "With all due respect, Lydie and Sebastian are not chess pieces. I say the best of luck to Lola for agreeing to stay with this guy for eternity!"

I raise my tumbler in a toast.

"Here's to a long life and a merry one. A quick death and an easy one. A pretty girl and an honest one. A cold beer—and another one! Cheers!" Chimes in Porter with his glass of Guinness stout.

"Agreed!" Morgan adds with his eyebrow cocked as he stares at my father.

"What are we toasting to?"

Our heads pivot to see Lola and the girls approaching. But I only have eyes for Haley.

Her curvy body makes the innocent lemon-printed bandeau bikini sinful. Damn, what a luscious body. So ripe for my picking. I'm sure it's tastier and more fragrant than the Sorrentine fruit.

Lola slips onto Baz's chaise lounge and gives him a kiss on the cheek. Then takes his drink for a sip.

"Aah… Refreshing! Cheers!" She laughs.

Everyone can't help but join her infectious happiness. Even Connor, who offers a small smile with a shake of his head. Undoubtedly wishing it were Lydie beside Sebastian.

"Oh, just wishing you and Baz the best. Really, you!" I roar heartily.

"Whatever, jerk," he throws his towel at my head.

Deftly catching it, I stand to offer it to my bathing beauty.

"Here, Haley. Your brother's aim is off. I'm sure he meant to give you a towel to dry yourself off..." I add, rolling my eyes at him over my shoulder.

Haley fidgets with her bikini top, then blushes as she peeks up at me, noticing my hooded green eyes locked on her tits. She stammers a thank you and something about going to the restroom. Then rushes off, wrapping the towel around her body.

Fuck. I hope I didn't upset her, I think as my sharp gaze follows Haley's retreating figure. When Lola goes after Haley, I turn to Baz with a smirk. Hopefully, he's not clued into my thoughts. Even if I was practically drooling over Haley.

"Race you to the pontoon, lovestruck!" I say to deflect.

We climb onto the deck and settle on an empty spot facing the beach. My muscles appreciate the hard swim, and I stretch my shoulders.

"Spill," Baz demands.

I jerk my head in his direction and scan his face to gauge his mood. I maintain a neutral expression. Damn, there goes that idea...

"What?" I rejoin.

"Do not fuck with me, Lachlan," Sebastian threatens.

He glares at me as though thinking I must have lost my mind. I know him well enough after these years, he's difficult on wankers messing with his kid sister.

But like I told my mother, I am no wimp and will not

back down from a challenge when I want something. And I want Haley. Mine!

"Sebastian, fuck off," my inner caveman snarls.

"*Ciao, ragazzi.*"

Two leggy Monica Bellucci lookalikes stand over us. Their minuscule bikinis barely cover their abundant assets. One reaches for my cheek, and the other grins at Baz.

He and I glance at each other. A nod sets our squabble aside to avoid. Without hesitation, we dive back into the azure waters.

As I sit aboard my Gulfstream G650 private jet for my return to Aberdeen, I leave a voicemail for Haley, asking her to dinner anyplace in the world she wants.

Baz asked me to be a groomsman, and Lola paired me with Haley.

I want an opportunity to meet with her on our own before their wedding in two months. She gets too nervous around her family and avoids me. Us alone should help her to relax and give me a chance to see if Haley truly wants more from me.

At least one can hope…

"*A*re you ready, Haley?"

I bite my lower lip and turn as I lift my gaze to Lachlan.

The bridal party lines up to enter the second ballroom at STEELE Dubai I for Baz and Lola's wedding ceremony. I knew this day was coming, but I'm not prepared for it still. For being partnered with Lachlan.

The past few weeks, I put off his requests to meet for dinner with work excuses I sent back as text messages. I couldn't bring myself to return his phone calls or Face-Times. My declinations didn't deter Lachlan, only made him offer more dates flexible for my schedule. Still no go.

Now, no more hiding from him and what he wants to talk about. Damn.

My eyes take in his masculine beauty—Cary Grant incarnate.

Lachlan is so handsome in his classic, bespoke black

tuxedo with boutonniere. Sable colored hair slicked back artfully. Emerald green eyes glitter in his tan, smooth skin. Strong jawline, cleft chin. So damn debonair.

I lower my eyes and peek back up at him through my thick eyelashes when he holds out his arm to me. I slip my hand around his elbow to rest my palm on his forearm. The corded muscles bunch beneath my hand as he squeezes my arm close to his side and smiles down at me.

"You look beautiful, Haley," Lachlan adds.

"Thank you," I murmur, distracted by his flexed muscles.

The Elie Saab custom creation is a dreamy halter-top column dress of silk organza layers in various shades of the orange and fuchsia hues that match Lola's color palette. I feel sexy and pretty at the same time. Lachlan's compliment makes butterflies flutter in my belly.

I wonder how we must appear to the three hundred guests as we walk down the aisle: a striking couple in love? For a moment I let my mind run free and pretend it's our wedding day. Now that's the best fantasy starring Lachlan. I shake my head as we take our places at the altar. Silly girl.

Lachlan's eyes never leave my face throughout the entire ceremony. A broad smile greets me when he extends his elbow again to escort me back up the aisle. Even during the photoshoot, he makes a point of never leaving my side. My face remains flushed the whole time, and the butterflies increase.

I make the most of the reception—more specifically, of the cocktails. So much so I miss out on catching the bouquet. Billie Chandler, Lola's West Coast personal assistant, snags it with glee. I shrug until Porter swats the garter away from him, so it falls into Lachlan's hand, who also looks dubious.

Well, I suppose there's no need for me to wonder about Lachlan's thoughts on marriage…

Instead, I continue to dabble in the cocktails and dance the night away with Lola—before she's whisked away by Baz—Leonie *The Lion* Beaulieu, her best friend and the megamodel, Billie, and Blair, Lola's other PA.

Even during our fun, I can't help but notice when women fawn all over Lachlan. He graces them with his charming smile and dances with some of them.

Ooookay…

After Baz and Lola disappear from their reception, I glance around for Lachlan. I spy him leaving the ballroom. Alone. Thank goodness, I breathe in a sigh of relief. I take one last glass from a passing server for liquid courage before I leave the reception intent on Lachlan's suite.

He wants to talk, well, we'll talk. Now.

Adrenaline pumps in my veins to provide fuel for my goal. Boldly, I press the doorbell on his suite.

It takes a few rings before he opens it and whammo!

Lachlan stands before me with damp hair, bare feet, and only a towel slung low at his hips. The eight-pack abs and the v-cuts of his Adonis belt on full blast. A feathery happy trail disappears below the towel. It directs my eyes to the outline of a long, thick cock with a mushroom head rests against his thigh, damn near to the middle of it.

My pussy spasms, and my ovaries explode.

"Haley?" He asks, unsure since I stand dumbstruck before him.

I blink and pick my jaw up from the floor.

"L—Lachlan," I squawk, then clear my suddenly parched throat and try again. "Lachlan, you wanted to speak with me."

Now *he* blinks but recovers quickly. With a slight nod, he opens the door further and steps aside.

I return his nod and enter the lion's domain—I mean Lachlan's suite. Thankful I don't collapse on my jellied knees, I make my way to a sofa. Remembering my finishing school pointers on being a lady, I sit gracefully and cross my legs at the ankles. My gaze lifts to Lachlan expectantly.

"Er... Give me a second to change," he says as he runs his thick fingers through his hair, biceps flex.

I nod and smooth my dress.

Lachlan tracks my movement, then swipes his hand over his face with a low groan before he pivots on his heel.

He returns in a black t-shirt that molds to his muscular torso and a pair of gray sweatpants that fail to hide his massive bulge. Unconsciously, I lick my lips as I stare at his crotch.

Lachlan coughs.

I drag my eyes up to his as I take in his flat stomach and pronounced pecs. Damn, this man is fine.

"Are you all right, Haley?" He asks with his head tilted as he observes me.

"Absolutely," I respond. "So, talk to me, Lachlan. I'm all yours."

My sassy demand makes him stifle a chuckle. He nods and sits on the sofa across from me.

I purse my lips at his choice of seating.

"I won't bite, you know. Well, unless…" I bait him with a flutter of my eyelashes. Damn, I'm a wild girl!

The corner of his mouth quirks up.

"I want to speak with you, but perhaps tomorrow would be better." Lachlan says and moves to the minibar. "Here, drink some water. You'll feel better."

I gape at him. Oh no, he didn't.

"You know what would make me feel better, Lachlan Jackson?" I query as I swat the bottle of water from his hand. "You! You on my lips, not some bubbly water!"

His eyes pop from their sockets like a cartoon character.

"You tease me with your heated gazes, then ignore me! Well, I'm tired of waiting for you to make a move, Lachlan! So, here I am. Fuck me!" I shout.

Now, his sculpted jaw joins his eyes rolling around at his bare feet on the silk carpet. Flabbergasted, he can't even respond to the gauntlet I dropped.

I sneer at him and rise from the sofa. Well, wobble.

If he still won't make a move, then it's up to me. Ladies first, as Queen Latifah says!

My fingers unzip my gown—albeit it after a few tries—and it puddles at my feet. Unsteadily, I step out of it and reach for the busks of my Lola's Coterie corset, determined to get this man's attention.

In the blink of an eye, Lachlan is on me. But not how I want.

He stays my hands with one of his and yanks his t-shirt at the back of his neck to put it on me. It hangs to the middle of my thighs, covering my matching G-string.

When an aggrieved whimper falls from my lips, he shakes his head and places a finger against them.

"Haley, you had too much to drink, and I would never take advantage of a woman's inebriated state. Especially not yours," Lachlan states.

My eyes fill with tears, and I slip my fingertips beneath my glasses to wipe the moisture from my face. I'm so distraught I threw myself at him, only to be shunned. I sag to the sofa and cover my face with my hands.

"Oh, My Baby Girl, do not cry," Lachlan croons as he sits beside me and pulls me into his brawny arms.

The woodsy scent of his cologne combined with his natural pheromones seeps into my nose as I bury my face in his neck. I take a deep inhale to imprint his intoxicating aroma on my brain in case I never get another chance to be this close to Lachlan.

I splutter words of him not wanting me and making me ache for him between hiccups. He rubs my back and brushes his lips against my hair softly.

"Hush, Sweet Girl. You do not know what you say," he admonishes me huskily.

Lachlan rocks me as my words give way to full-blown hiccups, followed by mouth-gaping yawns.

I have had no sleep so nervous about being with him for the wedding and unsure of his feeling for me. My body is on the verge of exhaustion. The liquid-courage-fueled adrenaline tank on empty. I burrow my tired body against her bare-chested warmth as my fingers cling to his broad shoulders.

As though privy to my thoughts, Lachlan scoops me up and carries me to the bedroom. Before he lays me on the bed, I stiffen.

OMG is this it? Will he make love to me at long last? I wonder to myself. I peek up at him, and he kisses the tip of my nose.

"I told you I will not take advantage of you, Sweet Girl. You need to rest," he says, then puts me to bed like a sleepy child.

Except he slips in behind me and pulls my back to his front with his large hand on my lower belly and one leg between mine possessively. He kisses the top of my head and murmurs good night.

My mind, body, and soul submit to his command, and I slumber in his warm embrace.

My Dearest Haley,

I hope you will understand me not being here this morning. I thought it best for

> you to awake alone to avoid any unease
> for you. I am sure you realize I want to
> speak with you about us. Whether you
> wish—as I do—to move our relationship
> beyond cousins, albeit not by blood, to
> that of a man and a woman who want one
> another.
>
> If your feelings match mine, meet me on the
> summit of the Eiffel Tower tomorrow at
> noon. If not, know that I will always
> respect you and your decision.
>
> Forever yours,
> Lachlan

I STARE in surprise at the note he left on his pillow. Tears of relief trickle down my cheeks as I hold his message to my bosom.

Lachlan knows me so well.

As I awoke, my mind replayed the prior night's events, and I feared he would think of me poorly. Or worse, never want to see me again. My heart skipped a beat when I noticed he was no longer wrapped around me, and the suite was silent.

But I should have known that's not Lachlan. No matter what, he's always been kind to me and had my best interest in mind. Case in point, his leaving me to avoid my potential embarrassment.

Gingerly, I slip out of bed, but not before I sniff his pillow where a trace of his scent lingers. Afterwards I take a soothing shower—a steam one to sweat out some of the alcohol…

Before he left, a thoughtful Lachlan must have called the concierge for a bit of shopping.

On the chair, I find a Diane von Furstenberg wrap dress and a pair of Chanel ballet flats to avoid a walk of shame in my bridesmaid gown. Interestingly, no bra or panties accompany my outfit. I put my corset back on and go commando. A quick call to housekeeping will get my gown and G-string cleaned and returned with my shoes to my suite.

A wide smile graces my face as I stride into the post-wedding brunch.

"Good morning, darling! Don't you happy!"

I glance to my right to find my mother standing with a wedding guest sipping Mimosas.

My cheeks heat. So busted!

Shelley excuses herself from the woman and loops arms with me. Along our way to a quiet corner, we greet more guests with smiles and nods. Obviously, my mother is on a mission and will not stop for small talk.

She gets another Mimosa from a server and hands it to me.

I take it knowing this conversation will require liquid courage, too.

"So, how are you and Lachlan? He came by earlier and said his goodbyes, but I couldn't get a read on him," my mother queries as she sips from her crystal flute. Dark brown eyes survey me.

I gulp down half of my Mimosa and close my eyes as it seeps into my system. The refreshing orange juice and Champagne prove the perfect hair of the dog for me.

"Fine. We're meeting noon tomorrow in Paris at the Eiffel Tower. We're going to talk about... us," I answer honestly, just as I did with Roger.

No point in hedging with my mother. We've always been close since I'm her only girl, and she acts as a buffer between my overly protective brothers and me. I only hope she won't find it odd I have feelings for Lachlan that extend beyond us being cousins.

With a hug, my mother dispels any doubt from my mind.

"Wonderful, Haley! I'm so glad the two of you came to your senses at long last! Lucie and I have a bet going whether the light would dawn on you during the wedding, or you'd put it off longer. With all the love in the air I said it would happen!" She exclaims triumphantly.

I can't help but to giggle and squeeze her tight. Then a disquieting thought comes to mind.

"Dad and Sebastian don't know, do they?" I ask, concerned my eldest brother will get angry with his best friend and attempt to keep Lachlan from me—little sister and all.

My mother purses her lips and shakes her head, her wavy black hair sways around her shoulders.

"I won't keep anything from your father—should he ask. And Baz has his own love life to focus on with his new bride," she responds and continues with a wink. "However, I will not allow either of them or your other brothers to prevent you from living your dreams. I've always known you had a crush on Lachlan. That summer night you fell, and he comforted you, confirmed my suspicions. You have my full support. And Lucie's!"

My heart soars.

Tomorrow, I'll fly to Paris and arrive at the Eiffel Tower well before noon, eager to be with my man and to live my life my way. No big Brothers will stop me.

LACHLAN

*F*uck!

I've never been nervous in my life. Always steadfast in all that I do from a multimillion-dollar negotiation to navigating my full-rigged sailing yacht—*Gorm Domhainn*—during a stomach-churning storm on the North Sea.

But this right here? Waiting for Haley to arrive?

I'm sweating bullets.

My eyes stay trained on the stairs, watching for the first sign of her as she climbs up to the summit at the Eiffel Tower. A jolt zings through me when I spy the top of an ebony-haired woman. I stride forward, only to apologize when a stranger gasps at my hand on her arm. I mumble an apology and take off my Tom Ford aviator sunglasses to wipe my face.

The ringing bells of several cathedrals nearby announce the high hour of noon.

No Haley.

Fuck.

I resume my watch in hopes she'll appear. Perhaps she's running late. A few women stare at me in interest, but I avoid them. Even if Haley doesn't show up, I still don't want one of them.

My mind fills with doubt after ten minutes pass and no sign of her. I glance down at my mobile. No missed phone calls or text messages. With a sigh, I tilt my head back and gaze up through the intricate work of the Iron Lady. A silent prayer moves across my lips.

Just as I push off from the railing to leave, my gaze lands on a woman whose head hangs as she hurries to the stairs. A curtain of wavy, ebony hair covers her profile. When she lifts her hand to her face, her hair parts as she slides a pair of glasses up the bridge of her nose.

I do a double take.

Haley!

She jumps like a frightened rabbit and spins in my direction.

Shit! In my shock at seeing Haley, I yelled her name out loud.

Her gray eyes shining with tears widen, and her lips part to form my name when she recognizes who called hers. Then the most beatific smile dawns on her gorgeous face.

My heart stutters in my chest, and I place my palm on it to steady myself.

We stare at one another, unable to move past a group of

tourists who follow a guide with a yellow banner on a stick.

Unable to bear the distance any longer, I push my way through them, offering an apology. Haley giggles and covers her mouth with her hand. As soon as I reach her, I scoop her into my arms and cover that full mouth with mine.

She gasps, and I slip my tongue inside to taste My Baby Girl finally.

The flavors of strawberries and cream—the contrast of sinful and sweet—tantalize me as I devour her. Soft moans and amorous sighs get swallowed as my tongue dances with hers. Then my Alpha Dom emerges, triggered by how quickly she submits to my passionate kiss.

I growl and nip at her lips, across her jaw, up to her ear, where I draw the lobe between my teeth. She yelps, and I soothe the pain with the flat of my tongue and a purr. Haley mewls and melds the soft curves of her body to the hard planes of mine. Including my cock that presses painfully against the zipper of my trousers, awakened by my Siren's Song.

"You are mine, Haley Steele," I growl as my lips brush the delicate shell of her ear.

She trembles in my arms and nods.

"Words, Baby Girl. I will have your words," I demand in full Alpha Dom mode.

She gulps audibly and nods, then catches herself.

"Y-y-yes, Sir," she says.

Fuck. Me.

Haley—My Baby Girl—Steele is a submissive.

My heavy balls damn near explode.

Then a thought occurs to me. One that has a red haze cloud my vision.

"Have you been in a D/s relationship, Haley?" I ask with narrowed eyes and flared nostrils. The caveman is none too pleased with that possibility.

She blinks behind her glasses and looks confused.

"What do you mean?" She asks.

"A Dominant and a submissive relationship," I clarify.

Haley's cheeks reddened, and she shakes her head vehemently.

"No! I haven't even been in any relations—" She slaps both hands over her mouth.

I cock an eyebrow and tilt my head in question. Now, she needs to clarify.

"Um, no. I've never been in a D/s relationship," Haley responds deftly avoiding the any relationship part.

I let it go. For now.

"Good," I smirk. "When did you get here? I've been waiting over there."

She grins sheepishly and says, "At 11:30. I wanted to make sure I wasn't late."

So all along My Baby Girl was just around the bend. And I did not need to stress out. All I had to do was look.

Fuck.

Her stomach rumbles, and she blushes.

"That reminds me. We have reservations at Le Jules Verne now. Shall we?" I ask as I offer my elbow to her.

"Yes! I'm famished," Haley giggles, holding my arm with both hands and grinning up at me. "I was too nervous to eat. I only had a couple of strawberries with fresh cream in my suite at STEELE Montaigne."

Well, at least I wasn't the only one scared...

THEY SAY the experience is dizzying 410 feet up in the sky surrounded by the panoramic views of the City of Lights. A dream-like state set within the heavens. Even more so as the soft shades of gray and cream blend seamlessly with the ironwork of the Eiffel Tower as we sit in Le Jules Verne, the one Michelin star restaurant

The chef exits his hallowed domain to offer our favorite dishes while the sommelier pairs them with their most esteemed wines. They fawn over My Baby Girl, much to her delight. Although to my chagrin she blesses them with her dazzling smile.

Once they leave to do her bidding, I reach across the table with my palm up. Haley places hers on top, and I clasp it while I rub the pad of my thumb over the inside of her slim wrist. Her eyes flutter at the intimate contact.

"So, your feelings match mine, Baby Girl?" I ask as I watch her face intently.

She bites her lower lip and glances down at our joined hands. A moment passes in silence as she contemplates my question.

I wait patiently.

Her eyes—made even more platinum by the colors of the restaurant's decor—meet mine.

"Tell me what you mean, Lachlan. I want to be very clear," she responds.

I take a deep breath and bare my innermost self to her.

"Until the summer of you sixteenth birthday, I only ever saw you as my little cousin, the baby girl of the Steele clan. My best friend's younger sister. You were a toddler, a girl, a teenager younger than me. Someone to tease, care for, and love, as I did with my own sister. Forbidden for more than one reason," I pause to formulate my next words.

Haley squeezes my hand to encourage me.

I smile at her and go on.

"But something changed between us that summer. I no longer viewed you as the kid sister of my best friend who tagged along wherever we went, stumbling, then walking tall. I tried to deny the difference, chastising myself for allowing my thoughts to stray beyond the cousin realm."

Another deep breath.

"I thought you felt the same, especially when you were so hurt by me kissing your friend at the beach."

Haley scoffs and pulls her hand back. I hold tight and cock my eyebrow. Instantly, she submits.

Fuck. Me.

I shift in my seat to adjust my reawakened cock before I continue.

"When you peered up at me with a look of such need after you fell, it pulled the last tie on the blindfold I put over my eyes to ignore my feelings for you. The jolt that ran through me as I touched your cheek confirmed it. Hell, I almost got into a fight with Baz about you later!" I admit.

Haley's eyes widen.

I shrug.

"He was being a protective big brother, so I can't be mad at him. *You* can't be mad at him either," I add when she protests. "So I gave in and left you be. For. Thirteen. Years. It was obvious your need to come into your own drove you to finish school and make your mark at STEELE International. But you have always been on my mind. Always, Haley."

Tears glitter in her gray orbs.

I squeeze her hand.

"In Positano, Lucie and Shelley drew out my confession and told me they think you feel the same way. With that in mind and their blessing, I knew the time was right to speak with you about us," I say, then brush my thumb against her wrist. "Do you understand, Baby Girl?"

Her lips part on a gasp, and her tongue darts out to lick the plump lower one. Pupils dilate as her cheeks tint a rosy hue.

I clamp down on my bottom lip to stifle a groan.

Her eyes drop to my mouth, and she mimics my move unconsciously. The way she's so unaware of her beauty and of her sensuality tempts me to show her the effect she has on me. Right here, right now.

The sommelier and server deliver our first course and break the moment.

Good. I need to control myself.

As soon as they leave us, Haley leans forward and reaches for my hand.

"Yes and yes, Lachlan," she says firmly as she rubs her thumb over my wrist.

I hiss as my cock jumps against the zipper teeth or may trousers.

"Excellent, Baby Girl. Now eat. You will need your energy," I command.

Once again, she bites that damnable lip and responds, "Yes, Sir."

WE FLEW through the streets in my silver-on-white Aston Martin DB7 Vantage headed to my penthouse in the *seizième*. The arrondissement is renowned for the ornate nineteenth-century buildings, wide avenues, prestigious schools, museums, and spacious parks. French high society has flocked here for their places of residence for years. The *seizième* is comparable to the luxurious Kensington and Chelsea neighborhoods in London. French popular culture has coined the phrase *le 16e* as association with great wealth.

The whole time, Haley stared out of her window and only glanced at me when I touched her thigh.

I worried she had a change of heart. But that concern dissipated when she took my hand in the garage and strode beside me to my private elevator. When I held her back against my front on our ride up, she didn't flinch. She leaned against me with a contented sigh and placed her hands over mine on her lower belly.

Now, we stand in my bedroom facing each other beside my king-size, four-poster, lattice-canopy bed, a cloud of fluffy white silk linens and pillows. And white silk ties on each post with toys in the nightstand. The duality apparent. I wanted it to represent our first time together.

"Baby Girl, are you sure?" I ask.

"Yes, Lachlan. I want this with you and so much more," she responds with a heart-stopping smile.

I don't hesitate.

"I will make love to you, Baby Girl. Then I will fuck you until *I* can no longer walk," I say.

She gasps and pushes her glasses up the bridge of her nose. Her nervous tell.

Then I remember her earlier admission: no relationship.

"Haley, have you been with a man intimately before?" I ask, trying not to let my possessiveness show.

Her eyebrows shoot to her hairline as her face flames red, and she averts her eyes.

My heart skips a beat as my dick jumps.

"Um… I… Um… I'm a virgin," she ends on a whisper.

Fuck. Me.

I damn near whoop and punch my fists in the air as I dance around my bedroom in my mind. Haley Steele will be mine all MINE!!! Yeah, My Baby Girl, yeah!

Haley mistakes my pause as disinterest and starts to babble.

I place my thumb against her open mouth.

"Suck it," I command.

She needs a distraction.

And I need to calm my racing heart.

Once again, her eyes widen. But the tip of her little pink tongue pokes out tentatively as she keeps her eyes locked on mine.

I wait, calling forth my Alpha Dom.

The natural sub in My Baby Girl senses her Dom. She wraps her tongue around my thumb and draws it into her warm, wet mouth. The sounds of her suckling my digit make a low rumble pour from my chest. She purrs.

"So responsive, Little Temptress," I croon. "I have something much bigger and more appetizing for you to suck."

Her eyes widen to saucers, but she doesn't stop suckling. She increases it with gusto.

"But first," I say as I withdraw my thumb with a pop. A string of saliva connects it to her lower lip. I groan at the sight. "I want you naked."

I place my hands on her hips, spin us around, and sit on the edge of the bed with her standing between my spread thighs. A squeeze to her hip points draws a yelp from her.

"Undress for me, Little Temptress," I command, and sit back with my palms on my thighs.

She nods, then remembers herself and adds, "Yes, Sir."

"Good, girl," I praise.

She beams.

More sure of herself, My Baby Girl slips out of the silk wrap dress she wears.

I notice it's like the one I bought for her. She must like the style, I muse, pleased. It's feminine and sexy since it hugs the ample curves of her D-cup tits and grip-worthy hips, then flares around her long, toned legs.

"Drop it," I answer her unspoken question when she glances around for a place to discard her dress.

She nods, "Yes, Sir."

The silk whispers to the floor beside her fuck-me heels. My hooded gaze skims up her calf to her thigh and over her bare mons, covered by a scrap of sexy black lace. I pause and inhale. Her arousal wafts through my nostrils like an aphrodisiac.

I growl and lean forward to bury my face at the apex of her thighs as I grab both ass cheeks.

My Baby Girl squeals and taps on her toes.

I cover a chuckle with a nip to the top of her slit near her clit.

A strangled cry slips from her mouth as her body bows, and she tangles her fingers in my hair before pulling on my scalp.

The pain goes straight to my throbbing dick. My fingers dig into her fleshy ass, and I grunt. A fresh wave of her musky arousal filters into my nose, past the lace. I rip the delicate material from her mound.

Nothing will come between me and My Baby Girl. Nothing.

I drape one leg over my shoulder and eat her out like a starved man. And as long as I waited to have her, I am ravenous.

"Oh… My… God… Lachlan… Fuuuck!!!"

She screams as her pussy walls spasm against my probing tongue. Her body collapses over me—damn near suffocating me—as her hips undulate to fuck my face. The tips of her fingernails dig through my suit jacket and shirt.

I continue my forbidden meal, grunting and growling like a feral beast as my fingers bore into her hips and ass.

My Baby Girl's moans morph into wails as I pull two more orgasms from her sensitive core.

When I've had my fill of her sweet essence—for now—I lower her limp form to the middle of the bed.

One of her hands covers her pussy while the other hides her eyes.

"Do not conceal yourself from me, Little Temptress"—I say as I move her hands above her head crossed at the wrists—"Especially while I have your pussy juices on my tongue. You bare all for me at all times"

She peeks up at me from beneath her thick eyelashes, pupils dilated and mouth slack. Her hairline slick with sweat. Face flush. Tits heave with each shallow breath. Tits that should be bare too.

Deftly, I unclasp the front closure of her matching balconette bra. Pillowy tits spill free, dark pink nipples puckered. She shrugs out of the bra and tosses it to the floor before she leans back against the mountain of pillows. Ebony waves fan out around her head.

"Gorgeous," I murmur.

A shy smile plays at the corners of her full mouth.

"Your turn, Sir," she purrs.

A smirk pulls at my lips.

"Oh really, now, Little Temptress," I chuckle while my hooded emerald eyes blaze a trail over her lushness.

She bites her bottom lip and nods. Gray eyes glitter like liquid platinum.

I pounce.

My mouth slants over hers, and I nip until she submits to my demanding tongue. I swirl it around, lapping at every inch of its warm wetness, just as I did with her pussy.

She mewls and dives her fingers into my hair. Nails scrape my scalp.

My Alpha Dom wants to punish her for dropping position, but I promised My Baby Girl I would make love to her our first time. So, I let her tangle my locks.

"Lachlan… I need you… Please," she gasps as I suck on the sensitive juncture of her neck and shoulder.

I grunt in response, not wanting to stop my mark goal. Only when I'm satisfied the skin will redden do I comply.

She follows my movements as I rise from the bed. With deliberately slow movements, I undress one garment at a time until I'm in my black boxer briefs. The bulbous head of my cock pokes out above the waistband. A drop of pre-cum glistens at the slit.

"Adonis," she breathes as her eyes scan my muscular body voraciously.

I palm my bulge and stroke its length, pumped by her delight in me.

"Please," she adds, arms outstretched, knees fall apart in welcome.

"I will take care of you, Little Temptress. Always," I say in a voice gruff with desire.

My boxer briefs drop to the pile beside me, and I stand erect.

She gasps and pushes her glasses up the bridge of her nose—nervous tell.

My knees sink into the fluffy cloud, and I prowl over her. I remove the glasses from her face.

She blinks at me as I put them on the nightstand, then plank over her.

Once again, I possess her mouth until she relaxes beneath me, hands squeeze my biceps. Her soft mewls let me know she's ready for more. *So much more.*

I spend the next minutes tasting every inch of her body, from her plump nipples to the round curve of her ass, along the backs of her knees to her big toe. By the time I brush the tip of my nose along her pussy slit, a puddle sits below it.

No way can I resist a taste and get my fill while I hold her hips to still her writhing body. Tugs to my hair bring me back from carnal nirvana. I kiss my way up her body and plant my forearms on either side of her head.

"Tell me. What do you want, Baby Girl?" I rasp as I drop my forehead to her damp one. I need to be sure she wants me—us.

"You... You, Lachlan. Now. Please!" She pants.

Thank fuck.

I fist my hungry cock and slide it along her soaking seam to coat it with her natural lubricant. My teeth clamp on my bottom lip for a bite of pain to stave off my urge to cum.

"Baby Girl, I am going to make you mine with nothing between us. Bare. Flesh in flesh," I growl as I drive my cock until fully sheathed within her tight virgin pussy. My eyes roll back from the erotic pleasure.

She cries out as my rigid ten inches claim her in one swift thrust.

I still my hips to allow her pussy to adjust to my girth. Our gazes lock: hers awed, mine enraptured.

At last Haley Steele is My Baby Girl.

MINE!

"You... You, My Lord. Now. Please!" I cry out, only able to pant my words.

I watch, mesmerized by each vein and ridge of Lachlan's massive dick as he grips it almost angrily and slides it along my dripping pussy. I mewl and toss my head from side to side when its tip hits my swollen clit, sensitive from his earlier ministrations.

Another climax seizes me in its powerful clasp. My eyes roll to the back of my head as a wail pours from my slack mouth—an erotic sound I never made before.

Nothing of what Lachlan has done to me is at all what I experienced before.

No sloppy kiss by a high school junior from Collegiate behind the bleachers at a dance.

No drunken pinching and twisting of my nipples by a Harvard frat boy at a kegger.

And especially not my magical wand...

The indescribable sensations Lachlan unleashes in my body shake me beyond my core; they touch the very depths of my soul. Thankful to be his at long last.

My hooded eyes flutter open to watch him as he hovers above me.

His teeth clamp on his kiss-swollen bottom lip. Eyebrows knit together in concentration as he continues to stroke my slick pussy with his cock. He raises his eyes to mine. The wild look in his nearly black orbs sends a shudder through my body. Goosebumps break out on my heated, damp skin.

"Baby Girl, I am going to make you mine with nothing between us. Bare. Flesh in flesh," Lachlan growls as he drives his ginormous dick deep inside of my tight pussy. His eyes roll back as he groans in pleasure.

I scream.

The pain as he rips through my virginity takes me by surprise. I squeeze my inner thighs against his narrow hips. My fingernails dig into his broad shoulders.

Fuck!!!

When air re-enters my lungs, I open my eyes to find Lachlan staring down at me with an expression of over-whelming emotion. Dare I think love?

A tear slips down my temple into my ear.

He gasps and wipes his thumb along the wet trail.

"Oh, Baby Girl… My Baby Girl," he croons as he covers my face with open-mouthed kisses.

His still hips give me a moment to acclimate to his massive dick.

I'm so full, it feels as though I'll split in two. His girth stretches me while his tip brushes my cervix. Even my ass comes into play with his heavy balls pressed against my lower cheeks.

Ever the geek, my brain reminds me I'm on birth control. Then it analyzes each ripple of my pussy walls along his dick, the way it flexes inside of me, and how within moments, I'm ready for more.

Instinctively, my ankles lock behind his firm ass and my pelvis tilts to give him more access, while my pussy clenches around his cock and my back arches from the mattress.

A wicked grin greets my carnal gaze. Then Lachlan drops those lips to my pebbled nipple. His mouth engulfs it, and he hollows his cheeks to suckle. Hard. His voracious appetite drives him to feed from my tits until they're wet and swollen, heavy from my arousal.

All along, his hips circle within the cradle of my pelvis. Not quite pulling in or out, merely reminding me of his presence. Sparks light with each rotation. I can never forget Lachlan's big dick inside of me. Impossible.

Heat pools in my lower belly, and my spine tingles. Another mind-blowing orgasm hurdles towards me.

Lachlan withdraws to his tip, and I growl in protest at the loss. Then cry out in wild abandon when he slams back in; the tip grazes my G-spot.

I buck beneath him. Another slow drag and quick thrust triggers my orgasm. My pussy quivers, and his cock jumps.

"Fuck!" He grunts. "Feel… so… good."

Each word punctuated with a drag and a thrust.

"Give me another, Baby Girl. Because I have so much more to give to you," he rumbles.

I break apart again, soaking his dick with my pussy juices.

Without separating our intimate connection, Lachlan rises to his knees and cups my ass; his thumbs firm on my hips. He tosses his head like a stallion to whip damp hair from his eyes. Neck, pecs, and abs taut with his biceps flexed, prepped to fuck me raw.

I shiver and mewl in anticipation.

Lachlan's nostrils flare as he inhales my musky arousal mixed with our pheromones. Then he's off, riding me with controlled, pistoning strokes. The bed creaks.

I dig my nails into the corded muscles of his forearms as I hold on. My tits bounce. I cry out with each toe-curling thrust of his velvet-covered steel.

"Uh. Uh. Uh. Uh."

Lachlan's eyes gleam feral.

"Only mine. Mine forever," he rasps. "Do you understand?"

I nod, too caught up in my emotions to respond verbally. But that's not good enough for Lachlan.

He spanks my pussy twice.

I hiss at the pain, then sigh in pleasure as a frisson of erotic bliss radiates from the punished spot. My swollen clit weeps.

"Yes, Sir!" I respond with a throaty moan.

"Good girl," Lachlan praises me, not slowing his pace.

He takes a nipple in his mouth and suckles as his hips snap. When he smacks my pussy again, I explode.

A deep passionate growl blows his warm breath against my wet tits. Lachlan sits back on his haunches, lifting me with ease onto his lap, legs wrapped around his hips, knees on the mattress. The new angle drives him deeper within my pussy. Once again, I'm reminded of the enormity of his massive cock. And of the carnal pleasure it ignites.

I throw my head back and keen when his upward thrusts impale me on his girth. I feel every vein, every ridge, every inch of him. Another orgasm takes me.

Lachlan swells within me. His dick impossibly harder and larger. He drives up as he pulls me down one last time. He sucks in a scant breath and stills.

I hold my breath.

Then hot spurts of his semen shoot from his pulsating cock to hit my womb, bathing my pussy. Lachlan marks me inside as his.

His roar punches the air.

His primal call forces a final climax from my greedy pussy as it milks him dry.

"You are mine, Lachlan Jackson," I say in a voice hoarse from my screams of passion.

He leans back. Blown pupils lock on mine.

"Yes, I am, Haley Steele," he responds gruffly.

I bury my face in his neck and lick the sweaty skin before I place my mark on him. He grunts but doesn't stop me. Instead, he holds me tighter in his embrace.

When I'm satisfied with my mark, I meet his eyes, and he kisses me breathlessly.

He carries me into the en suite bathroom and sets me in the extra-large claw-foot tub. I admire the all white, Carrara marble bathroom that has a walk-in shower big enough to hold four double vanities, and a separate water closet for the bidet and toilet. Sunlight streams in from the windows, sparkling off of the crystal chandelier and wall sconces and the brushed nickel fixtures. Thick fluffy towels rest on an antique straight-back chair.

Warm water fills the tub quickly as Lachlan adds essential oils of lavender and eucalyptus. I inhale and allow the fragrant steam to relax me. My eyes open when he slips in behind me.

He takes a sponge and dips it into the water before he squeezes it over my shoulders. Rivulets roll down and bead at the tips of my erect nipples. I sigh and melt against him when his lips ghost over my neck and collarbones.

"How do you feel, Baby Girl?" Lachlan asks.

I tip my head to the side to give him more access.

"Wonderful," I murmur. "And you?"

A blast of his breath blows tendrils of my hair as he chuckles.

"Me? Oh, Sweet Girl, you are a gem," Lachlan says as he wraps his arms beneath my breasts and squeezes. "*I* am fantastic, thanks to *you!*"

I giggle and kiss his smiling lips.

"Good!" I murmur against them.

We take turns bathing each other, even though I wanted

him again. He told me my body needs a rest from his sizable cock. But his full lips? They gave me immense pleasure…

I helped him to change the bedding despite my blush when our gazes landed on the spots of blood on the white sheet.

Lachlan crawled over to where I stood opposite him, beside the bed, and cupped my face. He thanked me for giving him the greatest gift and kissed me softly.

Now wrapped in fluffy robes, we sit on chaise lounges on the terrace while we sip tea and munch on tasty macarons. He was so thoughtful and had fresh ones delivered from Ladurée Paris on the Champs-Élysées—my favorite patisserie.

Lachlan offers me a taste of his orange blossom flavor, and I give him a bite of my pistachio one. When crumbs fall on his lips, I lean over and lick them off. He nips me then purrs to soothe the erotic pain.

"Nothing is as sweet as your lips, Baby Girl," he croons as his fingers slip inside my robe to stroke my pussy. "Both sets…"

I moan when he flicks my sensitive bundle of nerves, and I grind on his hand.

He chuckles wickedly. Two thick fingers pump in and out of my wet core. They flex and curl while his thumb presses against my clit.

I cum, back bowed with a strangled moan.

Lachlan sucks his digits into his mouth and groans around them. Emerald eyes dance.

"Délicieuse, Ma Douce Fille," he says.

Also fluent in French I understand him and purr in response.

This has to be the happiest day of my life, I sigh contentedly.

THE BLISSFUL WEEK passes in a blur of lovemaking, fucking while bound to his bed, and eating food and Lachlan, my absolute favorite treat. We never left his penthouse, preferring to remain in our own bubble.

While he's in the kitchen preparing breakfast in bed, I scroll through the messages on my mobile. I have a meeting at STEELE London tomorrow afternoon, so I want to be sure I have missed no updates from my administrative assistant Douglas Washington.

I come across a few things that need my attention, so I call him.

"Hi, Haley. I presume you saw my email?" Douglas says. "I'll load my notes to your system."

Harris and I are less formal with our admins and teams than our brothers are with theirs. My twin and I go by our first names, and everyone wears business casual. Although each team member has a garment bag with a business suit and the appropriate accessories in case we have an unexpected meeting to attend. Who wants to sit around writing code or monitoring the web in a stuffy tie and high heels? It's the techie in us.

I pick up my tablet when the notification for a file share appears. We discuss the details and the plan for tomorrow.

Distracted by our conversation, I don't notice Lachlan return to the bedroom until his tongue circles my bare nipple and suckles. I forewent clothes. Who needs them when entwined with a hunk like Lachlan?

I yelp and drop my mobile. Then scramble to pick it back up. I shoot Lachlan a not-so-irate glare.

He chuckles and bites into a chocolate-filled croissant.

I roll my eyes.

"Great, thanks so much… Right… See you then," I ring off.

"Who will you see soon?" Lachlan asks, eyebrow raised.

I make a show of scanning my tablet and respond nonchalantly, "Oh, that's just Earl. My other lover flew in to see—"

The air whooshes from my lungs as Lachlan wrestles me flat on my back. Through my hair covering my face, I see his emerald green eyes glitter with possessive fire. Oh dear…

"You have no other lover, Haley Steele!" He growls. "Now or ever. Do you understand, Naughty Girl?"

Oooh, punishment time! Who knew little sister was a pain slut?! Certainly not me, I giggle to myself and wiggle my hips.

In a flash, he flips me to my belly and binds my wrists by white silks to the posts. The resounding smacks of flesh on flesh fill the air when he spanks each of my ass cheeks. I squeal. Then he catches my flailing legs and binds my ankles to the other posts.

Once again, a curtain of hair covers my face, so I can't see him over my shoulder. But I sure do hear him.

"What did I tell you? You are mine and mine alone, Naughty Girl. Not even in jest do you mention another man to me," Lachlan rumbles in my ear, palms on either side of my head. His bare chest and black silk-covered legs press me into the mattress.

I squirm against his burgeoning erection between my stinging ass cheeks.

He nips my earlobe and straddles my thighs.

"Be… still," he says as he spanks my ass. "Twenty will remind you, only Lachlan. Thank me as you count. Miss and we begin again. Do you understand?"

I blow my hair from my mouth and respond, "Yes, Sir."

I've noticed how much it turns Lachlan on whenever I refer to him as *Sir*. It just came naturally to me. Now, I make certain to say it to get him amped up. I love the way I can make this dominant man lose some of his control!

But the first contact of his sizable palm on my ass brings me back to reality.

"One, thank you, Sir!" I yelp.

I make it to thirteen before I falter. Lachlan chuckles wickedly and rubs the hot, sore flesh with the calloused tips of his fingers. I hiss at the contact and bow my head. Damn.

We start anew. But his blows hold less heat until we get to fourteen. I guess he wants to give me a reprieve since

I'm new to all of this. But boy, do the last six remind me never to mention another man to him again. Whew!

The tender way he massages cool gel into my punished backside as he murmurs soothing words makes up for the pain. Even more so when two of his thick fingers caress the sopping wet seam of my pussy and tug on my engorged clit.

I climax with a wail across his muscular thighs.

Lachlan positions me on my hands and knees, then the whisper of silk precedes him plunging his ginormous cock deep inside of my spasming pussy. He grunts and growls as he pummels my pussy. Each thrust of his hips snap against my punished backside to reignite the bite of pain.

But I'm too far gone to feel it. My vision darkens and sound escapes me. If Lachlan did not hold me aloft, I would collapse to the mattress in a sated heap, mind blown by the carnality of our fucking.

Lachlan's roar of his release barely registers. Nor does his gentle touch rouse me as he cleans my body with a warm, wet cloth. Only the woodsy scent of his cologne combined with his natural pheromones permeates my haze. Innately, I recognize my mate and cuddle in his powerful embrace.

"Rest, Sweet Girl."

LACHLAN

"The Jackson Cabernet Sauvignon vineyard produced an exceptional harvest this year. The grapes impressed the vintner more so than usual. We expect to…"

Even though I know I should focus on my weekly executive team status meeting at Jackson Town House, my mind drifts back to the week Haley and I spent together.

I'm still amazed she met me, and we consummated our relationship finally. And boy, did we make us official. As I envision her bodacious virginal body writhing beneath me, bound in my silks, my cock hardens.

Fuck, My Baby Girl felt so good.

To hear her calling my name in pure ecstasy was the most enthralling of her Siren Songs yet. Followed by the little squeals and contented sighs from the pain of my palm on her plump pussy lips and round ass. My palm itches from the memory.

Now that I realize My Baby Girl is a natural sub and enjoys a bit of pain with her pleasure, I can introduce her to my world of BDSM. The silks and spankings are only a taste. I don't keep toys and such in my residences since I never bring my hookups home. Instead, my implements stay in my suite at STEELE Aberdeen and at the ones I maintain at LEVELS London and LEVELS Paris.

I am not a sadist.

It's the control and pushing of limits to bring the woman erotic bliss she's never known before that thrill me. My release is secondary to hers. I view making a woman come undone for me as an art form. One I take seriously and pride myself on.

To hone my skills as an Alpha Dom, I trained for two years as a sub to one of London's grandest Dommes. Even though I'm a Master, we still play a few times a year. Now we must ask My Little Temptress if she would take part as the sub while the Domme observes us play for her feedback on my Dom role.

I'm sure My Little Temptress won't mind me improving ways to heighten her pleasure.

"Mr. Jackson?"

I'm pulled from my musings to find all eyes of those gathered around the conference room table pointed in my direction.

"Pardon. Kindly repeat that last part," I say as I shift in my leather chair to adjust my bulge.

My Vice President of Liquor nods and tells me she thinks it's a good idea for a site visit to the vineyard in

Bordeaux. Her recommendation of next week conflicts with a rendezvous planned with My Baby Girl in London.

By the time my VP finishes the rest of her report, I decide to take the trip with My Baby Girl. LEVELS London or a château in Médoc? I'm sure she'll enjoy a week in the romantic locale.

I chuckle to myself at how I've turned into a wuss quickly. Especially after I teased Baz about him being gaga over Lola. My laugh stops just as fast as it started when I recall Haley's reaction to my request we keep our relationship private.

"A secret?! You want to keep me hidden?!" She screeches as she stands akimbo and shoots lethal platinum daggers at me.

I shake my head hurriedly and reach for her. She swats my hands away and steps back.

"Haley, not a secret or hidden. Rather kept to ourselves," I respond. When she scoffs, I add, "For now. Sebastian will lose his shit, and you know it. Let's have some time to ourselves before anyone tries to intervene in our relationship."

Realization dawns on her face. She knows her big brother—not to mention the other three and perhaps even Morgan—will not appreciate me fucking their little sister and daughter. She's off-limits. Despite me being so close to their family.

Above me being Baz's best friend who should remain hands off with his kid sister, their other major concern will be my Alpha Dom proclivities. Then there's Baz's probable assumption I lied to him all those years ago and since. Talk about a loss of trust. It could finish our friendship and impact our business partnerships.

Baz does not play with people fucking with him or his family. And I'm literally fucking his little sister...

So I wait for Haley to grasp the magnitude of our forbidden love affair. It doesn't take long.

Her shoulders droop as she lowers her hands to her sides in defeat. She won't meet my eyes as I walk towards her. Instead, she pushes her glasses up the bridge of her nose and crosses her arms over her breasts—nervous and defensive.

Already with no effort on their part, The Big Four create a separation between us. Great.

"Hey, it's okay. You are a forbidden fruit that tempts me beyond reason. And I will not stay away from you any longer. I just don't want anyone coming between us. Not so soon after we've begun. Do you understand?" I say as I hold her hips and stare into her stormy gray eyes.

When Haley cups my face and brushes my stubbled cheeks, I kiss her palm.

"It's just not fair, Lachlan. All this time, and we have to hi—I mean keep our relationship to ourselves. No one ever interfered with my brothers and all the women they've fucked over the years. Just because Baz finally settled down, doesn't erase his playboy ways!" She says vehemently.

"I agree with you, Baby Girl," I admit. "But you trust me to not hurt you, right?"

Her eyes search deep into mine, and I keep an open expression. No guile found. She nods.

"I do. So fine. For now..." she says with her head tilted and eyebrow arched.

"For now," I repeat for the second time.

She kisses me, and I know we'll be fine. For now.

We also agreed to meet somewhere in the world for a week each month. Just not in New York and in Aberdeen. Too many people know us in those cities. Not worth the risk. At all.

The times in between prove almost as steamy as our in-person week due to our vivid, no-holds-barred FaceTime calls. Whether My Baby Girl does an award-worthy strip-tease set to "Don't Cha" by the Pussycat Dolls, I jerk off naked in the shower, or we role play to my commands, both of us reach intense levels of climaxes. To say we're creative doesn't quite describe our video calls.

Still, I can't wait to get my hands on all of her luscious-ness. Not to mention kiss her silly and hold her close. Our post-coital bliss brings us closer with aftercare and spoon-ing. Nothing compares to the feel of My Baby Girl in my arms as she slumbers peacefully.

Next week is our first tryst. I'm glad for my VP's suggestion I meet with the vintner. The location poses no threat to Haley and me being together in the open. She will appreciate me showing her off at dinner with the team there and touring the vineyard and the surrounding area. I'm looking forward to it.

Once the status meeting ends, I thank everyone and head to my offices. I nod or chat briefly with high-ranking staff as I pass through the executive floor. Even though I'm the only full-time Jackson here, everyone keeps a suite of offices spread throughout the floor.

A sense of pride wells inside of my chest as I pass the portraits of past generations who founded and helped continue the legacy of Jackson Corporation. Starting with the founder who created the finest single malt Scotch Whiskey and set us on the path to the most renowned liquor company in the world. Then successors of each generation follow with my father last. The spot next to him remains blank.

He still harps on me taking over instead of Lydie. But we'll see.

I let my gaze roam. The executive floor has offices for our legal, finance, operations, and technology departments, along with various conference rooms. Our other divisions have designated floors below. The productive employees move about busy at their tasks. The hum of their conversations and activities mixes with the soft classical music piped in through the surround sound system.

The decor highlights the Old World feel of the landmark property built by our founders of the famous Aberdeen granite. Jackson Town House is the second largest granite building in the world. A palette of caramel and Bordeaux hues with gold accents reminiscent of our Scotch and wines blend with the dark mahogany woods and leather furniture, crystal light fixtures, and original artwork. The reception area has a spacious desk. Three attractive receptionists with headsets in their ears and custom-tailored caramel-colored dress suits and skin-tone heels that serve as uniforms sit behind it.

I greet them as I pass silently on the Aubusson rugs.

My steps continue until I reach my outer office where I have a reception area, conference room, and Gladys Sinclair and Isla Ritchie—my personal and administrative assistants, respectively—sit at their desks. Both smart and dedicated to their jobs, I count them as integral parts of my team.

"Mr. Jackson, I just put a call through to your voicemail from the general manager at Distillery No. 4. Not urgent, but he did request you to call at your earliest convenience. Your one o'clock lunch confirmed and will meet you downstairs in the bar of the Jackson Restaurant," Isla—the younger of the two in her late twenties—tells me. Gladys is in her early forties.

Talk about impact of generations. Lucien turned the restaurant into a three Michelin star eatery his first year as chef. His versions of traditional Scottish fare combined with skills he learned at Le Cordon Bleu earned him the recognition. It's one of my go-to spots to eat in all of Aberdeen.

"Thank you," I respond, then shift to include Gladys. "I'm going to Médoc next Saturday for a week. Kindly coordinate with the VP of Wine to schedule a tour, meeting, and dinner with the vintner and his team. I have a plus one. And book my jet. The crew can return home after they drop me off, then pick me up at the end of my trip. Thanks."

I leave them and close my office door behind me. My eyes go to the bank of windows that face Union Street. It's

Aberdeen's major street and shopping thoroughfare. Tourists and residents mingle as they go about their days. Cars and buses zip by for destinations known to their occupants. Normally, I take time to gaze at the sights.

Not now. I have a call to make. And not to the GM at Distillery No. 4...

"Hi, Baby Girl. Do you have a moment?" I ask after a few rings.

"Hold on," she responds breathlessly.

A muffled, excuse me a minute, and rustling fabric before she's back on the line.

"Hi!" She says excitedly.

It's infectious, and I grin like the Cheshire Cat.

Wuss.

"Hi! I know we're supposed to meet in London next Saturday, but—"

A disappointed sigh comes through.

I rush on.

"No, no, we're still getting together, babe! But I have to visit our vineyard in Médoc. I hope we can spend our week at the Jackson Château. We can tour the property, sample the new harvest, have—"

"Oh, Lachlan! That's a marvelous idea! I can't wait!" Haley exclaims in a low voice. "Text the details to me so I can have my pilot revise the flight plan. But I have to go. I'm training with Borya, and he's growling at me for being on the phone."

I growl and gnash my teeth at the thought of the giant

Russian Borya *The War Defender* Alexeyev—her personal trainer and former MMA champion—giving her shit.

"He better back the fuck up off you!" I snarl.

My Baby Girl has the audacity to giggle.

"Okay, Caveman, calm down. It's just Borya. Do you think Baz and Malcolm would let me train with him if they didn't trust him? You know he's one of Malcolm's best buddies," she says. "But seriously, I'm cooling down, and that won't do. Kisses!!"

I stare at the blank screen of my mobile.

She hung up.

Well, damn.

I grumble to myself as I send the details to her via text message. Then I send a GIF of a man uppercutting another so hard he flies through the roof. That's what I'll do to Borya. Like Baz and Malcolm only know what's best for *my* woman.

Besides, I can more than handle the MMA badass. From the time I could walk—all of us, in fact—I studied Scottish martial arts. So I'm no fucking lightweight. Bare knuckle fighting, fencing with the Highland broadsword and targe, and archery. Scotsmen don't mess about when it comes to their lasses and bairns. I'll open a can of Scottish whip ass on the Russian, as Laurent says.

Mine!

Immediately My Baby Girl responds with several laughing emojis in tears followed by winking kisses. I send back a kiss as I plunk in my desk chair and wake my computer.

Time to get back to work. Little Haley Steele has hijacked enough of my work time.

And I'd have it no other way.

Wuss…

HALEY

"*E*njoy your stay, Ms. Steele. We'll see you for your return in a week."

"Thank you. The flight was wonderful as always, captain," I respond to my pilot and crew as I deplane from my Gulfstream G650ER private jet.

We landed at Bordeaux–Mérignac Airport, and I cannot wait to see my man! I glance around the tarmac from the top of the steps. My heart races when I spot him.

My gorgeous man stands beside a stunningly luxurious Bordeaux-colored Rolls-Royce convertible with cognac leather interior. I can't see his emerald eyes covered by green lens aviators, but his full lips curve into a broad grin on his tan face. Lachlan strides on his long muscular legs covered by dark denim jeans that hang low on his narrow hips and end with his feet in black suede driving shoes. He pushes up the sleeves of his hunter green cashmere v-neck sweater; the corded muscles of his forearms flex. The gold of his Rolex Bao Dai—his favorite watch—glints in the late morning sunlight. He runs one hand through his longish, sable brown hair and waves at me with the other.

Lachlan is the epitome of a young, sexy multibillionaire whose power and virility draw people to him like a magnet. Everyone wants a piece of him. But he's mine all mine!

I wave back and skip down the steps gleefully. Before my feet reach the tarmac, he swings me into his arms. My bags drop from my hands as I wrap my arms around his neck, laughing.

Damn, it's so good to see him!

Lachlan slants his mouth over mine and kisses me as I dangle in his firm embrace. Our tongues dance as both of us groan in anguish, our bodies drawn together.

"Need you. Now," he murmurs against my lips.

I moan and nip at his lower one in response.

He growls.

I purr.

Another nip and he stands me on my feet before he grabs my bags. A nod to the crew, and we head to his convertible. He opens the passenger door for me to slip inside. I blow a kiss to him as he walks around to put my luggage in the trunk.

My palms smooth out my Diane von Furstenberg wrap dress. I bought a whole bunch of the iconic style since he likes it the most. Plus, it's easy on and off!

"How was your flight, my beautiful girl?" Lachlan asks

as he settles in the driver's seat and brushes his lips against mine.

"Smooth. I did some work during most of it, so I won't have any distractions from my man," I respond with a grin. "You know he hates not commanding my full attention."

Lachlan smirks, "He sounds like a man after my own heart."

We laugh over the purr of the engine as we drive off.

During the ride to the Jackson Château, Lachlan points out various sights. Even though I've been here a few times throughout the years, I enjoy the ride in and seeing the picturesque landscape. We chat and enjoy being together after weeks apart.

The time passes quickly and as ever, the vision of the Jackson Château takes my breath away. It's like I'm a fairy-tale princess who stepped back in time to my castle.

The majestic nineteenth century château is at once uniquely charming and romantic with its two emblematic turrets. It represents the vineyard's heart as the areas of vines spread out from it like arteries. Previously owned by a French baron whose family built it in the mid-1800s, the Jackson family purchased it after they expanded the company from Scotch to wine. They maintain its splendor, and the vineyard continues to produce award-winning harvests sought after around the globe.

I giggle when I recall my dreadful double date David expounding upon the greatness of Jackson Cabernet Sauvignon. Little does he know…

"What's so funny?" Lachlan asks as we stop before the

château.

I shake my head and laugh.

"This guy I went on a double date with tried hard to persuade me to order your Cabernet Sauvignon. I didn't bother to tell him I'm close with the family!" I answer.

Silence descends on the car's interior. My laughing stops, and I turn to face Lachlan.

He sits with narrowed eyes bright with the possessiveness of his inner caveman.

Oh, dear…

"I presume this was not a recent 'double date,' Haley?" He asks quietly with an undercurrent of dominance.

I nod.

His eyes sharpen on me.

"Well, then, I do not need to know about your past… interests, do I? Or their utter stupidity," Lachlan says.

"Um, no, I guess not," I reply, then chew on my lower lip as butterflies churn in my belly.

Damn…

A low rumble comes from deep within his chest.

I raise my eyes to gauge his countenance.

A scowl mars his gorgeous face.

Damn.

Not wanting our week together to turn into sour grapes before it even gets started, I clasp his face between my palms and kiss him. I pour all of my desire for Lachlan into it. Every. Single. Ounce. He groans. Then he takes control of the kiss, lifting it to another level of need and possession that makes my hungry pussy clench.

I mewl into his mouth, and he swallows it up on a groan of his own.

We make out like horny teenagers seated in the convertible right in front of the château.

I give zero fucks who's watching our passion. When in France and all that...

The Jacksons occupy the top two floors as a residence while the other two function as a luxury hotel, spa, restaurant, and special events space—typically weddings. I mean, who wouldn't want a fairytale ceremony set in this surreal place?

Lachlan loosens his grip on the nape of my neck and presses his forehead to mine.

"Promise me you will never mention your time—any time—with another man again, Baby Girl," he says.

"I promise, Lachlan," I vow.

He nods and steps out of the car.

The valet and bellhop who stood to the side pretending not to stare at our PDA greet Lachlan by name and take the keys from him and my luggage from the trunk.

Lachlan helps me from the car and holds my hand as we stroll towards the entry, arm in arm. We appear no different from the couples who mill about the grounds or in the central hall. The difference is we head to an area behind stanchions with a tapestry that covers an archway. As though is ordinary, Lachlan takes my bags from the bellhop and holds the elaborate piece that depicts the surrounding landscape to the side to usher me behind it.

We step into an alcove with a locked door. He enters a

code, and the door opens to a staircase. We climb up to the third floor and out into a grand room with corridors leading to other areas of the Jackson's private quarters.

"Come, we'll get you settled in my suite," Lachlan says as he takes my hand and leads me to the far end of the well-appointed space.

His set of rooms overlook the ornamental pool that stretches before the front of the château. The water's silvery expanse conceals an underground cellar with views of the water and of the sky. It's an architectural marvel people know the estate for.

As I stand before the windows, hands reach around my waist to rest on my lower belly and a firm chest presses against my back. I lean into Lachlan's embrace with a content sigh. Better than seeing him is being in his arms.

"I missed you so much, Baby Girl," he murmurs against the delicate shell of my ear.

His warm breath sends tingles down my spine to pool in my core.

"I missed you more," I reply.

Lachlan sighs and steps back.

The heat of his body goes with him, and I groan at the loss.

"I arranged for us to have an early lunch since you're probably hungry after your flight," he says.

I turn and place my hands on his chest.

"Only for you, Lachlan," I say. "You will fill me and slake my need."

His eyes flare with emerald fire.

"Well then, let us get you fed, Baby Girl," he says huskily.

He presses down on my shoulders.

I lower gracefully to my knees before him. His nostrils flare as I peek up at his face through my eyelashes.

"Such a good girl, Little Temptress."

He rubs my head as he praises me, and I arch into his body, eyes closed and a mewl falling from my lips.

The tug on my scalp as his fingers twine in my hair pulls my head back. My eyes pop open.

"Our FaceTime calls are nice and all. But I prefer the feel of your plump lips around my turgid girth," Lachlan says. "Now, you will take every one of my ten inches in your sweet, wet mouth. All the way to the back of your throat and suck me off without spilling one single drop."

Without the slightest hesitation, I reach up to unbutton and unzip his jeans to lower them past his hips. His bulging cock tents the black silk of his boxer briefs. I hook my fingers into the waistband and tug them over his dick and down his muscular thighs.

I heft the weight of his heavy balls and stroke them before I lean forward and lick the bead of pre-cum off of his bulbous tip with my tongue. I hum around his girth in mutual pleasure when he groans as I take him to the back of my throat.

I glance up again and smile, satisfied that Lachlan has his hands braced on the window frame, head thrown back, and mouth slack as more groans slip out.

I turn my attention back to his dick and really go at it.

Drawing him in deep with my lips pressed all the way down his shaft to press against his manscaped crotch. I pull back to swirl the tip of my tongue around his head. Then follow up with a long lick along the vein on the underside of his length to his balls. To add to the sensation, I suck his full sac into my mouth and stroke it with my tongue. Minutes later, the muscles in Lachlan's thighs tremble, and his cock grows larger, throbbing under my ministrations.

Lachlan grips my hair again to lock my head in place as his hips snap to fuck my throat. His eyes are wild and his lip curls, a guttural snarl ripping from his mouth as an abundant amount of his semen spews down my throat. I don't spill a drop as I seal my lips around his cock and swallow repeatedly.

"Damn, Baby Girl," Lachlan groans as his dick—still large, even when flaccid—slips from my mouth with a pop. He sinks to his knees, staring at me in amazement.

I grin. My goal is to master the pleasure I can give to Lachlan. So I did what I do best, I researched the Internet for videos and commentary on blow jobs. They don't call me a geek for nothing!

WE SPEND the rest of the weekend in his family's section of the château, not wanting to be disturbed while we catch up. On Monday, Lachlan and the head of the vineyard give me a tour. So many recent additions and updates since I last visited ten years ago. They impress me with their use of technology, and I offer suggestions to improve their systems.

While Lachlan meets with the team, I head to the spa. After all the hours of making love, my sore muscles need some pampering!

The facility is one addition made in the last few years. Rather than letting the extracts from the grape and grapevine during wine production go to waste, they recycle them for spa treatments—vinotherapy. Now, they produce skincare and haircare products sold to spas all over the world. I leave the spa feeling refreshed, buffed to perfection, and ready for dinner.

I take a last glance at myself in the full-length mirror, pleased with my outfit choice for tonight. A beige crocheted wool mini dress with a fitted long-sleeved bodice that has a flared bottom made of varying detailed ruffles starting below my breasts. It's flirty and feminine, yet sexy. I paired it with a black leather pouch handbag and five-inch black patent leather gladiator sandals. I left my hair flowing down my back in waves and simple makeup. Diamond hoops complete my look.

A wolf whistle makes me jump around.

Lachlan!

I didn't hear him come into the dressing room I use. He leans against the doorjamb in a navy blue suit with a white dress shirt and a green silk tie. His eyes rove over my body appreciatively, and I feel my nipples pucker against the wool of my dress. He smirks.

"Don't you look lovely, Baby Girl," he drawls.

I twirl and thank him with a smirk of my own.

"And aren't you a handsome devil," I tell him.

He chuckles and prowls towards me. He pulls a flat box from his trousers pocket and holds it up to me.

I glance from it to him with a raised eyebrow.

"For you. A memento for our time here," Lachlan says.

I press the cabochon closure and gasp at large earrings made of wine-colored clusters of diamonds set in yellow gold. The rare gems sparkle.

He slips them from the black velvet and holds them out on his palm to me.

"Lachlan, you shouldn't have—"

"Nonsense. You will accept all that I give you, Little Temptress. Every single thing," he says suggestively.

I bite my lower lip, still hesitant to accept such an incredible gift.

"Haley..." he warns.

To hell with it. They're incredible!

I slip my hoops out and place them on the center island. When I glance back in the mirror, my new jewels bring a smile to my face. I will forever remember our week here every time I wear them.

"Gorgeous, My Baby Girl," Lachlan murmurs as he stands behind me. Our gazes lock in the mirror's reflection.

I spin around and show him my appreciation with a passionate toe-curling kiss.

A girl can get used to this treatment.

For life.

"*Chérie*! Look at you! You glow like a woman in love! So tell me, who is the lucky man? And I'm sure your overly protective brothers can't possibly know!"

I gape, shocked Leonie sees a change in me. Her amber eyes glow like *The Lion* she's named after. I feel like a gazelle trapped in her steady, feline gaze.

Damn!

My stricken expression makes her laugh. The sound tinkles in the air around us as we have lunch at Le Café Marly in the Louvre. Her glossy mahogany mane shimmers as her shoulders shake. Leonie is more beautiful than the paintings and sculptures within the museum and more iconic than I. M. Pei's Pyramid in the courtyard.

Born to a Tunisian mother and a Parisian father, her stellar looks catapulted her to the stratosphere of a megamodel. Leonie became the most photographed face of fashion, signed multiple contracts including spokesmodel for Lola's Coterie, and editors named her Queen of the Catwalk. Now she splits her time between modeling and working at STEELE Paris part time as a junior designer. She completed her coursework and final project in interior design at the Paris American Academy a few months ago.

I'm working out of the Paris office on a project. So it's after our morning meetings we got together for lunch.

"Oh, don't look so surprised, *cherie*," Leonie says as she waves her hand. "I'll never tell! Even if Roger pleads with me. I promise. Us girls must stick together! So spill."

I'm torn because I'd love to share with Leonie and Lola, who have become close friends for me since they dated my brothers. But I gave my word to Lachlan I would keep our relationship private. So even though I'm sure Leonie wouldn't give me up to Roger, I can't tell her. A bummer, but the way it has to be.

I hate to lie, so I give a partial truth.

"My physical exertion has increased lately. It really gets my blood pumped and heats me up from the inside out," I respond with a straight face.

Leonie's lips quirk as her elegant eyebrow arches. She takes a moment to study my face.

It takes everything in me not to squirm under her intense assessment. She's picked up on Roger's habit of staring into your soul with his serious gaze—a trait from our mother. I hold firm as I press the pads of my fingers into my lap to keep them from sliding my glasses up my nose.

"Okay. Well, in that case, I need to sign up for *that* class!" Leonie laughs again.

Inwardly, I sigh with relief but maintain my composure. I take a sip of my Jackson Chardonnay and try not to think of my man. But I can't help it when I roll the liquid over my tongue and pretend it's his essence coating my mouth. Mmmmmm.

"Speaking of love, tell me about working with Roger in his Residential Division," I tell Leonie, going for the distraction.

She grins and claps her hands, shimmying in her seat—as she and Lola are wont to do when they're happy.

"I've always loved the aesthetically pleasing things in life. It's in my blood as the daughter of a long line of merchants thanks to my Beaulieu heritage," she begins. "Modeling just happened. One day I'm walking down the Rue Saint-Honoré and voilà! I'm on the cover of American *Vogue* at 16! But I never forgot my roots and my love of design. Work at STEELE is a dream come true! Even if my father still wants me to head Beaulieu Enterprises SAS when he retires in a few years."

She adds the last part with a forlorn expression on her face.

Beaulieu Enterprises is her family's multibillion-dollar company that specializes in antiques, antiquities, and fabrics. It was founded by her father's prominent Parisian family of merchants who date back to the Merchant Court of the eighteenth-century. From the French royal court to the grand bazaars of the Mediterranean Sea, they traveled seeking those aesthetically pleasing items. Leonie grew up surrounded by many of them in *Le Beaulieu Manoir,* their family's ancestral estate on the outskirts of Paris.

Her sadness turns into a smile as she raves about her new job and the projects she's working on. Only when she mentions some former classmates who work as interns treating her funny since she's dating the president does the light dim in her eyes. But the fierce lion she is roars back when she tells me how she bested the female classmate by impressing the project manager with her historical knowledge of the building they're working on.

While we chat, I enjoy my lobster salad Le Café Marly is renowned for, and Leonie eats the truffle fettuccine. The restaurant buzzes with the hum of other patrons' conversations and their cutlery on tableware. A few men do a double take and all but drool when they recognize *The Lion.* She's oblivious, so accustomed to fans and paparazzi. We end our meal with strawberry sorbet and fresh fruit with tea.

"I'm looking forward to Thanksgiving next month. Usually Lola would come over to *Le Beaulieu Manoir* and cook. My mother loves she has a daughter in the kitchen to share her family's traditional Tunisian recipes with finally. That is one who didn't burn water!" Leonie tells me as she cracks up.

I giggle, imagining her trying to cook. Not her forte… or mine!

"It's the Jackson's turn this year. You'll love the history and pieces in their collection at their family seat Jackson

Castle in Banff. It's just north of Aberdeen where their headquarters are located. Just as King Louis XV bestowed acreage on your ancestors, King James VI titled the Jackson family as Marquess of Huntly with their seat in Aberdeenshire. Uncle Connor and Aunt Lucie use their titles. But Lachlan—even though he's the heir apparent—and his siblings don't go all formal and use theirs regularly. But it's awesome to have!" I tell her.

"I cannot wait! Roger told me how Lucie met Connor while she was a bartender in one of their pubs in New York City. Now she's a marchioness! It's so romantic," Leonie exclaims. "Now that we're on the topic of romance, Lola and Sebastian return from their honeymoon soon. Two months of bliss!"

"It'll be good to see them," I say, despite the butterflies that take flight in my belly.

I'm so nervous Baz may figure out Lachlan and me. Consider how easily Leonie detected a change in me after five seconds... That's why I'm so glad he'll come to Paris and stay for a while to catch up on business then go to Jackson Castle.

At least that way, I won't have to see him face-to-face until Thanksgiving. I head to our offices in Singapore in a few days, then swing through Las Vegas before I make a stop in New York City, then fly to Scotland. No one will find it odd I'm visiting some of our global offices for system checks and client meetings. Harris just made a similar trip last month.

Fortunately, Lachlan planned a trip to Vegas to coincide

with my time there. We'll have a little rendezvous before we face our families at once. Whatever happens in Vegas stays in Vegas. And we need to keep our relationship under wraps.

After a while, Leonie and I return to STEELE Paris. Leonie goes to a meeting with her team, and we part ways with a hug and double kisses. On my way to my offices, I stop by Roger's. His assistant Françoise Faucher greets me and lets me know he's free. I thank her and knock on his door.

"Come in," he calls out, then stands with a grin when he sees it's me. "Hey little sis! How was lunch? Where's Leonie? Oh, right, she has a team meeting now."

I giggle at him, knowing her schedule by heart.

"Okay, silly, lovestruck boy!" I tease as we hug. "Stalker much?"

Roger's cheeks heat, and he lowers his head to hide his smirk. He leans his butt against his desk, then slides his hands in his trouser pockets. His intense gaze meets mine.

"I'll remember that, smarty pants," he says while the corners of his mouth curl up in a smile. "By the way, I noticed your busy schedule over the next few weeks. You're not staying in one place for long, huh? Any reason in particular?"

Now it's my turn to blush scarlet and drop my gaze to the floor. I lower myself into one of his leather guest chairs. Of course, Roger *The Responsible* would pick up on my itinerary. So much for stealth maneuvers…

I gather myself and go for the partial truth again.

"Hmmm, well, let me think… Oh, I know what could have me traveling to STEELE offices around the world… W-O-R-K!" I reply sassily with an eye roll.

Roger chuckles, "Cute, Haley, real cute. It is my duty to know all that happens with you, Harris, Malcolm, Sebastian, and now Leonie and Lola, in general. Even more so with Baz on his honeymoon and Malcolm and I in charge."

I feel bad. For a minute. Then grin at him.

"I know, Big Brother Number 3, and I appreciate you very much," I concede. "It's a knee-jerk reaction honed over the years of having not one but *four* overly protective brothers. Give a girl a break sometime."

"Don't you have a meeting in, oh… fifteen minutes?" Roger says as he glances at his Platinum Rolex Day-Date pointedly.

I jump up and kiss his cheek, then dash for the door. Whew! So close.

His laughter follows me.

I love my family and hate to not let them know. But I love—

The thought catches me off guard. My steps falter as I hurry down the corridor. A hand goes to my heart, thumping with the increase of my pulse. Well damn…

I take a moment to reflect.

All of these years Lachlan has been around me in some way, and I've always been attracted to him, even as a kid, before I realized what my feelings meant. It's always been as though I just knew we were destined to be together. So after two glorious months as a couple—albeit in secret—I can admit my love for him fully.

I, Haley Steele, love Lachlan Jackson.

And like him, it burns deep within me to not allow anyone to separate us. I take a deep breath to slow my heartbeat, certain a partial truth is worth not losing the love of my life.

I gaze at the world-famous view of the Las Vegas Strip at night. It sparkles like rare and exceptionally rare, fancy color diamonds through the floor-to-ceiling windows of STEELE Las Vegas Resort & Casino. The five-diamond property features two towers with the mall between them from the ground level to the third floor. A bridge comprising six floors for exclusive twelve penthouse suites connects the two towers. The Bridge Penthouses cater to high rollers and the über-wealthy clientele.

On countless occasions, I've stayed in Baz's penthouse for Guys' Getaways. This time I'm in one the rest of the family uses when they're in town for pleasure or for business. And My Baby Girl holds the key.

At first, I balked at staying in a STEELE hotel since I'd rather not risk us being recognized. But she told me it would be suspicious if she didn't stay at their property. Add us being amongst the sheer numbers of guests in and out of the hotel, it's unlikely anyone would notice us. I had to agree with her.

My flight landed earlier this evening. So Haley had the hotel driver who picked me up from McCarran International Airport bring a key card to access the private elevator and the penthouse. She explained I could bypass the check-in process for the Bridge Penthouses.

A walk through the main lobby led me to the etched-glass double doors for the separate foyer. The doorman opened them to allow me entry as I walked past the two security guards dressed in dark suits with transparent ear communications pieces. Since I had the key, I could whiz past the three reception and two concierge desks, four sitting areas, and walk to the bank of three private elevators.

Now I wait impatiently for My Baby Girl to arrive. I glance at my Patek Philippe—my lucky watch I inherited from my great-grandfather, when in Vegas and all that— even though I checked only moments ago. Her jet lands in twenty minutes plus ten to drive at the hotel. Thirty more long ass minutes to go. Damn.

With a disgruntled groan, I turn my back on the dazzling Strip and stride to the bar. I might as well have a drink while I wait. When I arrived, I ordered My Baby's Girl's favorite dishes from Lucien's New Orleans restaurant in the hotel: crawfish étouffée, asparagus salad, and a fresh-baked baguette with Bananas Foster for dessert. It's due in forty minutes. Enough time for her to change and to have a cocktail.

She'll need all the energy she can get. Once she's here, I do not plan to let her leave this suite for a minute. She'll count herself lucky if I allow her to get out of bed for more than a bathroom break. I don't care she's here for work. *We have unfinished business…*

I adjust my burgeoning hard-on commando beneath my black sweatpants. Then I push up the sleeve of my t-shirt to check the time again. Eight minutes passed. Grrrrr!

Drink in hand, I stalk back to the windows for the distraction of the fountains. It's time for one of their spectacular displays set to the classic tunes of Ol' Blue Eyes himself—the inimitable Mr. Frank Sinatra.

The first strains of "I've Got You Under My Skin" filter through the surround sound speakers in the penthouse. I snort as my lips touch the rim of the Waterford Crystal snifter with two fingers of Jackson Special Blend Scotch. Damn if that's not my relationship with My Baby Girl in a nutshell. I'm not going to resist. Damn Baz's warning voice in my ear.

Fortunately, he's been on his honeymoon, so Haley and I have had some peace. With his return next month, he'll have his Big Brother all-seeing googles on. The big test will be during Thanksgiving at Jackson Castle. My hope is Lola will prove such a distraction for him, Baz will have little time to pay attention to anyone else—really Haley and me.

I let the sophisticated amber liquid roll around on my tongue and touch every point of my palate. Perfection.

For a moment I allow my mind to stray to business. I have a new blend my Chief Distiller and I are working on. It's my pet project since I started in the liquor department nine years ago. The goal is a premium smooth Scotch. The longer the liquor remains aging in the barrels, the more the oak wood breaks down the coarser flavor in the alcohol. We went with a distinct smoky apple flavor combined with the malted barley and other proprietary ingredients. So far, we're pleased.

Arms wrap around my flanks to rest delicate hands on my lower abs and pillowy tits press into my back. The elegant and intense scent of Acqua di Parma - Gelsomino Nobile wafts into my nostrils. Warm, sweet breath blows against my ear.

My Baby Girl!

"Hello, handsome. Who's on your mind so deeply? Should I be jealous?" She purrs seductively as her fingertips trace the defined ridges of my eight-pack.

So engrossed in my thoughts, I didn't hear My Baby Girl approach me. She's early. Thank fuck!

Her fingers dip lower to tease my shaft with her nails. My cock lengthens and thickens under her erotic touch, pleased to feel her again.

My head falls back, eyes closed. A throaty groan slips from my mouth as my hips grind my groin into her hand. Blood rushes from the rest of my body to fill my hungry cock. Her continued erotic massage makes me hard as steel. Fuck! If My Baby Girl doesn't stop, I'll blow my load like a horny teenager. No longer in control like the thirty-three-year-old Alpha Dom I am.

I accustomed my body to regular release. Three weeks of whacking off doesn't slacken my need. At. All.

Plus, she's had a long flight and should eat. Food for now, that is…

"Babe," I groan as I turn in her arms and cup her gorgeous face in my hands. "You are the only woman on my mind. I miss you like mad. But you'll have me fucking you raw against this window if you don't stop now."

Her pupils dilate, making her platinum grays obsidian. She rises to her toes and nips at my bottom lip as she purrs seductively.

"Lachlan… don't tease me," My Baby Girl moans. One leg after the other wraps around my hips as she climbs onto me like a little monkey, arms around my neck. "I missed you so much. I need you. Now."

I close my eyes and take a deep breath in an attempt to calm my urges.

But when she humps her warm pussy through the silk of her thong against my cock, I lose it. Control be damned.

I spin us around, and her back slams into the window. Thank fuck it's reinforced.

"I won't be gentle, Little Temptress," I warn as I bite her plump lower lip between my teeth with a feral growl.

She doesn't even bother to respond—in words, that is. She simply yanks on the string of my sweatpants and dives her hand below the waistband to grab my junk.

If I weren't so far gone in a lust haze, I would chuckle at

the frown of concentration on her face as she shifts her hips up to align my cock with her bare pussy.

We groan in unison when I slide home in her creamy core.

The soft yielding of her feminine flesh intoxicates me as I tighten my grasp on her ass to hold her steady. I pull my hips back to draw out to my tip, then ram into her, possessing My Little Temptress fully.

"I miss you. I crave you," I murmur hoarsely in her ear as a strangled cry falls from her lips.

My body demands a relentless pace as I piston in and out of her more than willing body. She meets each of my thrusts with her own as her fingernails dig into my back.

"Oh, my God!!! Lachlan…. Fuck! Harder… Oh, yes! Just like that… Right there!!!" She screams when I change the upward angle to hit her G-spot.

The muscles in my thighs and ass flex, and my biceps bulge from my grip, strong enough to leave marks from my fingers on her soft skin.

Tremors from her pussy hint at the climax building inside of My Little Temptress. Her breath catches as her head falls back against the window with a thunk and her inner thighs squeeze my hips. Then she falls over the edge into erotic bliss. My name a moan on her parted lips.

Now, it's my turn.

I put her on her feet, facing the window, palms on the glass, and bent at the waist to a ninety-degree angle with her feet spread wide. One hand grips her hip while the other wraps around her throat. Held in place, I mount her in one swift thrust.

"Uh!" My Little Temptress grunts from the invasion of her dripping pussy by my girth. Her palm slaps the window as she drops her forehead to it.

I plunder her pussy as I growl possessively in her ear.

My words fuel her carnal passion. She bucks against my long strokes, arching her back to take me deeper.

Moan for groan, we go as I ride her through another toe-curling orgasm. As the last flutter of her pussy walls skims across my cock, I go for broke.

My groin pounds against her ass between spanks to each cheek. She gets wetter, and the squelching of her sopping pussy fills the living room. Steam from her hot breath clouds the window. The scent of our fucking surrounds us.

And I go on.

"Take me. Take every single inch of my cock, Little Temptress! You want me… Well, you have me… All of me!" I roar as one, two, three thrusts, and I barrel over the edge to carnal oblivion.

My vision darkens.

My hearing fades.

A jolt of lightning zips from the top of my head down my spine to shoot out the tip of my dick. It unleashes a torrent of cum deep within her womb.

My knees give out.

I wrap my arms around her waist, pulling her onto my lap as I drop to the floor.

Fuck. Me.

"Oooh! Lachlan, baby! How did you know I was craving some crawfish étouffée?"

A wacky grin spreads across my face at My Baby Girl's delight in her dinner.

It was sheer luck the server arrived after we showered. Otherwise, he would have seen us passed out on the floor in a post-coital coma.

Instead, I let him in while Haley dried her hair.

Now she beams at me as she shimmies in her seat at the dining table. We're wrapped in silk kimonos—hers, a floral print on a gray background and mine in black. I picked them up for us on white I was in Tokyo for a meeting. Although I'd prefer she walk around naked, we need a bit of clothing when out of the bedroom.

"I know everything to know about you, Baby Girl. Remember that," I tell her with a wink.

Lucien used recipes our mother remembered from her family in New Orleans. When she's ready to throw down, as she says, she heads to the kitchen to cook some of her favorites.

The gumbo I selected from the menu being one of them. The hearty stew over rice proves just what I need to get *my* energy back. We've only begun.

"How was your flight and business meetings?" I ask Haley.

The passion she displays for her work rivals that of our

lovemaking. Her platinum gray eyes light from within as she rambles on about a new program she's developing to prevent hacking through some backend method. I do not know what she's speaking about, but I'm impressed by her enthusiasm.

"And you? How was your flight in?" She asks as she tears a piece of the baguette off and dips it into my gumbo with a grin.

The sight of the sauce dribbling down her chin mesmerizes me.

She giggles and reaches for her napkin.

I stay Haley's hand and walk over to crouch at her side. I grip her chin between my thumb and index finger before I lean in to lick the sauce from her face.

She bites her lower lip as her eyes flutter behind her glasses.

"Mmm. Even better," I say.

Her cheeks flush, and I chuckle wickedly.

She thinks she's so experienced now, but she's oh so innocent still.

My Sweet Baby Girl.

THE BEAT PUMPS as the DJ spins a sensuous mix of songs at the nightclub in STEELE Las Vegas. Lights flash around the darkened dance floor to spotlight twosomes or three-somes as they pump and grind to the music.

We have one night left, so I promised My Baby Girl

time out of the penthouse besides her work at STEELE. Her idea? Clubbing. Something I did not know.

When the beam lands on My Baby Girl, I groan at the sight of her in a micro mini dress made of what she calls metal mesh in sky blue. Mile-long legs on full display with glittery, five-inch, fuck-me strappy sandals. When she waves her arms overhead, the curve of her ass peeps below the hem.

I refer to it as a Lachlan is going to have to knock someone on their ass tonight dress. Proven by the men who gawked at her as we passed on our way to the VIP section. A few of them averted their gaze when my eyes locked on theirs. Others raised glasses in salute.

Wankers.

When I told her it was too revealing, My Baby Girl glared at me and stormed to the penthouse's elevator. She tossed over her shoulder, "You are not my father, Lachlan! Do not *dare* to act like my brothers!"

Ouch.

Thankfully, we're beyond that blip.

She spins and backs against my front, gliding her palms down my leather-clad thighs as she lowers towards the floor, shoulders shimmying. On the way back up, she bends at the waist to grind her ass into groin.

Good gotdamn!

Automatically, my hands grip her hips.

My Little Temptress tosses her long ebony waves over her shoulder and glances at me with a sly smile. Shy Haley is *not* in the house!

"Dancing with you is like fucking," I growl in her ear when she stands upright again.

She giggles and wraps her arms around my neck, tangling her fingers in my hair as she bumps her ass against my painfully erect cock. At only three inches apart in height, thanks to her sandals, she aligns right with me.

"Yeah?" My Little Temptress purrs against my lips. "Hmmm… So I feel, Mr. Jackson."

"And what are you going to do about it, Ms. Steele?" I respond with a nip to her lip.

She spins in my arms, and my hands land on her lush ass.

"Whatever you like," she breathes against the shell of my ear.

Fuck if I don't tremble.

"Time to go!" I say as I grab her hand and lead her off of the dance floor.

Her giggles reach my ears as she comes alongside me and holds onto my arm with her other hand.

It's a race from the nightclub through the casino and lobby to the Bridge Penthouses' reception onto the elevator. My Little Temptress matches my long strides, and we're making out on the way upstairs in no time.

"If it weren't for the hidden cameras, I'd give you a blow job to ease your ache," she pants as I place open-mouthed kisses on her exposed collarbone.

I growl, "No one sees you on your knees or in any other way but me, Naughty Girl. I do not share you. Not even for my pleasure. Understand?"

"Yes, Sir," she moans as she squeezes her thighs together. My dominance is a major turn on for her.

The elevator doors ping open, and I take her hand. Damn near at a sprint, we rush to the bedroom where My Little Temptress does all that I like all night long. And into the next day until we part at the airport.

How in the *hell* are we going to get through Thanksgiving without jumping each other?!

Damn.

"Hey, Hal, what's going on with you?"

I jump as my head swivels in Harris' direction. My twin stares at me in concern, then sits beside me on the window seat.

Last night I arrived at Jackson Castle after everyone but my mother and Aunt Lucie went to bed. Lachlan sent a text message to say hi and good night, since it would be odd for him to stay up for me. This morning I skipped breakfast with the excuse of a last-minute video conference meeting. I didn't want to fake it so early in the morning. The idea of being around both of our families and having to lie—rather tell partial truths—makes me ill physically.

Instead, I came to the library with my laptop. It's my favorite room with its views of their land, especially with the first snowfall of the season fresh on the ground.

The baroque mansion built in the early eighteenth century

replaced the original fortified castle the Jackson family erected two hundred years earlier. The giant status symbol has a four-story center structure with two grand curved east and west wings of three stories each. Six staircases, elaborate fireplaces, and elegant formal entertainment salons along with an extensive art collection make for a splendid interior.

The landscaped grounds are just as spectacular with carriage drives and horse trails, walking paths, and a few ornamental buildings including a chapel. Over five hundred acres along the coast of northeast Scotland comprise the Jackson family seat.

I tuck my legs underneath me and adjust my glasses as Harris sits down. He raises an eyebrow expectantly.

"What do you mean?" I ask with a shrug.

He cocks his head and blows out a breath.

"Well, first off, you haven't answered my calls with an actual call opting to send a text. You fly in late last night, even though I know you could have arrived earlier or flown in with me. Now, you've hidden yourself in the library while everyone else hangs out in the lounge or went riding," Harris responds as he ticks off each one on his fingers. "What gives, Hal?"

I try for nonchalance and hold up my laptop.

"Oh, just a meeting and some work," I say.

"Bullshit," Harris states.

My mouth gapes.

He knows me too well as I know him. We can't lie to one another, which is why I didn't speak with him over the phone. He would tell by the sound of my voice or by my hesitation to answer something was on my mind.

And this scenario is the exact reason I do not want to hide my relationship with Lachlan. I can't continue to lie to my family. It's not right. And he and I are not doing anything wrong.

"Give it a rest, Hal. We always share the status of our projects, and you've been mum or give some generic update. You've declined most of my invites to hang out," Harris says, holding up his hand. "So what are you hiding?"

I push my glasses up and start to speak, but a cough from the doorway interrupts my response. Harris and I turn in unison.

"Pardon me, guys. We're getting ready for lunch in a few minutes," Lachlan says as his gaze moves between Harris and me.

"Well, if it isn't the Lord of the Castle himself," Harris chortles with a bow. "How say you on this fine, brisk November morning, milord?"

"Funny, Harris. Hilarious as always," Lachlan responds dryly.

I gather my laptop and mobile in my Chanel crossbody bag, then skirt around both men to head for the door.

"Haley, may I have a word?"

Lachlan's request catches me off guard. I didn't expect him to acknowledge me in front of Harris. As though hearing my thoughts, Lachlan turns to my twin.

"Harris, Laurent wants you to meet him in the study first," he says.

"Thanks, old chap," Harris quips as he claps Lachlan on the shoulder, then glances at me. "We'll talk later, Hal…"

I nod.

As soon as Harris closes the library door behind him, Lachlan pulls me into his arms and nuzzles his face in the crook of my neck. His warm breath fans along my skin, sprouting goosebumps in its wake.

"Baby Girl, I missed you so much. Why didn't you meet me earlier like I asked?" He murmurs against my closed lips.

I can't believe he will not address Harris' accusation. This is Lachlan's doing.

He nips my lip for entry, but I seal them shut. A frown mars his handsome face as he leans back to peer at me.

"What's wrong?" Lachlan asks.

Can he be that oblivious? He had to pick up at least the last part of Harris' conversation with me.

I shake my head and pull away. Lachlan tightens his grip on my waist with one hand, while the other holds my chin between his thumb and index finger. I avert my eyes, but he's not having it.

"Talk to me, Haley," Lachlan says. "Please."

"Did you not hear Harris asking me what I'm hiding?! My twin isn't stupid, Lachlan. He knows me well," I respond hotly as I snatch my face from his grasp.

Lachlan sighs and leans his forehead on mine as he stares into my eyes.

"Baby Girl, I heard him, but I didn't want to upset you

further. What can I do about it?" He asks. "No one knows anything about us."

My skin prickles as my anger detonates.

"That's your solution?!" I ask. "How's this, we tell the truth and stop lying! That's what you can do about it, Lachlan! It's been over three months already! I prefer not to tell partial truths. They're still lies."

He blinks, then opens his mouth to speak. Thinks better of it and shuts it. He steps away as he runs his hand through his hair. The conflicting emotions roll across his face.

"Secrets can hurt us, Lachlan," I whisper. "Do you want that?"

He pauses to scan my face, then shakes his head with a sigh.

"No, Haley. I never want to hurt you or us," he responds quietly. "But let's hold off for only a bit longer, at least not now during the holidays. It could turn into a mess and ruin them for everyone."

He takes my hands in his and squeezes them at his request.

I can't deny he's wrong. It could blow up badly. I'd hate to upset everyone at the most cheerful time of the year.

"Fine, Lachlan," I say, giving in reluctantly.

I just hope it doesn't bite me in the ass later...

* * *

"FIONA, my dear, you should get used to our Thanksgiving dinners. It's a tradition my wife shares with her best friend Michelle as we alternate the holiday between our families every year," Uncle Connor says to a fairy princess.

No exaggeration.

Princess Fiona the Fair. The willowy mythical creature with ash blonde waist-length hair, violet eyes, and a Scottish lilt stands an inch taller than me at five, nine. She even wears a flowy lavender silk midi dress with Swarovski crystal covered sandals. All she's missing is a circlet and a bow with a quiver full of magical arrows.

I nearly puke at Uncle Connor's suggestion to her.

When he and Aunt Lucie introduced us to Fiona Ridel, her parents, older brother, and younger sister, I assumed she was here for Laurent, who greeted her warmly.

Uh no…

Uncle Connor plans to match Fiona with Lachlan. My Lachlan.

It became clear who her intended was when Uncle Connor sang her praises. Graduated with honors from the University of St. Andrews with a degree in Art History; owns a successful art gallery in Aberdeen; daughter of an oil magnate. Perfect, as he said, for his heir apparent.

My heart sank as tears filled my eyes. I glanced down to will them away.

No wonder Lachlan wanted to wait to tell anyone about us until after the holidays. He has Princess Fiona the Fair on standby!

How naive am I???

"Dinner is served, My Lord."

The butler's announcement gave me the opportunity to excuse myself for the ladies' room. I staved off the tears with a cool compress and deep breaths. The flush in my cheeks also lessened with the damp cloth. I schooled my features and stalked to the dining room.

"Yes, My Lord. I have some American friends from university who invited me to their Thanksgiving dinners during school," Fiona responds, then turns to Aunt Lucie. "But your dishes far surpass theirs, My Lady."

Aunt Lucie gives her a smile that doesn't quite reach her eyes and nods.

"Thank you, Fiona. But they were only college students who wanted a semblance of home. I am certain they did their very best," she says.

Fiona—with a chastened expression—nods at Aunt Lucie's response.

"Now had they been *me*, the meal would have been exquisite!" Lucien *The Sexy Chef* adds with a wink.

The mood lightens, and everyone enjoys the meal while chatting amiably.

I can sense Lachlan's gaze, but I ignore him. It's bad enough I have to force some food in my mouth and concentrate on not gagging.

"Aren't you the quiet one, Ms. Steele?"

I glance up into the violet eyes of Fiona's brother Heath —another mythical creature. I sip my Jackson Chardonnay to swallow a piece of turkey.

"And are you so talkative, Mr. Ridel?" I ask with an

arched eyebrow. My second glass of wine loosens my nerves and my tongue…

He chuckles.

In my periphery, I notice Lachlan scowl at the laughter. So I join in as I lift my glass to her brother's.

"Touché," he says with a nod. "I understand you're a techie. I dabble in it during my off time from the company."

Oh boy, here we go. Another David Ross, well a Scottish version. But I smile and give him my full attention. Even more so when I see Fiona place her hand on Lachlan's arm and lean in to whisper in his ear.

He doesn't appear too bothered by her advances.

So fuck him! Two can play that game, buddy, I snicker as I take another sip.

"I must say you have the most unique eyes I've ever seen," I tell Heath and lean closer to peer into them.

He angles his face, and our lips almost touch, only a hair's breadth apart.

"Haley?"

I jolt and sit back. Heath remains in place, eyes locked on mine.

"Sorry, sweetheart. I didn't mean to startle you," Aunt Lucie says with a warm smile. "I was telling Fiona's mother about the program you developed to keep track of Lola's wedding planning. Do tell us more about it."

Again my heart sinks, and my cheeks redden. Et tu, Brute?

I chance a glance in Lachlan and Fiona's direction. She's

leaning forward, keen to learn all about it. He has a blank expression on his face.

My hand goes to my wineglass, and I take a generous sip. Fortification and all.

"Of course, Aunt Lucie," I respond. Then proceed to give them details.

Lola chimes in with how impressed she was with it. My mother who senses my distress changes the subject with it's not trademarked yet, so let's move on. I smile at her in relief.

"Smart and beautiful, Ms. Steele."

I stop my eyes from rolling and go along with Heath's flirtation. Hell, a girl needs a distraction after that conversation.

Once the dinner ends, the men move to the smoking room while the women go to the floral salon. Lydie loops her arm through mine and whispers, so only I can hear.

"What an absolute clusterfuck…"

I snort and nod. That's not even half of it, I muse. Then I collect myself. She doesn't know about Lachlan and me? Or does she? I wonder.

I peek at the eldest Jackson. She's a stunningly gorgeous woman an inch shorter than me, with waist-length sable brown hair, and intelligent green eyes. Eyes that flash emerald fire now.

"Poor Lachlan. Dad has been trying to get him paired off even more than his efforts with me. Dad wants the next generation of Jacksons started like yesterday. It's not about love, just the best business merger. I failed with Baz, so he's on to Lachlan," she continues with a shake of her head. "The Ridels? Well, that would be a coup: liquid gold and liquid oil…"

I falter in my step.

"Haley, are you all right?" Lydie asks, concerned, as she holds my arm tighter to balance me.

I nod, too sick to speak.

Fortunately, we make it to the salon without further incident and sit.

My relief doesn't last long.

Fiona and her sister come over to sit on the sofa across from Lydie and me.

"Oh, Haley! Your program sounds fantastic! I hope we can use it," Princess Fiona the Fair exclaims.

Her sister chimes in. But their words fade.

"Excuse me," I say as I rise from the sofa and head to the door.

My mother stands from where she's speaking with Aunt Lucie, Lola, Leonie, and Fiona's mother. I smile and wave my hand for her to stay.

Once out of the salon, I lean against the door, close my eyes, and take a deep breath.

Lachlan and Fiona will marry.

Well, I guess my ass got bit after all. No happily ever after with Lachlan for me. The Princess Bride got him.

LACHLAN

"Fiona, my dear, you should get used to our Thanksgiving dinners. It's a tradition my wife shares with her best friend Michelle as we alternate the holiday between our families every year."

Immediately, my gaze flies to Haley's.

She won't meet my eyes. But I can tell she heard what my father so annoyingly said since she stiffened and her nostrils flared. Then, her nervous tell, she pushed her glasses up on the bridge of her nose.

Fuck. Me.

Since Fiona and her family arrived—not that I knew my father invited them—Haley has avoided me completely. When she stepped away for the ladies' room, I tried to catch up to her, but she darted away. Then Fiona tapped my arm.

Torn between going after My Baby Girl and keeping up appearances, I hesitate. The hairs on the back of my neck rose, and I glanced up from Fiona to find Baz staring at me with an unreadable expression on his face.

Decision made for me, I escorted Fiona to the dining room and said a silent prayer Haley would understand once I explained I did not know my father invited the Ridels. Nor was I interested in a relationship with Fiona. Only My Baby Girl.

We just have to get through the meal and the after-dinner gatherings. At which point, I'll talk to her.

Easier said than done.

I seethe as I watch Fiona's brother blatantly flirt with Haley. He doesn't bother to hide his attraction to her. Undoubtedly realizing the coup to be made if he can snag the Steele heiress.

Over my fucking dead body.

Haley Steele is mine!

"Haley?"

It's a damn good thing my mother called her name at that moment. I was about to launch myself over the table and throttle Ridel for putting his lips within reach of My Baby Girl's. A snarl rumbles in my chest.

Fiona blinks, surprised by the animalistic sound coming from me.

I ignore her, then damn near lose it when my mother asks Haley about a wedding app. She looks gutted but responds. Not with her usual gusto when she speaks about her tech endeavors.

Fiona touches my arm and smiles up at me as though we share a confidence.

I plaster a stoic expression on my face and sip my wine.

How the fuck did this Thanksgiving go so left so fast? I grumble to myself. And here I thought my mother was Team Lachlan and Haley. Why the hell is she asking about a wedding app with Fiona seated next to me? Aunt Shelley eyes Haley with concern. At least her mother hasn't changed sides in all of this.

The rest of the meal passes, but not fast enough. I have to pay attention to Fiona since she keeps asking me questions about our liquor business and my likes and dislikes. It's as if she wants to get to know me better. Not necessary.

Between catching my father's eye as he observes my interactions with Fiona and me watching Haley with Heath, I sigh with relief when the dinner ends. At least this part is over.

I help Fiona from her chair and hold back a cringe when she takes my arm as I head for the doors.

"It was so good to meet you finally, Lachlan. I'd love to show you my art gallery," she says, staring up at me with violet eyes ablaze.

Not to be rude, I smile and respond, "It was nice to meet you, Fiona. Excuse me."

I nod and turn to follow the men to the smoking room. Fiona's soft sigh reaches my ears before she goes with the women to the floral salon. Then I sigh with relief again.

"Lachlan, son, tell Piper about the blend you're working on. I say it's good for a very special occasion, eh, lad?" My father calls out as I enter the room.

So much for relief...

"And what special occasion might that be, Lach?" Baz asks pointedly.

Wanker.

"Your guess is as good as mine, Baz," I respond evenly.

"Lach, looks like you… are… on… lock! Cla-clank!" Harris guffaws as he presses his wrists together in a hand-cuffed motion.

Laurent laughs just as heartily as his best mate.

Double wankers. Especially my brother, since he knows I have zero interest in Fiona Ridel.

Malcolm and Lucien snicker while Roger shrugs.

Uncle Morgan pours me a snifter of Scotch and smiles in commiseration.

"Well, I must say, your sister Haley is a beauty who's more than worthy of a special occasion."

You can hear a pin drop after Heath's comment.

The Big Four face him as one like robotic Stepford men. Uncle Morgan cocks his head to the side with a raised eyebrow.

"Pardon?" He asks just as Malcolm growls and Baz steps forward, fists clenched. Roger and Harris glare.

Heath glances from one to the other, then back to Uncle Morgan.

"My apologies, sir, mates. I meant no offense to your daughter or to your family," he stammers face reddened with embarrassment.

"Now you know," Malcolm *The Enforcer* snarls. "And count yourself lucky. I don't give a fuck who you think you are, *mate*."

Heath flinches.

I almost feel sorry for the tosser. Almost.

"Gentlemen, now that Heath has learned his lesson, let's have drinks and cigars," my father says as he beckons to the butler.

"Yes, forgive my son, gentlemen. Here's to alliances among friends," Piper says as he raises his Waterford Crystal snifter.

Everyone nods except for me—and Baz, who eyes me over the rim of his glass.

We move on to talk of sports, holiday travels, and much safer topics than marriage. After our conversations slow, Piper rises to end the evening. The butler goes to tell my mother the Ridels are ready to leave.

Everyone meets in the grand hall for goodbyes. I notice Haley isn't amongst the others and ask Aunt Shelley about her whereabouts. She tells me Haley retired to her suite earlier and pats me on the arm.

"Good night, Lachlan."

I glance down at Fiona. She smiles and tilts her head for a kiss on the cheek.

Thank fuck My Baby Girl isn't here to witness this, I think as I give Fiona double air kisses quickly. For the last one, she shifts her face and our lips brush. She giggles and squeezes my arm before she saunters through the front doors.

Oh fuck.

"Care to play a game of pool, Lach?"

I turn to find Baz and Malcolm standing together.

Great. Now it'll be longer before I can see about My Baby Girl.

"Sure, if you want your ass handed to you, cuz," I retort.

They chuckle, and we head to the billiards room with the rest of the boys after we tell our parents and Lydie good night.

It's NOT until over an hour later when Lola and Leonie wrangle Baz and Roger from the pool table do we call it a night.

I head to my wing, then double back to the guest wing where Haley's suite is located. It's after two in the morning, so I let myself in without knocking, knowing she's asleep. When I enter the bedroom, light from the moon filters through the window onto her bed.

Silky ebony hair fans across the pillow as she lies on her side. Her beautiful face damp with tears and eyelids puffy. Even in her sleep, eyebrows knit together as she fists the pillow. A low moan slips from her parted lips.

My heart stutters.

I promised My Baby Girl I would never hurt her, and now I have.

What a miserable sod I am.

She sighs, and I stop my pity party.

I toe off my shoes and socks, then strip out of my suit, dress shirt, and tie. As much as my erect cock aches to bury itself within her warm, wet depths, I need to console My

Baby Girl. So I leave my boxer briefs on as I slip under the covers behind her.

I wrap my arm around her waist and press my palm against her lower body to align our bodies. The other hand strokes her hair from her cheek. I lean over to whisper in her ear.

"Baby Girl. Oh, My Baby Girl, how I love you and only you," I murmur. "I'm so sorry. I didn't know my father invited them."

She stirs and calls my name. Even in her sleep My Baby Girl can sense me, want me.

I nuzzle her soft cheek and brush my lips over it.

"Lachlan? Is that you?" She asks as she turns her head, eyes still closed.

I kiss her lips, and she moans into my mouth. My tongue swoops in to draw hers out. I groan when the tip of hers touches mine.

"Haley," I breathe.

She jumps and twists around, eyes wide as she stares down at me.

Fuck, she's gorgeous.

"Lachlan! Wh—what are you doing in here?" She asks as she brings the sheet over her negligee covered breasts. Her peaked nipples press against the pink silk. "Hey! Eyes up here!"

I snag my lower lip between my teeth to keep from chuckling at her indignation.

"What time is it?" She asks, glancing around for her mobile on the nightstand.

I sit up and cup her face.

"Baby Girl, it's after two in the morning. I want to check on you—"

"Oh, please, Lachlan!" She says, snatching her face from my grasp and pushing on my chest. "Check on me for what? To gauge my level of embarrassment? To determine how silly I was to trust you? Oh, I know... To rub in my face your fiancée?!"

By the time she's finished, her fists pummel my chest and tears slide down her flush cheeks. I hold her hands to my heart.

"No! Let go of me, Lachlan!" She says as her voice rises with her distress.

"Haley! Hush! You'll wake everyone," I warn her.

She goes still.

"And you can't have that, can you, Lachlan? I'm the secret. Just the woman you fuc—"

Enough!

I slam my mouth onto hers and use my chest to push her onto her back as I cover her body with mine. I pin her wrists overhead with one hand as I wedge my knee between her thighs and bunch her negligee around her waist.

She squirms, tossing her head from side to side, and gnashes at my mouth as she tries to speak.

"No!" I growl into her mouth.

My free hand reaches inside of my boxer briefs and fists my cock. I rub my thumb over the tip to spread the pre-cum as I press it to her slick slit. In one thrust, I drive my cock in to the root.

She gasps at the thick invasion. I swallow her cry.

Slowly, I pull back, then slam forward.

She bucks and mewls. Her pussy contracts around my girth.

Another retreat and return, and she comes undone. Silenced except for the wail of pleasure, I gobble down. I rip my mouth from hers and stare down at her half-closed, hooded eyes.

"You are mine, and only mine, Haley. As I am yours and only yours. No Heath. No Fiona. No. One. Only us," I growl as my hips snap with each word.

Then my balls draw up. I cover her slack mouth with mine and roar my release as my cock spurts hot ropes of cum into her soaked pussy. It clamps onto my twitching dick to suck greedily. Emptied, I collapse on top of her, panting into her neck as our fingers entwine beside her head. Sweat drips down my spine.

Once our breathing slows, I lift my head and rise to my elbows to gaze down at her.

Despite us still being intimately connected, she wants nothing to do with me. She turns her head away.

"Haley," I rasp.

She bites her lower lip and shakes her head as a tear slips from beneath her thick eyelashes.

"Oh, Baby Girl," I groan. "Please look at me. Please."

She swallows audibly while I wait for her to face me.

When she does, I sigh in relief.

"I love you, Haley Steele. I love you more than life

itself," I say, then repeat my words from earlier. "I am so sorry. I did not know my father invited them. I promise you I want no one but you. Forever. Understand?"

A sob escapes her lips, and she nods as she blinks back more tears.

I raise my eyebrow.

"Words, Baby Girl. I will have your words," I tell her.

"It hurts, Lachlan," she says sadly.

My heart breaks. Fuck!

I kiss her face as I tell her how sorry I am and beg for her forgiveness. At last, she tells me what I've been waiting to hear.

"I love you, too, Lachlan. Forever."

My eyes close as I bow my head.

Thank you, I say in silent prayer.

Then I make love to My Baby Girl until no more tears fall from her gorgeous gray eyes.

LACHLAN

"*S*he's not going to fade away, you know."

I jerk my eyes away from My Baby Girl as she builds a snowman with Lola and Leonie, while Laurent and Harris build their version of a curvaceous snow woman in a bikini. Lydie smiles at me as she sits on a teak-wood chair.

It's Christmas week, and we're gathered to celebrate as one extensive family. Each year we rotate to a different STEELE property in the world. Sometimes hot and tropical for the beach and others snowy for skiing and more winter sports. For New Year's Eve, we do our own things now that we're older and want to party. So I have a surprise planned for My Baby Girl to bring it in with a real bang.

Now, Lydie and I sit on a heated deck of the contemporary timber and stone, twelve-bedroom mountain lodge the Steeles have within the STEELE Aspen complex of hotel, restaurants, spa, and residential properties. The gated private homes surround the hotel and have access to its amenities as a perk of being a part of the luxury resort. From their lodge, it takes only minutes to arrive in the center of Aspen or at the ski lifts.

It's not the panoramic views of Colorado's majestic snow-covered Rocky Mountains or of the ski resort that have me transfixed. My Baby Girl laughing with her close friends, twin, and cousin has captured my attention. Enough so I didn't notice Lydie beside me until she spoke. Who knows how long she's been there watching me watch Haley...

Damn.

"Oh, hey, sis. Well, at some point the sun will melt her away despite Laurent and Harris' best efforts," I say nonchalantly. My aviator sunglasses hide the exact spot I'm staring. So I go with the obvious—the snow woman.

Lydie snorts.

"Yes, that is true. However, I refer to Haley," Lydie says as she faces me. "And you know it, Lachlan."

I take my time to re-cross my long legs at the ankles in front of me. My gaze remains forward.

Lydie tilts her head to the side with an arched eyebrow and asks, "Oh, so no comment? Give me a break, Lach. I'm your sister, and I know you well. Don't forget."

When I make no effort to respond, she sighs.

"Listen, who am I to judge, huh? I made a mess with Sebbie—I mean Sebastian—so I'm in no position to say anything negative about you wanting Haley," Lydie says, then laughs mirthlessly. "At least you'll satisfy Dad's obsession with a permanent alliance between the Jacksons and the Steeles. And more importantly with someone you love."

I shift in my chair to face her and open my mouth. But she cuts me off with a flick of her hand.

"My advice? If Haley says she wants you, go for it. If she makes no verbal commitment, leave her be, and you marry Fiona, or whomever else. Trust me, it is *not* worth the heartache of waiting for someone to love you who never will," Lydie finishes quietly. Her gaze drifts to the others below us.

Even though she wears sunglasses too, I can tell she's looking at Lola who accomplished what Lydie couldn't—marry the eternal playboy, Sebastian Steele.

My heart breaks for my sister.

For years I wondered if she wanted more from Baz than the close childhood friend and business confidante relationship they share. Since she's working to take over the helm at Jackson Corporation from our father, just as Baz did with STEELE from his, Lydie has turned to Baz for advice. Especially since she craves approval from our father. Lydie will do anything to prove she's as good as a son to lead. Then it became clear she cared for Baz as a woman loves a man.

I consider Lydie's words.

She's not some woebegone, lovesick woman. She's second in command to our father in charge of a major corporation. And because her goal is to impress him enough to become CEO, she's a polished, well-kept, in-control woman. Lydie commands the boardroom and demands the greatest respect from other corporate leaders. So her advice is sound and based on experience.

"What makes you think I want Haley?" I ask.

Lydie smirks.

"You know I love you with all of my heart, right?" She asks, then continues when I nod. "You are a big ole sap with puppy dog eyes, Lachlan Jackson!"

Lydie can't keep a straight face and cracks up. When my mouth opens and closes like a fish gasping for breath, she doubles over, holding her sides.

"Whatever, Lydie," I harrumph, folding my arms across my chest and sliding down in my chair.

A burst of laughter from My Baby Girl brings my attention back to her. In the middle of her making a snow angel, Laurent has her pinned beneath him, shoveling snow in her unzipped white Moncler Grenoble parka. Her long legs covered in matching snow pants flail as she slaps at his hands.

What the fuck?!

"Aha! So long puppy eyes! Make way for the possessive caveman!" Lydie chortles as she wipes tears from her eyes. "Oh, and don't worry. Our baby brother has zero interest in Haley as a lover. She's the sister he can tussle with since they're a year apart. He knows I'm too old for such nonsense!"

I roll my eyes and snort.

"Lydie, you're thirty-four, a year older than me. How the hell are you too old?" I ask.

"Okay, too sophisticated then," she says with a shrug.

"Too sophisticated for what?"

We turn to find Baz and the rest of the guys back from snowmobiling. I had a video conference meeting so had to pass. Sure they called me the Grinch. But every last one of us knows it's work before fun. So they were only ribbing me.

Lydie laughs and responds, "For the likes of you chaps! I'm headed to the spa with mom and Aunt Shelley. Tootles!" She waggles her fingers and struts off.

Seconds later my mobile dings with a text message.

Your secret's safe with me, brother dearest ;)

I type a quick reply.

You're the best, Sophisticated Lady :D

"Do you see what those two yahoos made? A stripper snow woman! Tits, pole, and ass…" Malcolm guffaws as he heads down the stairs to join them. "Here, you forgot the C-notes. It's all about the Benjamins, baby!"

Laurent and Harris glance up as everyone laughs heartily. The rest of us follow Malcolm down the steps.

"Let me help you up, Haley," I say after I mush Laurent in the back of his head, then hold my hands out to her. "You should dry off before you get sick. Numbskull didn't think of that, did he?"

"Sorry, Hal, I just couldn't resist!" Laurent chuckles, then stutters when a snowball to the head by Harris surprises him.

Then Lola and Leonie squeal as more snowballs fly. Haley slips from my grasp and drops to gather snow. She laughs and throws some at me. Hitting me right in my mouth. I grunt and duck as one from Lucien zips past my head, only to get smacked in the chest by one from Malcolm.

"It's on," I say, followed by our Scottish battle cry. "*Gun eagal!*"

"*Gun eagal!*" Lucien and Laurent pick up our *no fear* clan motto.

"Oh, fuck that!" Baz yells as he throws a snowball at me.

We battle on until every one of us is soaked, red faced, and cold. Then troop inside through the mudroom. We strip down to silk flannel tops and pants.

I can't help but to ogle My Baby Girl's double Ds since her nipples poke the thin material. My cock follows suit to tent my pants. I grab a towel off of the heated rack to cover the evidence of my carnal thoughts before anyone notices.

A snicker from my side draws my gaze.

Lola smirks at me and glances at Haley.

Fuck!

But when Baz turns to see what has his wife's attention, she grabs his face and kisses him. Her hazel eyes twinkle at me before she winks and gives me the okay sign behind his back.

Damn… Can I be any more obvious? First Lydie, now Lola. At least they won't blab to anyone.

I glance at the others, but they're preoccupied. So I sneak another peek at Haley, and she bites her lips to stifle giggles as she stares at my partially hidden bulge. I pin her with my Alpha Dom stare, and she chokes back her laughter. With a smirk I stride through the doors, headed for my suite.

* * *

THE WIND WHIPS around us as we hop out of the helicopter that hovers over the pristine mountaintop. Aside from other peaks in the range, nothing but an expanse of fresh powdery snow, trees, and bright sunlight in a blue topaz sky surround us. The rest of the world is too far below to see.

For our Christmas morning run, the more extreme sports driven of us choose heli-boarding—Lucien, Laurent, Malcolm, Harris, Haley, and me. While the others ski one of the double-black-diamond runs. All of us—including Lola and Leonie—have skied since we could walk, and a few picked up snowboarding when it became popular, alternating between the two styles.

I've always felt protective of My Baby Girl when she tagged along as a kid on Baz's and my more adventurous activities. But now that she's mine, my heart skips a beat as Harris helps her from the helicopter. On the ride up, we didn't sit together, rather she opted for the seat beside her twin. Twice she flashed her gorgeous smile at me, and her light cleared my nerves.

Quickly we don our gear including avalanche airbag packs, satellite phones and tracking devices. When we gather for a pile on of hands before we head down the mountain, My Baby Girl stands next to me and places her hand on top of mine then squeezes it. I link my pinky finger with hers and nod.

"Let's do this!" Malcolm roars—the king of all extreme sports, along with Lucien.

One guide leads while the other takes the rear of our phalanx. We have only moments to appreciate the incredible views as we fly by on our snowboards. Adrenaline pumps through my veins, spurring me on. The sensation is unparalleled.

Aside from paying close attention to the steep cliff face, I monitor My Baby Girl ahead of me between Malcolm and Harris. She maneuvers her snowboard like an expert with nerves of steel—no pun. But I still won't relax until we're at the base.

Thirty minutes later, we complete the run with whoops and wolf whistles. We pose for photos to share with the others, then make our way to the helicopter.

"That was amazing!" My Baby Girl exclaims.

"Yeah, little sis. You should come with Lucien, Anton, Borya, and me the next time we go to Hokkaido," Malcolm says, grinning at her.

"Bet!" She responds, fist pumping with him.

I bite my tongue to keep from objecting. Japan has one of the most extreme spots for the sport.

Damn.

* * *

"Hey, Baby Girl."

She spins around and stares up at me as her eyes widen behind her glasses.

I caught her in the oversized pantry of the chef's kitchen, getting bags of popcorn kernels. Lucien is making gourmet munchies before our marathon of *National Lampoon's Christmas Vacation*, *A Christmas Story*, and *Die Hard* in the media room.

"Lachlan! You scared me," she says, clutching her hand over her heart.

I place my palm over her hand and lean in to kiss her pouty lips. We press together as she sighs and kisses me with equal fervor.

We've made love a couple of times and fooled around. But I ache to hold her in my arms and wake up with her head on my chest and my fingers in her mussed hair. That's why I cannot wait to leave in the morning. We'll be alone finally. Thank fuck!

"Ready for tomorrow?" I ask when we come up for air.

"Yes," she breathes with hooded eyes.

"Good, me too," I add with a nip to her lower lip.

I was able to get help from my mother and Aunt Shelley to arrange our departure in the helicopter alone before everyone else left. So no one will be the wiser.

Then we'll take my private jet. I still haven't told My Baby Girl our destination, only to pack bikinis, light dresses, and sandals. We'll spend a week together just as the others will on their New Year's trips. Again, our mothers helped me by quelling anyone's questions about Haley's whereabouts.

"Hey, Haley, did you find the popcorn kernels? They're on the middle of the left shelf."

Lucien's voice interrupts, canoodling with My Baby Girl.

"Got them," she calls out, then bites back a yelp when I swat her ass as she leaves the pantry. She shakes her round bottom as she goes through the door with a giggle.

Oh, My Baby Girl, you'll pay for your teasing... And you will enjoy it.

HALEY

"The chef stocked the kitchen pantry with your preferences, including the selection of Jackson Scotch and wines. He placed a list of recommended restaurants on the center island. The maid will arrive at your request. However, she put extra bedding and towels in the linen closet of the primary bedroom suite. The Range Rover has a full tank of gas. You may access the WiFi with the instructions in the office. Will you require anything else, madam?"

I shift from foot to foot as the butler for the opulent Casa Pararse in Ixtapa speaks to me after the property tour. Although I don't know how much *rest* Lachlan will let me have in this oceanfront mansion….

Lachlan's wicked chuckles reach my ears only as he stands behind me with his hand on my lower back on the terrace.

Even though I should oh and ah over the sublime view

of the Pacific Ocean's turquoise waters as they sparkle in the sunlight, I can't.

What I want to do is drop to my back on the tiles and spread my legs for Lachlan to fuck my sopping wet pussy while he plays with the plug in my ass.

I whimper.

As punishment for teasing him in the pantry last night, Lachlan refused me orgasms he built up only to deny me the pleasure of release.

The entire five hours of our flight down to Mexico from Aspen he kept me bound spread-eagle to the bed while he brought me to the brink of climax, only to stop before I fell over the edge. Again and again until my legs quivered and tears slide from beneath the silk blindfold down my temples. When I begged him to let me cum, he put my thong in my mouth.

And if that wasn't bad enough, he added a butt plug to the mix.

We've done a bit of anal play with his finger rimming my puckered hole or when his thumb pushed past the tight ring of muscles. But a full-on plug up my ass? Ah, no.

Lachlan dipped it in my dripping pussy to let my abundant juices coat the plug naturally. I moaned in plea-sure but sobbed at the burn and stretch of my bottom hole. With a pop he seated it fully within me, all the way to the flared base where my muscles clamped down on the neck.

I hate to think of how Lachlan got his experience. But he even made my body tingle with a plug up my ass. The pain morphed into erotic pleasure like I've never known—albeit in the four months I've had sex.

Before we landed, he warned me not to let the plug slip out or try to relieve the ache in my pussy. In the bathroom, I touched myself, only to have him barge in and spank my ass soundly as I leaned against the vanity.

The pressure of the plug jostling almost pushed me over the edge. But he stopped with a smirk as our eyes met in the mirror's reflection. A tap to the base, and he led me to the main cabin.

Sitting proved another challenge. I squirmed until Lachlan murmured in my ear, "Ten spanks to your pussy, Naughty Girl."

Now, I gaze at the butler without hearing much of his words. The need for release makes my breath come out in pants. My inner thighs squeeze together beneath my maxi dress. Surely Lachlan won't notice.

"Five more, Naughty Naughty Girl. Now, answer the man," he says with his lips behind my ear.

I whimper.

"N-no. No-nothing else, thank you," I stammer.

"Very well, madam, sir. Enjoy your stay at Casa Pararse," the butler says with a bow.

"Thank you," Lachlan responds as the butler leaves, then slips his arms around my waist. "So, Naughty Girl, how do you like your surprise?"

Once again, my gaze goes to the breathtaking view. The Pacific stretches endlessly to the distant horizon dotted with three mountainous peaks rising from its depths.

Below us to one side, waves lap at the rocky outcropping while on the other a private sandy beach has an inviting sunbed with an umbrella and tables.

I close my eyes with my head against Lachlan's shoulder and let the sun warm my face. A deep inhalation of the salty air fragrant with the tropical blooms along the sides of the terrace relaxes me. I meld into him further with a contented sigh.

"I love it, thank you, Sir," I respond.

"Ah, so you love the surprise. What about the man?" My Alpha Dom asks with a nip to the delicate lobe of my ear.

"Oh! I love the man… you!" I squeak.

He chuckles with his mouth to my neck as he sucks on the sensitive skin. His turgid length presses into my back. I rise to my toes—so much shorter than him in my sandals— to grind my ass against his crotch.

He groans.

"Strip and lean your palms against that table," My Alpha Dom commands with a slap to my ass.

A squeal pops out of my mouth, and I hurry to do his bidding. I shimmy the maxi dress up my thighs and over my head with an exaggerated wiggle to my hips. My lips twitch with a smirk at the sound of his growl.

As I pass a double chaise lounge, I drop my dress and glasses onto its terracotta-colored pad. My sandals slip from my feet as I bend at the waist over the elliptical-shaped dining table. Palms flat, I toss my hair over my shoulder to gaze at My Alpha Dom with dark hooded eyes, pupils blown with lust.

"Widen your stance, Naughty Girl. You know better by now," he chastises me with a tsk and a disappointed shake of his head.

My heart sinks at his dismay in my position. Quickly I make the adjustment and add an extra dip in my lower spine to lift my ass higher in the air; my forehead hovers over the table's surface.

"Better," he purrs silkily as he rubs my butt cheek. "The emerald on your anal plug glimmers so beautifully in the sun."

I mewl and press the pads of my fingers into the teakwood as he rotates the plug in a complete circle, first one way, then the other. My pussy clenches, hungry for his carnal attention.

Relief washes over me when his hand snakes around my flank to skim his fingertips along my lower belly before they slip between my wet folds. My thighs tremble in anticipation. I drop my forehead to the table. Yes!

THWACK. THWACK. THWACK. THWACK.

"FUCK!!!" I wail, as I rise to the tips of my toes to avoid the swats to my pussy lips.

"Oh, so you thought I forgot about your transgressions, Naughty Naughty Girl?" My Alpha Dom rumbles in my ear. His powerful chest presses me flat onto the table.

My breasts smash, nipples painful as my elbows drop against its surface. A breath bursts from my parted lips.

He leans back with bent knees to grind his groin into my ass. His rock-hard cock thumps against me. Fingers that exploded across my sensitive flesh now caress my engorged clit with tender strokes.

"Aaaahhh," I hiss as pleasure radiates through me from the delicious contradiction.

THWACK. THWACK. THWACK. THWACK. THWACK.

A garbled cry replaces the brief moment of respite. My confused pussy gushes against his palm as he grinds it onto my throbbing clit.

"Nine more, Naughty Girl," My Alpha Dom warns with a nip to my shoulder.

My entire body lights up, alternating between erotic pain and pleasure with each precise smack. By the time my punishment ends, my juices coat my thighs and drip to the tiles below. Swollen and needy my core contracts around three of his thick digits as he finger fucks me ruthlessly.

"Cum for me. Cum for me now," he commands with a pinch to my clit.

Fireworks explode behind my closed eyelids. Palms slap the table as my back arcs and my toes curl. Heat fills my lower belly as the muscles in my ass clamp the plug with a vice-like grip. A low and guttural scream rips from the very depths of my soul as my climax rolls through me.

My sweaty body collapses, spent and sated.

"GOOD THING we don't have any neighbors, Baby Girl."

The sound of Lachlan's chuckle greets me as I rouse from my post-coital coma.

I lengthen my arms languorously over my head as my back arches and my feet point for a full-body stretch. Damn, if my body doesn't hum with gratitude, I muse as I purr like a contented kitten.

"That good, huh?" Lachlan says with another chuckle.

"Mmmm… Abso-fucking-lutely," I groan, then open my eyes to his handsome face. His stunning emerald green eyes dance with mirth. "Thank you."

His mouth quirks into a smug smile as he stares down at me.

"But did you learn your lesson, Naughty Girl?" He asks back in Alpha Dom mode.

Now my eyes glint with mischief as I bite my lower lip to hide my salacious grin.

"Well, I may need another lesson, Sir…" I respond.

He snorts.

"Oh, but of course. I replaced your anal plug with a bigger one after I cleaned you with a cloth. Later my cock will take its place," he says, once again smug.

My mouth gapes, but my nipples harden to little peaks and my pussy weeps.

Lachlan chuckles with a knowing smirk.

Well damn…

* * *

"Harris knows."

"Lydie figured it out."

Lachlan and I speak at the same time as we float in the

infinity pool. Its edge meets the Pacific Ocean for a continuation of infinite blue hues.

We face each other in surprise.

"How did she—"

"What did you tell—"

Lachlan raises his hand and says, "You tell me about Harris first."

I nod while my mind reels. If we haven't fooled Lydie, does Uncle Connor know? Did she tell him? Or did Aunt Lucie slip up? Nerves make my stomach hurt. I push my glasses up the bridge of my nose and take a deep breath.

Lachlan rubs my arm.

"It's okay, Baby Girl. Don't get upset," he soothes me.

Again I nod. This time I recount my conversation with Harris after Thanksgiving.

"Okay, Hal, give it up. And do not even attempt to lie to me," Harris says as we ride horses along a bridal path at Jackson Castle.

Suddenly I'm overly warm in my padded short jacket, silk turtleneck, insulated riding breeches, and fleece-lined tall boots. Even the brisk wintry breeze off of the North Sea fails to cool my flushed face. Automatically, I reach up to adjust my glasses, forgetting I wear googles instead. I shift in my saddle to face him.

Harris shakes his head.

"I haven't lied to you, Harris," I respond.

"Okay, so what have you kept from me, Haley?" He asks.

An internal debate rages. Should I confess? Is it better to deny? Or should I just not answer and deflect?

"You know you and I are closer to each other than we are to

any of our brothers. We shared the same womb, for fuck's sake, Haley. If you feel you can't trust me with whatever goes on with you, then just say so. But do not insult our connection with partial truths. And I know that's what you've given everyone recently. So don't bother to deny it, Haley," He continues.

"Just tell me if you're in any trouble or aren't safe," Harris adds with an expression of concern mixed with sadness.

He's right. We share a special bond, and I trust him implicitly. I can't do this to him.

"Lachlan and I are in a relationship," I confess, then rush on. "I've always loved him. Out of respect for his friendship with Baz and for the closeness of our families, Lachlan didn't act on his love for me until after I approached him at Baz and Lola's wedding. We still don't want to upset him or anyone else. Only mom and Aunt Lucie know. In fact, they're Team Lachlan and Haley. So for now, please don't tell anyone. It's for Lachlan and me to share. When we're ready."

In silence, Harris studies me with an unreadable expression on his handsome face. So like Baz, I feel as though I speaking to him instead of to my twin. But then the jokester in Harris comes through.

"Well, milady, your secret is safe with me"—he says with a bow, then he turns serious—"However, should Lord Lachlan hurt you, I won't challenge him in a duel. I'll let The Enforcer have at him. And good luck to Lord Lachlan with worming his ass out of that situation."

Lachlan—whose expression remained guarded while I spoke—rubs his hand over his face and chuckles.

"Although I won't hurt you and can go head-to-head with Malcolm, I'm glad Harris supports you—"

"*Us.* He supports us," I interject with a cheerful smile. "Now, tell me about Lydie. Before a panic attack overtakes me."

Lachlan pulls me through the water closer to him and kisses the tip of my nose before he tells me not to worry. After he finishes recalling his conversation with Lydie, I sag with relief.

"Well, at least we have four for us. Technically, six, us included," I say thoughtfully as my gaze goes back out to the Pacific.

The fiery ball of the setting sun streaks brilliant oranges and golds at the horizon to mix with the blues of the sky above reflected in the ocean below. Day and night merge for a moment in time before night overtakes day.

I liken it to my relationship with Lachlan. I give a silent prayer we can blend harmoniously without losing one to the other or losing our families.

For this moment in time, I nuzzle my cheek against Lachlan's brawny chest to draw on his strength as he holds me close in his arms.

"Hey, babe. It's always a pleasure to see you even via FaceTime. But aren't you in flight to Mozambique?"

Lachlan asks as he sits up and runs his fingers through his tousled sable brown hair. The sheet falls to his hips to reveal his muscular chest and eight-pack abs with a happy trail to his delicious cock.

"What time is it?" He asks with a yawn.

I grin like a loon at my sexy as sin boyfriend who even half asleep still looks like a movie star. I'm way too distracted to answer right away.

He rubs the stubble on his cleft chin and asks, "Um, Baby Girl? Everything okay?"

I nod and grin.

"Now that I've seen your face, yes. And yes, I'm on my jet headed to Buenguerra Island and will land in a few of hours," I answer. "I'm so excited to see my girls! Starr has an entire week of sessions scheduled, after we'll hang out after her clients leave."

Lola met Starr Knight when she hosted her first international fitness retreat on Laucala Island in Fiji and raved about it. She owns Starr Light Fitness & Wellness Beverly Hills and branched out to retreats overseas. She also wants to have a center in the Caribbean. Lola told Malcolm since he's the President of STEELE's Entertainment Properties Division that focuses on our casinos, hotels, resorts, and beach clubs.

Starr has become a close friend of ours along with Blair and Billie—both of whom are as much friends as they are Lola's personal assistants—and of course, Leonie. So not only will we support Starr with her second fitness retreat, but we'll also make it a Girls' Getaway, too. We're bound to have a blast.

Plus, Starr's body is ah-mazing! She's five feet, six inches, and her Pilates and yoga keep her fit without losing her curves. I'll do whatever she's putting down to stay in shape!

"So tell me again how many guys signed up to watch you in your tight leggings or those barely there yoga shorts?" Lachlan grumbles.

I giggle and wave my hand.

"I have no idea, Lachlan. Besides, I have new shorts you haven't seen yet and bikinis I bought for this trip. Oh, and we can go topless on the beach!" I tell him.

"What the fuck?!" He roars, and his mobile drops amidst the bedding.

When he picks it back up, his face is beet red.

"Oh, hell no! You will not prance around naked, Haley Steele! My eyes only!" Lachlan rumbles.

Now awake fully, he storms around his bedroom while he yanks at his hair and rants on and on. He scowls into the camera as his tirade about my clothing—or lack thereof—choices are unacceptable.

I let him go on as I stifle more giggles before I pretend to lose the connection and end the video call to his yells.

Good! Leave him hanging, and let him wonder, I laugh out loud.

The rest of the flight, I do work and return calls and emails. On the drive to the resort, I scroll through the many missed calls and texts from my angry caveman. Ooh… He is mad at me! I send a message to Lola to let her know I arrived, then drop my mobile in my tote bag. Lachlan can wait, I grin as I watch the tropical foliage go by.

Starr chose a five-star luxury beachfront resort on the island off the east coast of Africa in the channel between Mozambique and the Indian Ocean. I can realize why as I spot several pristine, white-sand beaches and clear turquoise waters. I get an overall tranquil vibe from the island.

The property we're staying at is the most exclusive of the resorts with only three cabanas, ten casinhas, and one large villa scattered across eleven acres of beachfront and lush tropical vegetation. Starr's retreat participants and her staff along with us secured the entire resort. It's our private oasis.

Lola, Leonie, Billie, Blair, and I claimed the villa since it features five large bedrooms with sitting areas, living room, dining room, and kitchenette. The outdoor areas include a pool, deck area with thatched-roof cabana and chaises, plus chaises down by the ocean. It's stunning and peaceful.

Starr chose a casinhas since she's working more so than relaxing. She needs more space for her staff to meet and for her one-on-one sessions with guests. It's through the palm trees on one of the sandy paths that crisscross the property.

As the Range Rover SVAutobiography stops outside of the villa, Billie saunters out with two cocktails in her hand.

"Hey there, Haley!" She says in her sweet Southern belle accent. "Look what I have for you, honey!"

Her bright green eyes twinkle. She reminds everyone of a petite Tyra Banks with her wavy, medium-blonde balayage hair, and pecan-colored skin. Skin that's flush. More than likely from the cocktail she holds out to me. Billie is a self-professed mixologist. So I know I'm in for a treat.

"Hey, girl!" I respond as I take a sip. "OMG! This is fantastic! What is it?"

She grins devilishly.

"Well... the base is Tipo Tinto R&R rum, the iconic Mozambican liquor. But I added my special twist to it," she winks. "Come on. Everyone's out by the beach."

The maid takes my luggage as I loop arms with Billie. We chat as we pass through the villa to the terrace facing the sparkling water.

"Hey, little sis!"

"She's here!"

"Let's get this party started!"

"Oh, *chérie*, you made it!"

My girls raise their cocktails in the air to welcome me as we hug. I drop onto a chaise lounge and grin at Starr.

"I am so ready for your yoga and meditation sessions. My body needs to relax!" I exclaim.

Starr claps her hands and shimmies on her chaise.

"By the end of this week, you'll be a new woman. I promise!" She says. Her dimples deepen in her heart-shaped face like mine.

"Me, too!" Blair pipes up. Her cerulean blue eyes glitter as she sips her cocktail.

"Don't forget me, *chérie*! I've been working so hard!" Leonie chimes in. "School, project manager, modeling. A girl needs a break!"

We raise our glasses again to celebrate the start of a great week. Time for us to reconnect with our minds, bodies, and friends. Perfect.

* * *

"Let us end our practice with three oms together. Inhale through your nose gently, hold it for a heartbeat. Then slowly release your breath back through your nose. Let us begin."

Starr's entrancing voice guides us through the last part of our yoga session. We started with breathwork for five minutes to prep us for a vigorous, forty-five-minute flow sequence. After savasana Starr ended with a ten-minute meditation.

"Namaste. The light in me honors the light in you," Starr intones.

We bow to each other with palms pressed together at our heart centers. We remind ourselves of the good energy and intention we set forth in our practice. As we sit up and open our eyes, Starr beams at us. Her love of helping others reach their best mental and physical potential shines from her sorrel brown eyes.

"That was transcendental," Lola breaths out in awe as she sits cross-legged on her mat beside Leonie.

She nods and whispers, "*Oui.* She's amazing."

"I agree," Blair leans over to whisper.

I stretch my arms overhead with a contented sigh. All the muscles Lachlan worked out melt and shout out a big namaste to Starr!

"This is the best I've felt in a while," I breathe.

"Yes, she's still the best yoga teacher I've ever had a session with," Billie adds as she wipes down her mat.

We follow suit and clean ours, then hang them on the wooden racks inside the beachside, open-air pavilion. Other students gather around Starr to glean more of her sage advice. Two of her assistants offer adjustments for those who want more instruction.

Starr glances up and waves at us. We wave back before we walk down the steps to the sandy shore. Two other assistants offer us frothy shot glasses filled with refreshing juice made from local fruits. The delicious concoctions cool us down and fill us with energy.

"It has ashwagandha in it. An Ayurvedic herb that many studies show increases energy and reduces stress and anxiety," the assistant with a curly afro tells us.

Blair smiles at her and says, "This is tasty."

We nod and thank Starr's assistants for the elixirs as we place the empty glasses on the table. Our next session for Pilates isn't for another two hours. So we stroll along the empty beach to our villa. The sun glistens on the water between the island and the Mozambique coast. The allure of the waves as they splash on the sand beckon.

As I glance at it longingly, Lola claps to get our attention.

"Hey, I'm going to change into my bikini and go for a swim!" She declares.

We agree it's a good idea and a great way to wash away the sweat from our yoga class. The flecks of gold in Billie's moss green eyes glint as she peeks over her shoulder at us. Then she skips ahead.

"Last one in is a rotten egg!" She shouts mischievously.

We race ahead, each one of us determined to be the first to dive into the crystal clear waters. Quick as I can, I strip from my yoga shorts and tank top into a string bikini—

with the top, despite what I said to my angry caveman. I grab my towel and jog down to the shore.

"Damn supermodel! You're used to quick changes!" Blair says as she splashes Leonie, who beat us.

"*Absolument! Ma chérie!*" She giggles as she sweeps her arm through the water to douse Blair.

I duck to avoid the spatter.

Lola's laughter as she beats Billie into the water by a hair's length draws our attention to the shore.

"Ha, ha! You lose, Billie!" She shouts. "*Piu*, you stink like a rotten egg!"

Billie laughs and ducks under the water.

"Tell her not to worry about it. Patrick thinks you smell divine!" Blair laughs.

Billie captured the heart of Patrick Rockett, her new Scottish billionaire beau. Sebastian nearly had a fit when he found out Billie was dating the CEO of STEELE International's biggest competitor, Rockett Construction. Lola had to calm him down when she reminded him Billie signed an ironclad nondisclosure agreement and she swore her allegiance to Lola.

When I spoke about who was attending the retreat to Lachlan, I mentioned Billie and her having a Scottish boyfriend. Lachlan and Lydie know him along with his younger brothers from Saïd Business School. He had good things to say—outside of the STEELE competition—about Patrick. So I'm happy for my friend.

"You got that right, honey!" Billie's cheeky reply. "And my brawny babe cannot get enough!"

We crack up as her Southern drawl switches to a Scottish accent flawlessly.

I hold my breath, hoping they won't ask me about my love life.

My mother, Aunt Lucie, Harris, and Lydie may know. But Lachlan and I agreed to hold off a little longer. We want to keep our love positive in its early stages. It's our honeymoon phase, and I don't want anyone to tarnish it. In time, we'll share with our families.

And I'm more than certain Sebastian wouldn't want anyone stomping on his newlywed love with Lola. So I won't allow him to do it to mine. Even if Lachlan and I aren't married. Yet.

"Your turn, Blair! Leonie and I were on the hot seat last night. Billie fessed up. Do share..." Lola says, splashing Blair.

I sag with relief and lower into the warm waters as I send a silent prayer of thanks.

Meanwhile, Blair splutters as her face reddens. Her cerulean blue eyes dart everywhere but at us.

"Yes, Ms. Secretive!" Leonie teases. "How are things with *Le Renard Argenté*?"

Blair floats onto her back and closes her eyes before she responds.

"I don't kiss and tell—"

The three of us cover her in a deluge of seawater as we shout at her for being so prim and proper. She flips over and dives under the water, resurfacing a few feet away. She flips her chestnut brown hair over her shoulders, then stands akimbo.

"I won't let you bully me into saying a word!" She declares but can't hold in her laughter.

After a moment, she wipes her eyes and saunters back over to us.

"You know cheese, wine, leather… They all age well… But not as well as my Silver Fox Luc Montaigne!"

She ends her pronouncement with a two-armed sweep of water aimed at us. We retaliate, and it becomes an all-out, every woman for herself water war. We laugh hysterically while trying not to drown as we jump around, splashing in the warm, tropical Indian Ocean.

* * *

"How did you like the retreat?" Starr asks as we sit at the outdoor dining table surrounded by fragrant torches.

It's only my girls and me at the resort since her clients and staff left yesterday morning. Yesterday we went for a long hike through the verdant patchwork of forests on the island. We followed it with a rejuvenating swim in one of the crystal-clear freshwater lakes.

Now, we're on the villa's terrace for an appetizing dinner of flavorful local favorites prepared by a chef on the outdoor grill and cooktop. The aroma is mouthwatering.

I sip my Tipo Tinto à la Billie Chandler and grin at Starr.

"It was the best I've ever been on! Fantastic!" I say as I rise to give her a standing ovation.

"You did such a superb job, Starr! I can't wait for the next one," Billie answers as she clinks glasses with our hostess.

"Indeed! I thought nothing could top your first one on Fijian Laucala Island last year. That private paradise is surreal," Lola chimes in.

"Sign me up for all of them! I feel incredible, thank you very much!" Leonie exclaims.

"Me, too!" Blair says as she raises her glass. "A toast… Here's to good friends, good loves, and good times!"

Everyone cheers and clinks glasses. Lola pauses and peers at Starr.

"What's the latest on your conversations with Malcolm?"

Interestingly, Starr avoids Lola's probing gaze. Starr shifts in her chair and pretends to straighten the napkin on her lap.

Lola won't give up so easily.

"Well?" She demands with an arched eyebrow.

Starr clears her throat and returns Lola's gaze. Defiantly, Starr lifts her chin as she responds.

"Malcolm Steele is an arrogant, self-focused cretin!"

Oh, boy, here we go with my brothers and their escapades… I cover my ears, not wanting to hear a damn word.

But Leonie, Billie, and Blair gape at Starr's heated reaction.

Our normally quiet calm, namaste, om, center your mind friend now flustered completely. Their gazes dart between her and Lola in shock. I whistle to block any sound.

I see Lola pull back from the table, doubling over in glee as she bursts out laughing. Her last sip of Tipo Tinto comes out on a snort.

The sight is too comical. We can't help but join in—even Starr.

Once Lola gathers herself, wiping tears from the corners of her eyes, she straightens. She lifts her left hand and waggles her fingers. Her engagement ring and wedding band shine in the moonlight.

"That's the same thing I said about his doppelgänger brother, Captain Caveman… Now look at me, my friend!"

Starr looks as stunned as the rest of us. But Lola keeps giggling. She definitely knows something Starr is clueless about. When the girls question her, Lola shakes her head and sips her drink, laughing to herself.

I CREEP into the primary bedroom of the President's Suite at STEELE Mayfair. Lachlan lies asleep on his back, muscular arm draped over his face. My dress slips to the floor as I step out of my flip-flops beside the bed. Gently, I crawl over his body and brush my lips over his.

He stirs but doesn't open his eyes.

I lick from the cleft in his clean-shaven chin up to his lips.

His arm lowers to rest his palm on my bare ass.

"Margaret? Is that you, baby?"

I jump back and land on my butt, legs sprawled on either side of his hips.

"WHAT?!?!?!" I shout incredulously.

Lachlan jolts and stares at me with wide eyes.

"Oh… Haley… Fuck…" he stammers.

My heart drops as tears well in my eyes.

No fucking way!

I crab crawl backwards away from him, unable to pull my shocked eyes from his guilty ones.

Lachlan jumps up and traps me beneath him.

"Baby Girl! I was only teasing! Please don't cry. I'm so sorry. Please," he says, entwining our fingers beside my head as I thrash about.

I stop and stare up at him.

"Only you, Baby Girl. I just wanted to get back at you for teasing me about being topless around all those guys," he says remorsefully. "Hell, I don't even know a Margaret."

I bare my teeth at him and jerk against his hold.

"You *ass*hole!!!" I shriek.

He doesn't move but lets me swear at him until I'm breathless. Then he slams his mouth on mine.

It's not until that point I feel his fat dick pressed between our bodies. I squirm halfheartedly, also aroused by the need to claim my man.

"Your jealousy makes my cock painfully hard, Baby Girl," he growls as he grinds his pelvis into mine.

I nip his lips and growl right back as I spread my legs to cradle him between them. My ankles lock behind his ass, then I pull him closer to my heated core.

"You are mine, Lachlan Jackson. Do not fuck with me again!" I tell him.

He clamps my wrists in one hand and fists his dick with the other before he enters me with one brutal stroke.

"And you are mine, Haley Steele. Do not fuck with me again," he repeats as he thrusts.

It doesn't take long to reach our release as one, as our cries of pleasure blend.

"I love you, Baby Girl," Lachlan breathes in my ear.

"You better," I retort.

His wicked chuckle and still hard dick let me know we've only begun.

And I'm more than ready for my lover.

LACHLAN

"*O*MG! What did he say he wanted? Did he sound suspicious? What did you do to make him ask?! How far away are you? Aargh! My stomach hurts—"

Haley's rapid-fire questions started the moment I told her Baz asked me to meet him for a game of squash and dinner. I can imagine her wide eyes, flushed face, and glasses readjusted on her nose. My poor Baby Girl.

I don't suspect Baz knows anything about us. This is more of a fishing expedition. We're both Alpha males protective of our families—especially of our sisters. So I know how the game plays.

Hell, plenty of times I pissed off Lydie when guys came by for their dates with her. I gave zero fucks she's a year older than me and the guys ranged from one to three years older than me, with some of them more muscular. I'd answer the door before our butler and polish my dagger while the guy and I waited in the library for Lydie to come downstairs. Sure she groused about it. But oh well.

So I don't harbor any bad sentiment toward my best friend for his Big Brother Syndrome with Haley.

What I have to do is strike a balance between Haley being my girlfriend and Baz as my best friend for our entire lives. It's really fucked up when I think about it. Baz has his woman. Why should he prevent me from mine? Sure, My Baby Girl happens to be his baby sister. But damn!

My fingers run through my hair as I sigh in frustration.

"Baby Girl," I cut in. "Listen, did you forget Sebastian and I are best friends prior to you being my girlfriend? So, he and I hang out. That's what we do. Especially when I'm in New York or he's near Scotland—"

"I know! But it's awfully suspic—"

"Haley. Enough. Take a deep breath and let it go, babe. You're freaking out over nothing. Come on… Breathe with me," I interrupt. My girl needs to relax.

"You there?" I ask when silence descends on our call.

She sighs.

"I just don't want any drama, Lachlan. We just celebrated our six-month anniversary," she says. "Six months without The Big Four going buck wild. I want to keep it that way."

My heart clenches at the sorrow in her voice.

It's not how I want her to feel. And I definitely don't want her to feel pressured to please her family or me over the other. That would only lead to trouble.

"I mean Baz has Lola; Roger's with Leonie. Why can't I have my happily ever after?" My Baby Girl mutters.

My driver stops my Black Badge Rolls-Royce Cullinan, and the doorman opens my door.

I slide off of the back seat and nod a thanks to him.

"Babe, I arrived. Don't worry. I'll call you later," I tell her. "I love you, Baby Girl."

"I love you, too," she replies.

We disconnect the call as I walk into the opulent lobby at the Union Club of the City of New York on tony Park Avenue. I slip my mobile into my trousers pocket to avoid the faux pas of an openly held device in the common areas of the club.

Baz—as with the other Steele men of each generation— has been a member of the one hundred-eighty plus year old exclusive social club since its founding as the first of its kind. Despite the club's history of being notorious for denying membership to sons, they granted Steeles access at all times. One could say having a Steele as a founding member doesn't hurt their chances...

Suitably attired in my bespoke Saville Row three-piece suit, custom dress shirt, tie, and A. Testoni Oxfords, the concierge checks me in as a visitor. Had I arrived in a t-shirt, jeans, and flip-flops, he would have security show me to the service entrance. Did I say a posh men's social club?

I poke fun. But the Steeles and their relationship with the Union Club does not differ from the Jacksons' founding member status we have at the equally notable Royal Northern & University Club Aberdeen. However, we one-up them since Queen Victoria granted our club royal status after her visit.

Once I thank the concierge, I continue through the lobby to the main elevator for access to the men's locker room. My leather duffle bag holds the required all-white clothing of a collared shirt, shorts, socks, and sneakers for squash.

"Hey, cuz. Glad you could make it."

I glance around the open locker door to find Baz grinning at me as he twirls his goggles around an index finger. He's already dressed for squash in pristine whites. Platinum gray eyes shine with his competitive nature on full display.

"Ready to get your ass handed to you?" Baz smirks. "Because I sure am ready to do it."

I pull my Ralph Lauren Polo shirt over my head and past my abs before I respond.

"Good to see you too, cuz," I say then slip on wrist sweatbands. "As far as asses go, you tell me since I plan to win."

I pick up my racquet and goggles, then clap him on the shoulder as I pass.

"What are you waiting for? Scared?" I rib with a smirk.

Baz chuckles, and we stride out of the locker room to the squash courts. With a nod of his head, he indicates the second one as reserved for us.

"Best of five games, or do you want to wimp out at only three?" Baz taunts.

I snort and respond, "Well, you are the old man here. Do you need me to go easy on you?"

"Ha! Five, fucker!" He responds. "Bring it!"

We maintain a ferocious pace throughout the match while we talk smack. Forty minutes later, we're sweaty and ready for showers. We gulp down bottles of coconut water to replenish our electrolytes as we return to the locker room.

"Okay, you may have won this match. But before you skip town, we'll be back here for round two," Baz says.

I bark a laugh and respond, "It'll be my absolute pleasure to serve you your ass again, cuz!"

He rolls his eyes—sore loser—as he heads to his personal locker in the members' section.

"I'll meet you in the lobby," he calls out over his shoulder.

I nod and chuckle to myself.

My Baby Girl had nothing to worry about.

"BROTHERS, cousins, best friends, they're great to have. We can make special bonds for life. But sisters? Sisters rank even higher. Especially baby sisters."

I control my reaction to Baz's comments even though they take me by surprise after our chummy conversation in the SUV.

During the ride out to Williamsburg in Brooklyn for dinner at the one Michelin star Peter Luger Steak House, our conversation was casual. I rubbed in his loss with recaps of his misses and my scores. We moved on to brag-worthy business deals before we got into the Knicks' basketball game we'll attend tomorrow night in the STEELE International box at Madison Square Garden. We jumped out of my Cullinan, cracking up about the hijinks we'd get into as teens and in our twenties.

I should have known Baz's trip down memory lane wasn't by happenstance…

"As the eldest of my siblings I have a responsibility to care for them—a third parent, if you will. I prioritize their wellbeing equal to my own and now to Lola's," Baz continues conversationally as he slices into his dry-aged porterhouse steak.

I play the game and take a bite of mine with an at-ease expression on my face, as my eyes never leave his.

It reminds me of our game as kids where we'd stare unblinkingly at each other until one of us gave in. Now I put it to good use. I don't speak. To explain without cause proves a clear sign of a guilty conscious.

And I am far from guilty.

Baz and I are no different. I take the same stance with my siblings and have always counted Haley amongst them. From cleaning her scraped knee when she fell down the treehouse ladder to sitting in the living room with her prom date while Baz read him the rules.

The urge to care for and to protect My Baby Girl never waivers. It's grown over the years. And now she's mine.

"I love Lydie—like a sister—and could never see her as more than that. It pains me my negligence to recognize her interest in me beyond cousins hurt her," Baz goes on. "Once I found out, I made it clear the close connection our families share prevent me from wanting more from her. She's my younger cousin. Nothing beyond that relationship despite her mistaking our closeness as something more."

My hand remains steady as I bring my glass of Jackson Cabernet Sauvignon to my mouth. Meanwhile, my heart races with indignation.

His situation with Lydie is far from mine with Haley. I want her, and she wants me. Baz never desired Lydie. For him to come up with this shit pisses me off.

"You and I are best friends, Lachlan, as close as our mothers. Their friendship carries over into STEELE International and Jackson Corporation's affairs quite positively," Baz says before he spears a piece of steak with his fork and stares at me. "I would hate for a lack of trust and loyalty to cause an abrupt end to our business. How can one build a partnership without those two factors?"

Fuck. Me.

He did not go all the way there. Baz's behavior hits wanker territory. It's one thing to get pissed I'm with his little sister. But to threaten our business relationship goes to a whole other level.

"Sebastian, either spit it out, or shut the fuck up with this long ass dialogue," I respond, my temper held back by gossamer.

He takes a slow sip of his wine as he watches me over

the rim of the glass. Unblinking platinum gray eyes meet my emerald fired-up ones. A moment later, he nods.

"Is there anything you want to spit out to me, Lach?" Baz asks.

My molars grind hard enough to send a sharp pain through my jaw. This wanker! I'm tempted to tell him about Haley and to back the fuck up. But then her worried face pops into my mind along with her concerns to keep peace. I take a deep breath.

"No. So move on, Baz. How's your married life?" I counter. Let him worry about his relationship, not mine.

He backs down with a nod.

The tension abates, and our conversation returns to normal. By the time we cross the Williamsburg Bridge to the FDR Drive in Manhattan, jokes replace cloaked accusations. We part in the lobby of The STEELE Tower as I head to the residential elevators for my full-floor flat on the forty-ninth floor. Baz strides to their family's private elevator with a reminder about the Knicks' game.

On my ride up, I loosen my tie and run both hands through my hair with a tug. I pace to burn off the pent-up agitation. Once in my primary bedroom, I stride to my en suite bathroom, stripping off my clothes as I go.

A steam shower eases the tightness in my body. The warm water sluices from my head down my pecs and abs. Multiple massaging shower heads direct water to my back, ass, legs, and feet. Satisfied the coils unfurled, I dry off with a heated towel and pick up my mobile from the sofa.

Plunking down on the bed, I stretch my naked body out and dial My Baby Girl.

"Lachlan!" She cries out when the FaceTime call connects. "How did it go? What did Baz—"

"Babe, hold on. I'll tell you everything," I cut in, not wanting her to get wound up again.

She nods and sits back against her headboard.

How I wish we were in bed together and not a floor apart. Ironic how she's just above my bedroom. I'm tempted to put a firefighter's pole between them. No one would see it on her floor if she put a rug over the hatch…

I chuckle.

"What?! Tell me!" She demands.

I recount the entire conversation as she sits rapt. When finished, she bites her lower lip.

"Listen, we continue as *we* planned. No one—not even Sebastian—will change how we want to live our lives. Understand?" I tell her.

She nods again. This time her eyes wander over my bare chest. The gray gives way to obsidian as her arousal takes over from her worries.

Good.

"Now, put your mobile on the headboard and kneel on your bed. I want you to strip for me, Baby Girl."

HALEY

My nerves peak as I wait at the conference room table of Baz's office suite at STEELE New York. He's running late from an external meeting due to traffic for our STEELE Technology and Cyber Security biweekly status update. Harris met with him earlier today since a client needed me to handle an unexpected project on site.

Now it's my turn. Alone. Without Harris as a buffer.

I swivel in my leather chair to take in the city through the floor-to-ceiling windows of the modern, gray-tinted glass fifty-seven story mixed-use skyscraper. We're on the twenty-ninth floor for the executive level where besides Baz, my father, Malcolm, and Roger have offices suites with more for our finance and legal departments. Along with STCS, our other divisions have designated floors below.

The Manhattan skyline stretches out before me with

201

views for miles in every direction. Central Park to the north, the Hudson River to the west, the East River opposite, and the rest of Manhattan to the south from Midtown to Battery Park. Ordinarily the panoramic sight gives me solace—a way to clear my head of code. This late afternoon? Not so much.

Lachlan left a few days ago for Chicago. While he's in the States, he's visiting Jackson Corporation offices and liquor distributors, followed by time in Asia before he returns to Aberdeen in six weeks. His last night we met up at the St. Regis Hotel New York's Presidential Suite.

We had a beautiful night of passionate lovemaking and cuddling since some time will pass before we see one another again. I leave tomorrow morning for an extended trip to Latin America to connect with our clients and to spend time at our properties in various cities. We'll meet in Paris for a little rendezvous...

"Penny for your thoughts?"

So lost in thought, I didn't notice Baz enter his office and sit across the table from me.

I spin in my chair to face him, heart racing from the surprise.

"Oh! Ha! Sorry, I didn't hear you come in," I sputter as I grip the arms of the chair. "Enjoying the view, so no bank, sorry!"

Baz's platinum gray eyes sparkle as he chuckles.

"My dear Haley, you undervalue yourself," he says with a shake of his head. "I apologize for my tardiness. Let's get started."

"No worries," I respond before I go into detail on each of my projects.

Despite not being a techie, Baz understands more so from a CEO's viewpoint. He asks questions and makes suggestions. It's good to get his perspective since he's not immersed in the minutiae. He allows Harris and me to run our division with little interference. Baz's two requirements: keep clients happy and generate revenue. Fortunately, since Harris and I started STCS it's been profitable with clients satisfied and referring others.

An hour later, Baz sits back in his chair and finishes his bottle of water. I gather my laptop and tablet before I turn off the flat-screen television used for my presentation. While Baz scrolls through his mobile, I check mine and smile at the photo Lachlan sent via text message.

"Sure you don't have bank for me?"

The grin slips from my face, and I school my expression. No way can I give Baz a hint as to the nature of my message. Particularly since it's a photo of a tented sheet…

With a straight face I quip, "Well, this thought would double your account. But I don't think you could handle it."

Baz throws his head back and barks a laugh.

"Come on, let's go to dinner," he says. "Lola and Harris await us in the lobby."

As we stride through the corridors, I take in STEELE's interior as it reflects the metal our name represents. The decor—as sleek as the exterior—features platinum silk wall treatments, ebony wood floors, dove gray and white leather furniture, crystal light fixtures, Lucite tables, steel accents, and original artwork. A spacious desk with room for the three daytime receptionists anchors the reception area. The woman on the evening shift sits behind it with a headset in her ears and a custom-tailored light gray dress suit and skin-tone heels.

I can see why STEELE makes an impression on visitors from the moment they cross the threshold of the elevators. Even I'm not jaded by its beauty and power. It makes me proud to be a member of our clan.

"Good night, Mr. Steele and Haley," the evening receptionist says with a smile and a wave.

"Good night, Sheila," we respond in unison and tell the security guard at the elevators the same.

As we ride down, I get a phone call from our mother I put on speaker so Baz can hear too.

"Hi, sweetheart! What plans do you have for tonight?" She asks. "Your father and I just arrived home and are ordering Thai food from your favorite place. Do you want to join us?"

I love my Mom! She knows I'm bummed on not seeing Lachlan for a while and wants to cheer me up. They were in Mykonos on *Serendipity* and came back early.

"Hi, Mom! Thanks, but I'm with Baz and we're going to Kurumazushi with Lola and Harris. If I'd known, I would've hung out with you and Dad!" I giggle, glancing at Baz.

"Whatever, Haley… Hi, Mom. How was Greece?" He asks as he nudges me with his arm. "You look nice and tan."

"Oh, hi, honey! It was marvelous! Your father surprised me one night with dinner in the square decorated with fairy lights, flowers, and lanterns and a trio performed. It was so romantic!" She gushes.

I love how in love my parents are after thirty-six years of marriage. My father showers her with gifts at random from a crystal bird for her collection to a suite of rare pink diamonds or a simple dinner on a Greek isle. Sure they have their disagreements. But in the end, they make up and move on.

That's what I want. And I want it with Lachlan.

It's been six months without a mention of marriage or our future. He tells me I'm his, and he's mine. We've exchanged the important three words. But nada.

Me?

I can already visualize our wedding with our families and closest friends at Jackson Castle—a true fairytale with an earl and a countess. Even Lachlan in a traditional kilt of their clan sans boxer briefs, of course! A ballgown spun from the softest silk with a cathedral-length veil for me. I'd love to have children at least three, maybe four, to keep them even. A couple of Gordon Setter dogs—a Scottish breed known to be protective of children—to round out our happy little family.

We'd live in—

"Uh, Earth to Haley…"

I blink, and my dream dissipates like mists on the Scottish moors as the sun rises.

"Oh, sorry," I respond to Baz. "What did you say?"

"Are you sure about those pennies?" He asks with a smirk.

"Haley, sweetheart, I said go enjoy dinner with your brothers and Lola. I'll book a spa day with lunch for tomorrow. Ask Lola if she wants to join us," my mother says.

"It's Saturday so I think she's free," Baz adds as the elevator doors open. "She's here, let's find out."

Lola smiles and returns his wave as Baz and I approach her and Harris.

"Hi! I'm so ready for some sushi!" She says as we hug.

"Well, are you ready for a spa day? Mom is planning one for tomorrow and wants to know if you'll join us," I tell Lola as I gesture with my mobile.

She claps her hands and takes it from me.

"Hi, Mom! Absolutely count me in!" Lola says into the speakers.

The four of us make our way through the plush lobby to my Bentley Bentayga, where Gary opens the back door and helps Lola and me into the third row. Harris and Baz slide onto the second row, and we're off.

Lola and I chat with my mother about the treatments we want to book and our meals. The boys ramble on about some playoffs for some team or the other. In no time, we arrive ten blocks away at Kurumazushi off Fifth Avenue.

We take our seats on a corner of the sushi bar. The head

chef greets us with a bow as he performs an art-like preparation of sushi with his filleting knife. Each of us request *omakase* where we leave the meal selection up to the chef. It's the ultimate way to experience Kurumazushi. While we enjoy sashimi, the server brings us various sakes to heighten the flavors in the appetizers.

"Man, I could live here," Harris says. "Every time I come, the food only gets better."

Baz raises his sake glass and inclines his head at the chef.

"I couldn't agree more," he adds.

Lola snorts and says, "Well, you could always ask to put a bed in the *washitu* room. Meanwhile, I'll stretch out in ours. Without. You."

Baz chokes on his drink, and we laugh as his face turns red.

"Well, that could work," I tease. "They say absence makes the heart grow fonder."

Baz grunts as he catches his breath. Lola rubs his back and kisses his cheek.

"Aaawww. Will you miss me, babe?" She asks sweetly.

He leans over and whispers in her ear. It's her turn to turn crimson.

"Oh brother. Let me guess... Alpha Dom talks shit, huh?" Harris chuckles. "Give us a break already, Baz."

Lola and I giggle as Baz chuckles.

Dinner progresses, and we sit in awe of the mastery the head chef has over the fish as he transforms them into incredible works of art. The presentation is so fine, I hate to touch my food once the plate sits before me. Silence descends upon us, only broken by our sighs of pleasure. It's almost orgasmic.

Over fresh fruit and tea, talk returns to our weekend activities. Lola offers to make Sunday brunch since our parents are back. I tell her I'll pick up a Principessa cake from the Italian bakery Sant Ambrœus as my contribution. She giggles, knowing how I hate to cook as much as Leonie.

"Well, count me in for the wine," Harris says.

"Speaking of wine, Lachlan has a big multi-city trip ahead of him. He's like me before I got married. Work ahead of love," Baz states out of the blue. His bright eyes turn to me.

"Oh, so first you want to move out. Now you're reminiscing over the old days. What's up, Sebastian?" Harris deadpans.

As they stare at each other, I hold my breath. I know Harris used his jokester ways to deflect for me. I also know Baz doesn't want to hurt me and is fishing since he didn't get anywhere with Lachlan. So I face Lola and grin.

"Girl, what's up?" I tease.

Lola turns to Baz.

"Yeah, Sebastian, care to explain?" She asks as she crosses her arms over her chest. The petite spitfire's amber eyes gleam.

Baz raises his hands, palms out in surrender. His wide eyes dart from one of us to the other.

"Okay. Okay. I do *not* want to live anywhere but at

home, and I have *no* interest whatsoever in my old playboy ways," he starts and slips his arms around Lola's waist. "You've made me a better man, Mrs. Steele."

Lola grins and pats his cheek.

"Good answer, Mr. Steele," she says. "Now, take me home."

Baz grins wolfishly and pulls his wallet from his suit jacket pocket. The server appears to take the proffered American Express Centurion Card. Moments later he returns, and we leave.

During the ride back we laugh and joke. Thankfully, Harris did a great job of changing the course of the conversation. Baz doesn't make any further comments, and Lola talks about her upcoming photoshoot for a new collection of evening gowns.

We part ways when the elevator doors open on my floor. I give everyone a hug and tell Lola I'll see her tomorrow. Baz gives me an extra squeeze before I step out. Over his shoulder, Harris winks at me, and I grin.

As I walk through my quiet penthouse, I wish Lachlan was here with me. I want to come home to him every single day. Go to bed wrapped in his powerful embrace each night. When I reach my bedroom, I sigh at the sight of the big, empty bed.

Absence does more than make the heart grow fonder. It reminds you of what you don't have.

I may not have Lachlan here right now. But I intend to have him forever.

LACHLAN

"Leonie, it's so good to see you well."

I place double kisses on her glowing cheeks. And indeed she looks fantastic at three-months pregnant.

Along with Leonie, Roger, and the Beaulieus, the rest of the Steeles, Luc, and Blair gather in the solarium that overlooks the rear rose garden of *Le Beaulieu Manoir*. I flew in last night from Aberdeen for business at our Paris offices this week. Roger invited me to Sunday brunch since he and Leonie plan to make a special announcement about their pregnancy.

First Baz, now Roger.

I'm happy for my cousins. They've got their girls, and Leonie is having Roger's baby. Only Malcolm and Harris remain single of The Big Four. Who knows when they'll settle down. Although I noticed a certain brown-eyed yogi has caught *The Enforcer*'s dove gray eye.

Hopefully, all of their action will distract them from My Baby Girl and me. One can hope…

Roger growls possessively when I kiss his woman. I chuckle and drape my arm around Leonie's shoulders.

"Calm down, Papa Caveman! I'm off the market!" I say with a wink.

A stricken sound behind me makes us turn.

My Baby Girl stands staring at me. Her gray eyes widen behind her glasses. Scarlet flushes her cheeks as she turns away quickly.

Damn!

What I thought would be a funny joke to throw Baz off results in upsetting her. And on top of that, drawing their attention as proven by the stoic expression on Baz's face and the intense stare I sense drilling in the back of my head from Roger. A quick glance to the side reveals a scowling Malcolm and Harris shaking his head in dismay.

My gaze returns to My Baby Girl's retreating figure as she stalks towards the sideboard. She takes a flute filled with a Mimosa and gulps half of it. Her reaction trips up my usual Alpha Dom bravado. I can only stare. Fuck! I want to bite those words back.

The sound of Roger clearing his throat pulls me from my pity party.

I face him again, and he cocks his head questioningly.

Damn.

I avert my gaze and squeeze Leonie's shoulders before I step away. I'd like to ask My Baby Girl what's wrong, but that would attract more unwanted attention. We can wait.

"Mon Cœur? Are you ready?"

Fortunately, Leonie's question reminds everyone of why we're gathered. She and Roger go on to share their exciting news. After cheers and hugs, we enjoy the delicious dishes arranged on the buffet. The tantalizing aroma of savory and sweet foods fills the air. Leonie's mother Josy blends traditional Tunisian and French fare of meats, vegetables, and baked goods for a mouthwatering collection of delights.

As we enjoy our brunch, the conversation stays lively with everyone chatting about the happy couple's upcoming preparations. Their decision to find out the sex sparks a gut-punching comment from My Baby Girl.

"We need more girls!" She declares. "We have more than enough testosterone and overinflated egos to last a lifetime!"

I wince at her declaration. Once again Baz and Roger share a glance. The All Seeing Ones. Great...

My Baby Girl dodges my eyes as she continues to chat with her girls about Leonie's fairytale nuptials. A fleeting wistful expression crosses Haley's face when Baz teases Lola about the little amount of time he gave her to prepare for their wedding.

It's at that moment My Baby Girl peeks at me.

When our eyes meet, she chews on the corner of her lower lip thoughtfully. It's as though she's gauging my reaction to all the talk of babies and weddings. My expression remains blank since we're surrounded by her brothers, and

I don't want to spark their ire at Roger and Leonie's special time.

Instead, I try to relay my love for My Baby Girl through my eyes. I almost laugh out loud when I recall her telling me she smizes à la supermodel Tyra. As Haley told me, she has to do more for people to see her eyes since she wears glasses. I took them off and kissed each eyelid before I made her more than smize...

"—Lachlan? Did you hear me, sweetheart?"

The sound of my name interrupts my musings. I glance across the table to find Aunt Shelley's brown-eyed gaze on me. Her knowing look makes me squirm in my seat.

"Pardon me, Aunt Shelley," I respond sheepishly. "What did you say?"

A soft smile plays at the corners of her mouth.

"Oh, sweetheart, no worries!" She responds. "Lucie tells me you've had a busy travel schedule and working nonstop. Any chance of settling down soon?"

I nearly choke on my Jackson Chardonnay. Without meaning to, my eyes swivel to My Baby Girl. Her body angles forward slightly as she watches me with an intense stare, enough to rival Roger's. I dab my mouth with the linen napkin from my lap and clear my throat.

"Mom always worries about me. Business called for a few weeks away from home, but nothing unusual," I start, as my gaze never waivers from Aunt Shelley. "I'm back in Aberdeen for a while now."

"Ah, yes, you mentioned being 'off the market.' So who's

the lucky lady to snag the Earl?" Baz asks as his platinum gray eyes sparkle with devilry.

"Oh, do tell," Malcolm adds with a raised eyebrow.

"We're all ears," Roger says.

Only Harris remains silent. However, he cocks his head, eager to hear my answer.

Now I'll have to say more shit that will upset My Baby Girl. I take a deep breath and send a prayer up she won't run from the solarium screaming.

"Fiona Ridel," I say.

In my periphery, Lola glances at Haley and Leonie's mouth gapes. My Baby Girl sits stiffly as she concentrates on her plate of food.

"The woman from Thanksgiving?" Baz asks for confirmation. "Interesting. I'm sure Uncle Connor must be pleased with that match—oil and liquor. How will they mix?"

"Well, whomever Lachlan chooses to spend the rest of his life with is of no concern to you, boys," Aunt Shelley says. Her elegantly shaped eyebrow arches as she pins each of her sons with her cut-it-out-this-minute expression. The same one she used on all of us as kids.

If this wasn't such a fucked up situation, I'd crack a joke and laugh.

"Or would you like to discuss *your* marital options, Malcolm and Harris?" Aunt Shelley adds.

It's not My Baby Girl who concerns me may run from the solarium screaming. Now it's her brothers. Their faces flush crimson as they lean back in their chairs and cast their eyes to the doors, longing to escape.

First I chuckle, then the others join in. The tense moment passes, and we go on to enjoy the rest of the afternoon. During our stroll through twenty acres of manicured park-like grounds, Leonie points out paths to the stables, tennis court, and the swimming pool with cabana. Her family's ancestral estate is a peaceful respite from the bustling city.

I watch My Baby Girl as she walks arm-in-arm with Lola ahead of me. Baz's conversation about a new deal registers barely. My only focus giggles at something her sister-in-law says.

When we make our way back to the palatial French Rococo mansion, we bid Guy and Josy adieu. Everyone gets into their vehicles and leave the couple waving as they stand before the front doors to their home.

The engine of my Aston Martin DB7 Vantage purrs as the tires crunch the gravel of the driveway. I press the phone button on the steering wheel.

"Call My Baby Girl," I state.

The sound of the car mobile rings through the interior. With each long ring, my stomach sinks. When her voice-mail picks up, I disconnect the call.

She's in a chauffeur-driven Rolls-Royce Corniche alone, so she could answer her mobile. If she wanted to, that is…

I maneuver through the streets of the *seizième* to my penthouse close to their mansion. My mind on overdrive as I wonder what Haley is doing. We planned to see each other tomorrow evening. Now what?

A sigh slips past my lips.

I turn the corner onto the street for the garage entrance. My heart leaps.

My Baby Girl's sedan sits at the curb. The back door opens, and she steps out. The wind catches her glossy ebony waves. She slides a loose tendril behind her ear and raises her hand to greet me.

I pull my car right up next to her and jump out—engine running still. In a flash, she's in my arms. Her laughter fills the air as I lift her from her feet and swing her in a circle. Without a backward glance, I carry her to the passenger side of my car. She slips onto the plush leather seat and smiles up at me as I close the door.

"Haley, I'm so sorry to upset you—" I begin when I sit in the driver's seat.

She places her index finger over my lips as she shakes her head. Hair falls around her heart-shaped face, and I run my fingers through the strands to expose her natural beauty. My mouth slants over hers, and she opens to me on a sigh. I swallow her soft moans like a thirsty man in the desert.

"I love you, Baby Girl," I say against her full lips, then pull back to look into her eyes. "No Fiona Ridel. Only Haley Steele. Understand?"

"Yes, Lachlan. It just surprised me. But I get it," she replies sadly. "I just wish my brothers would back off—

rather Sebastian, Malcolm, and Roger. Harris gets it too. He just doesn't want me hurt."

I nod and promise I won't ever hurt her. After she confirms she understands, she motions for me to drive into the garage.

Happily, I rev the engine and take My Baby Girl home.

On the ride up in my private elevator, I stand behind her with my arms wrapped around her waist and my lips on the side of her neck. The sensitive juncture at her shoulder calls for me to mark her. My lips blaze a trail of heat along her skin. Goosebumps prickle in the wake of my open-mouthed kisses.

She purrs like a content kitten.

My cock punches against the back of my trousers zipper, eager to bury itself balls deep in her pussy. It's been way too long since we made love. Way. Too. Long.

"Missed me much?" My Baby Girl teases as she wiggles her hips provocatively.

I place one hand on her hip and the other on her throat. As I bend my knees and squeeze her hip bone, she jolts, then groans from the pressure of my hard cock against her lush ass. My groin grinds into her, and she arches her spine as she pushes back into me.

"You tell me, Baby Girl," I rumble in her ear then nip the lobe.

She gasps. Her palms go to my muscular thighs for support as her knees turn to jelly.

The ding of the elevator doors opening disrupts our passionate make-out session. With a growl, I scoop My

Baby Girl into my arms and carry her through to my penthouse. I make no stops until we arrive at my bedroom.

She giggles as I toss her onto the middle of the bed. Her D-cup tits bounce beneath her silk wrap dress, exposing the black lace of her bra. Long legs splayed over the bed reveal more of the sexy lingerie at the apex of her thighs. Her bare mound peeks between the delicate fabric, enticing me like a red cape before a bull.

When My Baby Girl leans back on her elbows and toes off her fuck-me heels, she beckons me with her finger.

"Show me how much you missed me, My Lord," she purrs.

I grin wolfishly and strip.

Her hooded eyes caress my body as she takes me in from head to toe. She parts her lips and darts her little pink tongue out to swipe it along the bottom one. When she pulls it into her mouth with her teeth, I pounce.

"Oh *my*, My Lord!" My Little Temptress giggles as I plank over her, hands grip the headboard and toes planted in the mattress.

My massive cock points at her undoubtedly soaked pussy like a dowsing rod above a hidden well of water.

I follow her heated gaze to my dick. A wicked chuckle falls from my mouth when she gasps at it flexing.

Her eyes fly to mine, and she giggles nervously.

No matter how many times we make love, her tight pussy has to stretch to accommodate my girth. And as erect as I am now, my cock appears twice its size.

"Oh, you will take every veined inch deep inside of your greedy little pussy, Little Temptress," I growl.

She mewls.

I tighten my ass and thighs to brace myself as I use one hand to pull the bow of her belt. My much-anticipated gift unwraps before me.

She shrugs out of her dress. The tops of her tits jiggle above her demi-cup bra. Pebbled rosy nipples poke at the black lace.

My mouth waters.

"Off!" I command.

My Little Temptress scrambles to open the front closure of her bra, then shimmies out of her G-string.

Before her hips lower back to the mattress, I drape her thigh over the crook of my elbow and raise it to her right shoulder. My palm plants on the bed beside her head, and I thank Starr for the virtual yoga sessions My Baby Girl takes with her four days a week.

"Put my cock inside of your pussy," I growl as I widen my feet. Prepped to rock her world, I groan when her little fingers fist my dick and guide me to her slippery core.

Our eyes lock on our connection.

In one quick thrust, I bury myself within her from tip to root. My heavy balls slap her ass cheeks, and her juices drip down to coat my sac.

"So. Fucking. Good..." I grunt.

"Oh, yes, My Lord," My Little Temptress moans. Her eyes close in carnal bliss.

I drop my hungry mouth to her pebbled nipple and lave

it with the flat of my tongue. Her back arches from the bed when I suckle. Hard.

My hips move in gentle circles for my ten inches to touch every part of her pussy, drawing more of her juices from her core. Her soft moans spur me on, and I increase my ministrations to her tits. When she cries out as her pussy walls clench around my girth, I bring her other thigh over my left arm. Her orgasm continues with flutters along my length as I drive in and out of her pussy in a steady rhythm.

"Give me another one, Little Temptress," I command.

Once again, she clamps down on my cock as a wail falls from her slack mouth. Her fingernails dig into my biceps. Trembling, she rides out her climax on my pistoning dick.

I pull out and flip her onto her hands and knees—ass up, head down. My fingers grip her hips, and I slam back into her creamy pussy again and again.

"Fuck. YES!" I roar as my release rips through me.

My mind blanks, but my body goes on autopilot. More strokes follow until every drop of my seed coats My Baby Girl's womb.

In my rattled state, the thought of her carrying my baby rises to the surface.

Could we have it all, like Roger and Leonie? Baz and Lola?

My body follows my mind and collapses over Haley's back. I wrap an arm around her waist and lower us to our sides, still attached intimately. Spooned, we drift off, sated.

The unanswered questions float away.

The loud metal clang of Highland broadswords hitting targes rings out in the open-air court-yard of the Scottish Arts Center With Ewan Kerr. Now that I'm back in Aberdeen for a stretch of time, my HEMA sessions start again with Ewan—my trainer and a world-renowned master of Historical European Martial Arts. He's helped actors prepare for their action roles and consults with the Scottish Olympic fencing team.

Ewan puts his extraordinary skills to task on me since my mind won't stop drifting back to my last night in Paris.

"We'll make it a Guys' Night Out with the added benefit of tasting my latest creation," I tell Roger on the phone. "I'm sure Leonie will give you permission to hang out with your mates for a few hours."

Roger barks a laugh at my taunt.

"Nice try, Lach. But I'll grace you with my presence anyway," he says. "I'll tell Joel to join us. He's a Scotch connoisseur."

"Good, the more the merrier, cuz. Lucien said he has some guests too," I add.

We end our call, and I turn to my computer. My calendar is pretty packed with meetings from now through this afternoon. So I look forward to some downtime with friends. The intercom rings with my Paris administrative assistant announcing my next appointment. Work now; play later.

"Good evening, Monsieur Jackson. I'll see you to your private tasting room. Your guests have not arrived yet. So I will bring them to you once they come, sir."

I nod at the voluptuous, redheaded hostess at Jackson Smoke&Scotch Lounge Paris. It's a new lounge Lucien opened five months ago on Rue Saint-Honoré.

The legendary Place Vendôme/St. Honoré area is the place to see and be seen. Where money is no object for the people it attracts. Old society, fashionistas, and celebrities frequent the nearby high-chic spots to shop, drink, and dine.

It's the latest addition to Jackson Corporation's luxury establishments created by The Sexy Chef. His team slated locations in London, New York, and Los Angeles for over the next six months. Another hot property for the company to add to our roster of fine eateries and establishments.

"Kindly follow me, Monsieur Jackson," the hostess all but purrs as her eyes travel over my body surreptitiously.

Outwardly I smile; inwardly I roll my eyes and make a mental note to tell Lucien to have human resources speak with her about flirting with us and our patrons. Human resources will correct her behavior or replace her. Jackson Corporation prides itself on providing a reputable and a responsible environment within its establishments. We will not abide by staff wooing us, or our guests. This is not a brothel, nor are our employees anything but professional and respectable.

"Thank you," I respond.

She smiles and steps from behind the hostess station. Seductively, she sways her hips as her long legs—emphasized by fuck-me heels—carry her through the lounge towards the glass-enclosed tasting rooms along the perimeter. The form-fitted, black calf-length dress molds to every curve of her body.

Several male patrons turn to ogle her as she passes by them seated on vintage leather club chairs around low tables or near the fireplaces. One even lifts his Baccarat snifter and tips his head to acknowledge the hostess. I can't see her face, but I notice the preening of her body as her shoulders go back and her hips sway more.

I whip out my mobile and shoot a quick text message to Lucien. No time like the present to inform him of his hostess' unbecoming antics. I add a recommendation to send an email to the lounge's subscriber list to act appropriately with the staff. Keep the reprimand equal and all...

After I hit send, my gaze takes in the rest of Jackson Smoke&Scotch Lounge Paris.

The atmosphere is Old World, similar to our headquarters in Aberdeen. Lucien and his team want to recall the European smoking clubs of the past. They incorporated rich burgundy, hunter green, and burnished gold hues; parquet floors with hand-knotted silk-wool area rugs; elaborate plaster crown moldings and trims; and decorative pillows and accessories. Ambient lighting from crystal wall sconces and chandeliers with floor and table lamps enhance the sumptuous feel.

The modernization comes with the advance ventilation system that filters the air from the Jackson Cuban Cigars and the locking mechanisms created by STEELE Technology and Cyber Security for members' private humidors and cubbies. Not everyone comes to smoke, and no one wants others sneaking into their treasured cigars and bottles of Scotch.

"Here you are, Monsieur Jackson."

The hostess' purr draws my attention back to her as she stands before the tasting room's door reserved for our Guys' Night Out. With a smile, she pulls the door open and gestures for me to continue inside. A soft snick sounds behind me. I turn to find the hostess smiling like the Cheshire Cat.

"Do you need any additional assistance, Monsieur Jackson?" She asks.

I take a deep breath and channel my Alpha Dom to nip this shit in the bud really quick.

"No, thank you. You may return to your station. Now," I respond.

Then, without further communication, I pivot and stride towards the high table to set up the tasting. My purposeful actions discourage further unwanted attention.

With an audible sigh, the hostess says, "Very well, Monsieur Jackson."

As the door opens, on second thought she pauses and offers, "Should you need anything at all, please let me know."

I place my carrier on the table and keep my back to her as I *nod. The denied hostess leaves me in peace. Sorry, lass, My Baby Girl is the only one who will call me sir and I respond with interest. And the only one I need.*

After a while, the fellas arrive one after the other.

"Hey, Lach, let me introduce you to Joel Bailey," Roger says then goes on to tell me how they met at a business function years ago. Joel is a successful investor in real estate. His girlfriend is an attorney who specializes in commercial property law.

With an outstretched hand I respond, "A pleasure to meet you, Joel."

"Same here, Lachlan. Roger tells me you're the President of Liquor for Jackson Corporation. Your brands are top-shelf, mate," Joel responds with a firm handshake. "I appreciate the invite to your tasting. Looking forward to your new blend."

"Thank you kindly," I say. "Do share your honest opinion of tonight's creation. I could use the feedback of someone who's familiar with our brands."

"Let's get this party started, bros!"

We turn to find Lucien with three beautiful women dressed provocatively. He smirks.

Roger mutters under his breath as he shakes his head.

The Sexy Chef has a way with food and drink as much as with women. The Alpha Dom enjoys a bevy of them. His more the merrier leans towards ménages. And not many women will decline an invitation to spend the evening with him.

Tonight proves no exception. Lucien has invited a few ladies to what I started as our guys-only Guys' Night Out. They preen as much as the hostess, which makes me wonder whether he would have a problem with her behavior. But then Lucien has his limits and an employee going beyond their duties would push them.

In the past, sexy women would hold my attention. Now I suppress a roll of my eyes.

No more than the hostess do these three pique my interest. My Baby Girl wins again. She's my bonnie lass.

I clear my throat and return to the high table. Time to move the evening forward.

"Now this is my latest creation. No one but the craft team has tasted it. You, my brothers, will be the first beyond the walls of Jackson Corporation to experience this exquisite blend of—"

"Give us a damn snifter already!" Joel interrupts my introductory speech with a chuckle.

"Here, here!" Lucien adds as he picks a Baccarat crystal snifter off of the tasting table.

I chuckle and let the boys have at it. Being the gentleman I am, I hand snifters to the three women and smile.

"Enjoy, ladies," I say, then go over to Lucien to discuss his employee matter.

As we speak, two of the women meander over. The four of us converse about mundane things before I sense someone's stare and glance around the room.

Roger has me in the crosshairs of his intense platinum gray stare.

I can only imagine his interpretation of me speaking with these women. They fawn over Lucien. But I made it a point to not allow them to get too close to me. When one wrapped her fingers around my forearm and leaned up to whisper in my ear, I extracted myself from her hold and shook my head.

Obviously Roger missed my dismal and only witnesses us standing in a cluster, as shown by the I-see-you chin bob he gives to me before he tips his snifter of Scotch to his mouth. Great.

Slowly, I return his nod. Yup, I know what Roger is thinking exactly. And it's not good.

When will the day come My Baby Girl's Big Four will back the fuck up?

"Oomph!"

The counterblow Ewan aims at me lands on my targe with enough force to make my step falter backwards.

"Wake up, man! Or else I'll *gie ye a skelpit lug!*"

Ewan's Scottish accent thickens as he threatens to hit me on the ear. He shakes his head in disgust and goes on.

"Do you know what would happen on the battlefield if a warrior had his head in the clouds?!" He bellows. His red hair glints with copper streaks and his navy blue eyes gleam in the afternoon sunlight.

"Get it together or go take a nap. These double-edged swords draw blood, *dhuine*," he finishes as he flicks a button off of my shirt deftly for emphasis.

I nod and gather myself.

"Let's go," I respond as I resume my fencing stance.

We continue for another twenty minutes before our session ends. Ewan grouses some more but admits I made up for my earlier blunders. After we confirm my next session, I head to the locker room, my mind on a good steam and shower.

"Oh!"

I collide with a smaller figure as I round the corner. Automatically, I reach out to steady the woman.

"Whoa! Pardon me, lass!" I exclaim as my hands grip her tiny waist, and she clasps my biceps to prevent her from landing on her bottom.

Violet eyes peer up at me.

Fiona Ridel. Fuck.

I drop my hands from her body as though she were a hot metal rod. She stumbles but rights herself.

"Oh, Lachlan! I didn't see you… Pardon me," Fiona says as she brushes her hands down her slim thighs encased in tight pink leggings.

I track her movements, then catch myself and glance back up at her face. Her violet eyes sparkle, and my face heats from embarrassment.

What the fuck?!

"I'm glad to run into you, Lachlan. In a few weeks, my gallery hosts an event for a new painter who has attracted a good following. I'd love for you to come," Fiona says.

I've declined multiple invitations from her since Thanksgiving and now almost floored her, so I can't very well come up with an excuse. I'm not that callous.

"Sounds interesting, Fiona. I welcome your invitation, thank you," I respond with a decisive nod.

A dazzling smile blooms on her otherworldly face, and she claps her hands.

"Wonderful! I'll send it to your offices on Monday," Fiona says, then eyes me up and down appreciatively.

"Well, it appears as though you finished a vigorous workout. I'll leave you to shower while I head to my session."

As she passes me, I pivot.

"I haven't seen you here before. Is this your first time?" I ask, curious.

Her cheeks pinken as her eyes dart away from mine.

I frown at her hesitation. Then I realize my faux pas. Fuck! I scramble to find a way to backtrack as I rake my fingers through my damp hair.

Fiona places a delicate hand over my frantic heart to still me. I blink down at her hand and back up at her. She shakes her head.

"The center is a special place, but not that special," she says. "Today is my first day here. Since you seem more experienced, perhaps you can show me more another time."

With that cryptic response, she pats my chest and saunters away. I watch until she turns another corner. Her ass-long ponytail switches with each step. She's the type of woman I chose before Haley: blonde, willowy. But Fiona is bright and not someone I would fuck randomly. She could have been a match for me under different circumstances.

I shake my head to clear it since I don't know what the fuck just happened here. But I refuse to read any more into it. I will simply attend the event and call it a night. Then my obligation to see Fiona's art gallery visit will be complete.

My hand runs over my head again as I stride into the locker room, more confounded than when I arrived.

"Sebastian has told me such wonderful things about your cyber security and technology division, Haley. I am glad you will meet with my team to discuss my company joining your roster of corporate clients. In fact, I would like you to take me on as an individual, if you do not mind."

Claudio Venturi's stunning golden eyes fringed by thick blond eyelashes pierce my gray orbs as he stands before me at Café Altro Paradiso.

Baz told me he had a potential corporate client for me. He invited him to dinner the night before our meeting with his team at STEELE for me to have a chance to see him in a less formal setting. Funny enough, Baz didn't invite Harris…

When I arrived at the SoHo trattoria with its sleek and sexy, moody atmosphere and saw a gorgeous specimen of an Italian man chatting with Baz and Lola at the bar, I knew this was a total setup.

Dammit, Sebastian Steele! Must you meddle in my love life?!

I took a deep breath, channeling my inner Starr to calm my racing heart and to get my head together for what will undoubtedly be a chess game of a night.

As I neared the trio, Lola glanced up and spotted me. She waves happily.

"Hi, Haley! I love your dress!" She gushed as she hugged me, then held me out at arm's length to inspect my outfit.

I wanted to keep it professional and nice for a night out —a fine balance. So I opted for a red floral ruched silk mini dress with long sleeves and a v-neck paired with red bow-front mules. My hair hangs down my back with minimal makeup and diamond studs as my only jewelry. Sexy and sophisticated. Perfect.

"Thanks, sis!" I responded. "You look marvelous, darling!"

Lola twirled in her off the shoulder yellow silk mini dress. The loose fit and flouncy ruffle floated around her toned legs as she spun in her strappy crystal sandals. She piled her long ebony waves into a topknot and colored her full lips with a matte red lipstick. They widened into a bigger smile when Baz slipped his hand around her waist and tucked the petite beauty into his side.

"Hi, Haley. I would like to introduce Claudio Venturi, the CEO of Venturi Ventures S.r.l. Claudio this is my sister

Haley and the Co-head of STEELE Technology and Cyber Security," Baz said.

Claudio—who could pass for a sculpture by Michelangelo—graces me with a smoldering smile.

My face flushes as he speaks.

Baz jumps in when I fail to answer quickly.

"Ah, Claudio, you can trust Haley with your company and your personal tech needs," he says. "Come, let us take our seats at the table."

"I am sure," Claudio replies as he gestures for me to precede him. His voice skims over me, and I bow my head, confused by my reaction to him.

Dammit! What's the matter with me?

We follow the maître d' through the restaurant to settle into a corner table of the long leather banquette that lines the front wall below the giant windowpanes. Baz and Claudio sit in the wooden chairs opposite Lola and me. After the server takes our beverage order and shares the evening specials, Claudio picks up where he left off.

"So tell me, Haley, what made you start your division focused on tech?" He asks once again, focusing on me as though no one else exists around us.

This time I'm better prepared and launch into my story. Claudio listens raptly and asks questions—real ones and not those he thinks will impress me or over flatter me. I take a moment to pause while the server sets our cocktails on the table.

Claudio and Baz speak fluently in Italian to place our orders with the server. Lola and I chat since we speak

French and not Italian. So we leave the guys to take care of our meals. With the mouth-watering menu, they won't be able to pick a bad dish.

"I hope you're not mad at me for this," Lola whispers, so only I can hear.

I raise my eyebrow in question. So she continues.

"Baz told me Claudio would make a suitable match for you romantically. I mean, the business part is legit," she adds when I frown. "Baz just thinks it could lead to more."

I. Knew. It.

Dammit, Sebastian Steele!! Back off already!

Inwardly I fume, but I turn a bright smile on Claudio when he begins to tell me about his varied business holdings. A multibillionaire—obviously single—from a prominent Milanese family. The eldest of four boys. I gauge his age at thirty-two or -three and his height of six feet, five inches. His build that of a male model—long with lean muscles. Highly educated at the best schools in Europe. The total package. For the right woman.

If not for Lachlan being my teenage-crush-cum-boyfriend-Dom, I would be receptive to a pairing with Claudio. As far as my carnal reaction to him, what red-blooded woman wouldn't respond to his absolute masculinity?

With that in mind, I sit back and enjoy dinner and his companionship. His tales of travels to exotic locales to fulfill his wanderlust intrigue me. It's apparent Claudio prefers to do things his way and does not hesitate to go after what he wants in life.

And since Baz has given him the green light by way of this pre-meeting dinner, Claudio doesn't rev forward like a glitzy Lamborghini, rather he's more subtle, like a classic Alfa Romeo. Smooth and stylish.

At the end of the evening, Claudio takes my hand in his sizable one and brushes his lips over my knuckles as he pins me with those golden eyes again.

"Haley, it was a genuine pleasure to get to speak with you before our meeting tomorrow. I prefer to know my partners on a more intimate level before I give them access to my family's company," Claudio says. "I look forward to the morning."

I nod, robbed of speech for a moment, then muster up the words for a verbal response.

"It was a lovely evening, Claudio. I expect you will find STCS the right fit for your needs," I reply in a steady voice.

His smile brightens his golden eyes even more than before.

* * *

"This concludes our presentation. What questions do you have?"

Harris stands at the head of the conference room table at STEELE International and brings his gaze to Claudio, who sits at the other end flanked by his team.

"Bravo. Quite impressive as I knew it would be, Harris, thank you," he says.

His CTO and COO murmur their agreement along

with the other three members of the Venturi Ventures' team.

"We will confer amongst ourselves and provide our decision to you by the end of day today. *Buono*?" Claudio states as he glances from Harris to me.

"Excellent, Claudio. We will await your decision," I answer as I rise from my seat and extend my hand to him.

Briefly, a smile plays at the corners of his lush mouth before he shakes my hand.

"Indeed," he murmurs.

"Great, I will walk you to the elevator."

Harris appears at my side and extends his hand to Claudio, effectively ending our little tête-à-tête.

Claudio flicks his mesmerizing eyes to my twin and back to me, then lets my hand go to shake Harris' proffered one. A nod to the rest of the team, and Claudio strides beside Harris through the double doors of the conference room.

I sag in relief as the others file out.

"Well, Haley, it pleases me to inform you Venturi Ventures S.r.l. will partner with STEELE International, Inc. to handle our technology and cyber security needs."

Claudio's voice booms over the speakerphone as I sit at my desk in my office.

Harris had another meeting to attend, so I waited for the call.

"Fantastic news. We appreciate the opportunity to work

with your company, Claudio," I respond with a smile. This new deal will satisfy Harris and Baz, I muse.

"—dinner with me tonight."

With my mind on my brothers, I only hear the tail end of Claudio's sentence. But dinner and tonight catch my attention.

"Pardon, what did you say?" I ask.

A deep rumbling comes through the line. His chuckle resonates around me.

"Ah, Haley. I would like to have dinner with you tonight as a celebration of our newly formed partnership and to discuss my personal account," Claudio says. "Do say yes."

I push my glasses up my nose as my eyebrows knit together.

Dammit! What do I do?

On one hand, we could score a second deal and with the high-net-worth individuals he knows get the word out on our services and procure more clients. On the other, I know he wants to discuss more than business with me…

To hell with it!

I have my boyfriend, and I do not have a modicum of interest in another man—no matter how attractive he may be. I am also a grown woman who has a division to run profitably. Not to mention Baz will question my hesitancy to date…

"I'm happy to join you for dinner, Claudio. Where shall I meet you?" I respond with confidence.

"*Buono!* However, my mother raised a gentleman, and I would disappoint her if I were to leave you to make your way to the restaurant. I will come to the lobby of your residence at eight," he responds.

We end the call, and I sit back in my chair.

My mobile chimes with a text message. I glance at the screen and see it's from *My Lord*. A smile spreads across my face as I unlock my mobile.

Hi, Baby Girl. How was your meeting? I'm sure you closed the deal. Who wouldn't want to partner with you?

I bite the corner of my mouth. Is Lachlan psychic or what???

Hi, My Lord. We got it!!! :D So excited!!!

I don't have to wait long for his response; my mobile rings with his call.

"Congratulations, Baby Girl! I knew you'd get the deal! Venturi is no match for you!" Lachlan exclaims. "I can't wait to see you next week in Malta and to show you just how very proud of you I am."

I giggle and sit back in my chair. We talk for twenty minutes. It's late in Aberdeen, and I need to get changed for dinner. So we end the call with an exchange of I love you.

As I make my way from my offices to my family's private elevator for our residences, my mind clears of any doubt of my attraction to Claudio Venturi. I have none.

Lachlan Jackson is the only man for me. And I'm the only woman for him.

Mine!

LACHLAN

"Ladies and gentlemen, I am Fiona Ridel, and I welcome you to Ridel Art Gallery this evening. It pleases us to share the wonderfully innovative paintings of Byron Thorndale, a native of our very own Aberdeen! The natural beauty of River Don and its riverside nature preserve at Donmouth inspires Byron's works. You will note his interpretation of the wildlife including the seals and waterfowl as they inhabit the pristine area. Byron has a few words for you. Enjoy the evening!"

Fiona turns to Byron and beams at him as she squeezes his hands between hers. He double kisses her porcelain cheeks, rosy from her exuberance. She steps to the side and glances around the gallery filled with Aberdeen's high society and those in the art scene. When our eyes connect, she beams at me and walks in my direction through the crowd.

Several patrons stop her, and she chats with them graciously. As attentive as she is to them, Fiona raises her gaze to mine and smiles. Once she's before me, she tilts her head for a kiss.

I balk but recover quickly to double kiss her cheeks and not her proffered lips.

"Lachlan, I'm so glad you could make it! When I didn't see you earlier, I thought you changed your mind. Again…" Fiona says. Her easy tinkling laughter floats around us.

Other patrons turn in our direction, captivated by her ethereal beauty.

Her ash blonde waist-length hair parted in the middle cascades down her back to frame her face. The paleness of her hair and smooth skin heighten the intensity of her violet eyes. Fiona wears a dusky rose patterned strapless dress that falls in gentle pleats to her mid-calf to end in strappy sandals on her feet.

As Fiona laughs, she sways, and her dresses flutters around her.

"But never mind all of that, Lachlan. You're here now and that's what matters!" She says as she waves her hand in the air to dismiss her complaint. Then loops her arm through mine. "Come, let me show you around. You may find something you'd like to take home tonight."

We take glasses of wine from a bar before we stroll from one painting to the other in the large airy space well lit to showcase the artwork. Fiona gets kudos for the cases of Jackson wines and Scotch served and displayed throughout the gallery.

She points out interesting facts and her knowledgeable views of each piece. Fiona impresses me as much as the artist and his eye for detail and color combinations.

As Fiona predicted, I find a couple of pieces to add to my collection and let her know.

She claps her hands and rises to the balls of her feet as she leans in to kiss me on the cheek.

"How fabulous, Lachlan! Show me which ones!" She says, then winks. "I'll give you a good deal. I promise."

"Thank you, Fiona. I will remember your kindness and return it at the appropriate time," I tease with a smirk.

Her violet eyes shimmer with her giggles as she sweeps me through the gallery toward the first painting.

"This one... How do you say it? *Speaks* to me," I tell her.

Fiona signals to an assistant who rushes over to give her a sold sticker.

"How many stickers do I need, Lachlan?" She acts sweetly.

I chuckle and shake my head.

"One, perhaps two more, Fiona. There's another my mother would like. She can put it in her sitting room at Jackson Castle," I respond.

"Ah, yes, the marchioness. Perfect! Thank you, *My Lord!*" Fiona exclaims as she links our arms again. "On to the next painting."

As we continue through the gallery, my mind drifts to Haley at Fiona's reference of me as *my lord*. A flash of guilt jolts me from the playful repartee she and I share. Not that I'm doing anything wrong. Haley has my heart.

I'm merely fulfilling my obligation to see Fiona's art gallery as I agreed months ago. Especially since my father still harps on me getting married and producing the next Jackson heir. This way he can see a bit of progress even though it's a facade.

After I complete my purchases and arrange for the deliveries, Fiona's assistant whisks her away to engage with other patrons interested in other paintings. Fiona offers her apologies and pecks my cheek with yet another kiss.

"Don't you dare leave without saying goodbye, Lord Lachlan!" She demands with a wag of her finger. "I won't let you slip away so easily now that you're here."

I bow and agree, then watch Fiona saunter away. Her dress flutters around her slim legs. Before the crowd swallows her up, she glances over her shoulder and waves at me with a broad smile.

"Hello there, Jackson!"

A man with a full beard, wire-rimmed spectacles, and shoulder-length hair appears beside me with an attractive woman who has arms covered in colorful tattoos. I recognize him as the owner of several popular pubs and a one Michelin star restaurant who's on my Jackson Tasters Circle.

"McFarley, good to see you, mate!" I respond as we clasp forearms.

He introduces the woman as his wife. I go along with them as they stroll through the gallery and select paintings they intend to purchase. Along the way, Fiona joins us and completes the sales.

"My wife insisted I come out, and I must say it was a good use of my time," McFarley says. "I'd like to invite you to dinner at my restaurant. The chef is working on a new menu, and I could use your feedback. Game?"

I open my mouth to respond, but Fiona beats me to it.

"Oh, what a lovely idea! How can I deny my newest clients?" She says as she links her arm with mine.

McFarley chuckles and gestures towards the front of the gallery.

"Well, lass, let us go," he says.

Fiona beams up at me, and I force a smile.

Fuck. Me.

I had not planned on dinner. This was supposed to be an in-and-out situation only. However, I can't very well back out when a tier one Jackson Liquor client extends the invitation and Fiona goes and accepts it.

Outside, my driver Theodore steps out of my Rolls-Royce Phantom Extended at the curb and opens the back door.

"We'll see you there," I tell McFarley as I place my hand on Fiona's lower back to guide her to the sedan. The flash of cameras nearly blinds me. I figured we would have escaped the ones in the gallery.

Fiona shifts on the back seat to face me when I slide inside from the opposite door.

"Oh, Lachlan, please don't be upset with me for saying yes to dinner. It's a great business opportunity to spend time with the owner of so many popular eateries. He and his wife selected some of the larger paintings to hang in them," Fiona pleads with wide eyes.

I take a moment to answer. Let her sit in discomfort as a lesson, My Alpha Dom decides.

"Mr. Jackson, where to, sir?"

Theodore's question gives me an excuse to let her wait longer.

"The Moonfish Cafe on Correction Wynd, thank you, Doyle," I respond, then press the button for the divider to ascend.

"Lachlan?" Fiona whispers.

I face her and say sternly, "Fiona, I can appreciate your eagerness to engage with clients. However, you cannot answer for me. So as not to create an uncomfortable situation, I will comply."

Chastened, she nods and sits back in her seat, head turned to the window.

I remove my mobile from my trousers pocket and send a text message to My Baby Girl. I need to reconnect with the woman in my life.

Hi love, heading to a business dinner. I'll call you later. Naked in bed...

No response for a couple of minutes leads me to believe she's not available or with one of The Big Four. I scroll through emails until an alert pops on to the screen. With a grin, I switch apps and open the text messages.

A video loads. An NSFW video.

I glance over to Fiona. She's distracted by her mobile. Thank fuck...

On screen, My Baby Girl sits on her office chair with her feet on the desk edge. Her dress bunched at her waist and two fingers in her mouth. Slowly she lowers her hand to her red silk-covered mound. Damp fingers slip beneath the thin material until her palm presses against the lingerie. Her head falls back as her fingers pump in and out. When her thumb presses against her clit, she explodes soundlessly. As her body shudders, she narrows her eyes at the camera and blows me a kiss with soaked fingers. The screen goes black.

Holy shit…

I swallow a groan and pull the side of my suit jacket over my burgeoning erection. Another quick glance at Fiona finds her typing on her mobile's screen, oblivious to what transpired.

I close my eyes for a moment and say a thankful prayer for my frisky Little Temptress.

The sedan stops, and Theodore hops out to get my door while the valet opens the one for Fiona. We step out, and I round the back—surreptitiously adjusting my cock. Fiona offers me a wan smile and holds her hands in front of her —not reaching to link arms as she's done all night.

Thank fuck.

For a minute there, I felt as though her ethereal presence entranced me. Haley's video was all the reminder I needed.

I nod at Fiona, and we stride into the restaurant just as McFarley and his wife enter behind us.

"Excellent timing! We'll sit at the table in the kitchen.

The chef will plate the dishes straight from the pans," he says as he leads the way.

As expected, the tasting provides tantalizing dishes. Small samples of prawn and sesame toast, roast scallops with salsa verde and rice, beef bavette steak, and pearl barley risotto with duck egg for the appetizers and main courses. The chef follows them with buttermilk panna cotta and bananas with dulce de leche and burnt white chocolate for dessert. Of course, the sommelier pairs the dishes with Jackson Liquor brands.

Throughout the meal, Fiona and I praise the chef and offer our feedback. Mine more focused on the liquor than the food. She gives a few suggestions the chef appreciates. McFarley's wife adds her recommendations particularly on the names and descriptions since she handles their marketing.

As McFarley and I sip digestifs made from Jackson Special Blend Scotch, his wife and Fiona chat about classic arts and digitally made graphics.

"So which team do you think will win the Guinness PRO12? Edinburgh Rugby or Glasgow Warriors?" I ask McFarley, remembering he's an avid fan of Edinburgh's team.

"Aha! I tell you, my Edinburgh will beat the eleven other clubs to win the cup!" He responds exuberantly.

He spouts stats and predictions. We continue until Fiona interrupts.

"Pardon me, gentlemen, but it's late, and I have to get home. Lachlan, do you mind if I leave?" She says. Then adds, "No need for you to end your evening early for me. I can call for my driver."

"Of course. I will take you home, Fiona," I tell her and turn to McFarley as I rise from my chair. "Thanks to you and your chef for a delicious meal. Next week, I'll send a case of the blend I mentioned to you."

"Thank you, my friend," he responds, as we clasp forearms. "Fiona, it was a pleasure meeting you. I'll walk you out."

Once we're in the car, Fiona turns to me.

"Lachlan, I apologize and hope we can move past my faux pas. I meant no harm. Truly," she says sincerely. Her violet eyes deepen to a navy blue in the dim lighting as she searches my face for a hint of forgiveness.

This time I don't make her wait. It appears as though her lesson worked, as she was on her best behavior during dinner. Her sole focus was on charming McFarley and his wife. Only interacting with me on a companionable level. Perfect.

"Apology accepted, Fiona. I wish you the best with your art gallery. I will recommend it to my family and to my acquaintances," I respond. Remembering a business opportunity, I add, "I noticed you served Jackson Liquor brands. Let me know when you schedule your next event, and I will send a case of our limited editions."

She nods and thanks me.

The rest of the ride, we carry on small talk until we arrive at her residence. I walk Fiona to the elevator and bid her good night. Instead of a tilt of her head for a kiss, she extends her hand. We shake before she steps into the elevator.

A wistful expression appears on Fiona's face and her eyes stay on mine as the doors close.

I sigh in relief and stride back to the sedan.

When I arrive at my building, the concierge hands a small package to me with a note: *Take to Bed. ~ MBG.* I thank her and continue to the private elevator.

Once I enter my penthouse, I strip and drop a trail of clothes behind me in my haste to get in bed, naked as promised. My thick cock lengthens down my thigh as my heavy sac swings with each step. After I place the package on the nightstand, then crawl onto my bed and lean back against the headboard.

"Why hello there, My Lord…"

My Little Temptress answers my video call wrapped in a floral-printed silk kimono. Her long ebony waves cascade around her shoulders, the tips of her tresses curl around her full tits. Their puckered nipples press against the material, begging for me to suckle them.

I lick my lips. She's more tasty than any morsel a Michelin-starred chef can create any day.

"I have something for you," she continues in a purr, then reaches off camera and pulls a tiny black remote into view. She waves it in the air.

"Open your gift," My Little Temptress commands.

I scramble for the nightstand and snatch the package off of it.

"Good, boy," she purrs. "Now open it."

Torn paper falls to the mattress followed by the box lid. Nestled inside rest a tube of lubricant, a quilted black sleeve made of stretchy silicone, and a purple remote. In one end, a long gold bullet sticks out while the other end has a hole.

"What is this?" I ask, flipping it over. I glance up to see My Little Temptress smirking.

"Put some lubricant on your dick and slip the sleeve over it," she responds, then leans forward. "I want to watch."

I angle my tablet on a pillow between my knees. A fist around my slippery cock guides it into the hole. I use both hands to pull the sleeve to the root with the rim on top of my balls. The snug fit reminds me of her tight, wet pussy. A groan slips from my mouth as I close my eyes and lean my head against the pillows.

"Oh, fuck!!!" I shout as I jump up.

My eyes fly open, and I glance down at my vibrating cock.

My Little Temptresses' giggles draw my gaze to the tablet screen. She waves the remote, and the vibration changes from a rumble to two short and one long pulse pattern.

"Now that you get the gist of it, time to up the ante," she purrs.

A tug on the kimono's belt and it opens to reveal her pillowy tits and flat belly. The silk robe pools around her hips as she sits cross-legged. Her bare mound gives an unrestricted view of her glistening pink pussy lips and engorged clit.

So distracted by the erotic vision, I don't notice the purple egg massager until it touches her seam. She slides it up to her clit.

"Use your remote, My Lord. I need you," she says before she bites her lower lip and leans against her headboard.

I grin like the Cheshire Cat and fiddle with the purple remote until My Little Temptress writhes on her bed.

We alternate bringing each other to the edge and back before we explode as one. My fist pumps my sleeve-covered cock with the vibrations set to an intense level. Great ropes of creamy jizz shoot into the air to splash on my chest and dribble onto my hand. I roar my release.

My Little Temptress squeals as the egg massager pulsates inside of her pussy pressed against her sensitive G-spot. She jerks as her body reaches the pinnacle of her climax.

Sated, we stare at one another with half-closed eyes.

"I miss you, and I love you, Baby Girl," I murmur huskily.

"Ditto, My Lord," she replies as she stifles a yawn. Flushed and limp, she's a beauty who captivates me like no other.

I sigh contented as we continue to cuddle from afar.

Even miles away, my tech wiz girlfriend creates a means for us to make love.

I cannot wait until we can be in each other's arms forever.

"And when I call, you will take your position on the edge of the bed naked with your ass on your haunches, back straight, palms up on your spread thighs. The blindfold over your eyes. In total silence. Understand, Little One?"

My still thrumming body shudders with erotic desire from My Alpha Dom's directive.

I arrived in London at STEELE Mayfair earlier then expected to find Lachlan stepping out of the shower. He was on his way to a breakfast meeting, and I kind of waylaid him. Two hours later he's headed to his rescheduled meeting.

"Yes, Sir," I purr as I stretch my arms overhead and arch my back from the rumpled bedding. A moan slips out of my mouth at the soft suckling of my nipple.

My fingers run through Lachlan's sable brown hair as I hold him to my breast.

"Oh, baby, I wish you could stay and cuddle," I pout.

His warm breath blows across my wet skin as he chuckles.

"When I get back, we'll cuddle for as long as you like. Well, after we make up for the last few weeks," Lachlan replies before he stands to his full six feet, four inches.

If looks could fuck, it would capacitate me. His heated, lust-filled gaze leaves no doubt as to his carnal need for me. Nor does the bulge along his inner thigh visible clearly beneath his bespoke trousers.

I lick my lips and groan with my own need. My fingertip circles my areole before it slides between the valley of my breasts, down my belly. A growl from Lachlan stops my movement. My hand hovers above my mound, itching to finish its quest.

"Behave, Naughty Girl. If I return to find you sated, I will spank your pussy with my paddle, then find my satisfaction in your tight bottom hole. Do you understand, Naughty Girl?" My Alpha Dom warns with eyes narrowed sparking emerald fire.

I shudder and mewl.

"Y-yes, Sir," I whisper.

He nods and pivots on his heel. Long legs make quick work of the distance to the bedroom door. Moments later, I hear the snick of the suite's lock.

Worn out from our romp and jet lag, I curl onto my side with my head on his pillow. The woodsy scent of Lachlan's cologne mixed with his natural pheromones wafts into my nose as my eyes flutter close. Pure bliss.

. . .

"Hɪ, Mom... Yes, I landed safely... He had a meeting but will be back soon. I'm going to do some work in the meantime... No, I'm not sure... Okay, I will... I love you, too. Kisses!"

We end our call, and I head into the bathroom for a shower. No need to divulge my sexual activities to my mother. Although I'm sure she's got an idea...

I decide on a bubble bath instead. My achy muscles could benefit from a soak. As the tub fills, I unpack, then pick up a couple of magazines from the living room's coffee table to flip through.

The warm water with essential oils blended in fills the air with lavender and bergamot—the perfect combination to calm me and ease my sore body. I pile my hair atop my head with a Scünci and slide into the tub with a contented sigh.

The first magazine is a quick read about what to do in London. Fine for tourists who stay in the President's Suite but not for me. I drop it off the side and pick up the next one. The articles prove more interesting with what's happening amongst the international glitterati as Leonie calls the chi-chi jet set—of which she's a member...

Towards the back of the glossy magazine, photos from recent events in the U.K. splash across the pages. A section labeled "From The Granite City" catches my eye. Since I can't exactly visit Lachlan at home in Aberdeen, I can see what's happening from afar at least.

A caption heralding a new exhibition at Ridel Art Gallery sticks out from the rest. I sit up to get a clearer view of the images.

"Hhhmmm. What's Princess Fiona the Fair up to?" I muse aloud.

Of course, she looks as ethereal as ever in a breezy linen midi dress with an empire waist and sleeveless neckline that shows off her flawless pale skin. Impossibly stick-straight pale blonde hair and those enchanting violet eyes once again make her appear fairy-like. Ugh!

"Fiona Ridel owner of Ridel Art Gallery and heiress to the Ridel Oil fortune hosts another successful opening for upcoming painter Byron Thorndale… Blah, blah, blah. Yada, yada, yada," I read aloud. "Well, congratu-fucking-lations, Princess Fiona the Fair. *She rides off into the sunset of the Scottish Highlands moors, never to be seen or heard from again!*"

I giggle and scan the page for more images of her. It's the masochist in me.

My gasp echoes in the marble bathroom when a photo of Lachlan leaning down to kiss Fiona makes my heart skip a beat. Another photo of them with their arms linked as they laugh, strolling through the gallery has my hands shaking. The sight of them outside of the gallery with Lachlan helping Fiona into his car has me leaping from the tub.

Water sloshes to the marble floor and drips from my body as I hurry from the bathroom. Tears fill my eyes, blinding me as I pace in the bedroom.

"How could you, Lachlan??? How could you do me like this?" I cry out as I throw the offensive magazine across the room. It hits the chair and drops to the hardwood floor.

My body shakes uncontrollably as adrenaline course through every cell. I squeeze my eyes shut, but the images burn into my retinas. I can't get them out of my head.

I yowl like an injured cat as I crumple to the floor. How much time passes before I notice the drop in my temperature, I don't know. The shivers drive me to get warm. With a pounding head, I drag myself to my feet and into the walk-in closet.

Then my mobile rings.

I jog to the nightstand and grab it up. Lachlan!

My mind clears and one thought emerges: get the fuck out of here before that lying fucker returns!

It's the fastest I've ever packed. Fully dressed and towing my luggage behind me, I rush to the suite's front door. It opens.

"You did not answer your mobile, Naughty G—"

Lachlan stops cold. His emerald eyes take in my messy hair, red puffy eyes, and mismatched outfit. When he spies my luggage, his mouth drops open.

My heart hammers in my chest.

Even pissed at him, I can't help but react to his dominant presence. My nipples pebble and my pussy clenches. My submissive brain wants to please him and take my position. But one flashback of the images hardens my resolve.

I step forward, intent on pushing past his hulking frame.

"Whoa, Haley! What's wrong?" Lachlan asks as he grips my shoulders.

I jerk at his touch with a stricken cry and pull away. Each time I attempt to sidestep him, he blocks my path.

On our last tango, he raises his hands palms out and says, "Hold on, Haley! I won't touch you. But tell me what happened to upset you. Is everyone okay?"

Did he just ask me if everyone is okay?! I scream in my head.

Lachlan flinches, and I realize I spoke aloud.

"Haley?" He asks quietly.

"Get out of my way, fucker!" I growl, channeling Harris. Then rush forward only to collide with the wall of Lachlan's powerful chest.

He wraps his arms around me and holds tight. I tremble and sob.

"Haley, Baby Girl, please talk to me," he pleads. "Tell me what's wrong?"

I blubber against the front of his dress shirt. Tears stream down my cheeks. When he strokes my back, I hiccup and pull away, only for him to grasp my upper arms. He bends down to level our eyes and cocks his eyebrow.

"Tell me, Haley, what happened?" Lachlan asks in his Alpha Dom voice.

Is he serious with me right now??? I question internally.

"Fuck *you*, Lachlan! Do *not* go all alpha on me right

now! *You* are the one who should tell *me* what happened!" I shout.

He flinches, then shakes his head.

"I do not know what you're referring to, Haley. Give me a clue," he says.

A growl rumbles from deep within my chest. I stalk to the bedroom and retrieve the magazine from the floor. Lachlan follows me. I slap through the pages until the art gallery shots appear. Then I shove the open magazine in his handsome face.

"Tell me, *Lachlan*, what happened?" I sneer, mimicking his earlier question.

He blanches as his eyes scan the pages.

"Haley," he starts, nervous eyes flick to mine. "It's not what you think…"

A roaring increases in my ears as a red haze fills my vision. I no longer hear Lachlan's sorry ass. He lied to me. He used me. He. Is. Not. Mine.

I spin and rush from the bedroom.

Before I make it to the front door, sizable hands lift me from my feet and easily toss me over a shoulder like a sack of potatoes. My legs flail as I pummel his firm ass with my fists. He jostles me as he strides back into the bedroom, where he drops me on the bed and straddles my hips with my wrists in his firm grasp.

"Haley, you will hear me out and not leave here until I finish. If I let you leave at all," Lachlan growls.

He sits back and holds my wrists on my lower belly.

"No, nothing happened between Fiona and me. Yes, I

went to the art gallery. Yes, I double kissed her cheek in greeting. Yes, she linked arms with me, and I allowed it. No, it meant nothing to me. Yes, we left together but only because a client of Jackson Liquor who purchased paintings invited us to a menu tasting at his restaurant. No, Fiona and I did not fuck afterwards. Yes, I went home. Alone. Business only."

Lachlan stops his confession and stares at me.

I bite my tongue to keep from speaking. I'm a Steele trained in the art of war by the best—my father—and honed my skills on my four older Alpha male and Dom brothers. Lachlan doesn't stand a chance.

We continue to stare at one another. Neither willing to give in first.

Lachlan breaks.

"Haley, do you have anything to say?" He asks.

I relax in his grip and smile up at him.

"Business only, you say, Lachlan? So it shouldn't bother me you spent time with a woman who wants you for her own?" I ask.

He nods, then shakes his head.

I shift beneath him, and he scoots back to let me sit up. Face-to-face, my smile broadens.

"Well, that's a relief, huh?" I ask, then continue when he nods again. "Good, since I had dinner with Claudio Venturi to celebrate our new partnership and to discuss me handling his individual account. Business only."

Instead of blanching as he did before, Lachlan's face flames red, and his nostrils flare.

"What. The. Fuck. Haley?!" He breathes through clenched teeth.

I lean forward to touch the tips of our noses together.

"What. The. Fuck. Lachlan?!" I repeat.

When he growls, I continue, "Oh, doesn't sit well with you, does it, Lachlan? Well, guess what? It hurts me too."

I sit back and scan his face.

"Eleven months of us hidden—a secret. Never able to be seen together as a couple. As lovers. No photos to link us to be found. Nothing," I say, then raise my hand to stop him from speaking. "Yes, I know I agreed not to tell anyone to avoid damaging your friendship with Sebastian and upsetting everyone. Then just wanting time for us to develop our relationship in peace. So I played my part in the secret. But it sure hurts like hell when a woman I know your father would like you to marry and to bear Jackson heirs can prance on your arm for the cameras and I cannot. So excuse me when I get upset enough to walk out of your life forever."

A gust of air blows my messy hair in my face.

Lachlan grimaces—mouth a perfect circle—as though Borya punched him in the stomach. No longer crimson, Lachlan's face turns ashen. He slumps as I crumpled moments ago and runs his hands over his face.

I wait for his response.

He takes a ragged breath and opens his eyes to stare at me.

"H-Haley," Lachlan croaks, then clears his throat. "Haley, I'm so sorry. I promised to never hurt you, and I did. Please forgive me and don't give up on us. Don't leave me."

Fresh tears fill my eyes as his shine with wetness. We're caught in a web partially of our own making, and now it tangles us. Lachlan and I both feel pain from our inability to be free.

I close my eyes to collect my thoughts.

Without a doubt, I sure as hell don't want to give up on us or to leave forever. The pain was so intense I couldn't breathe. Now that I know nothing happened and witness his reaction to us breaking up, I can't just go. No.

"Where do we go from here, Lachlan?" I ask as my eyes open to his stricken face.

He shudders from another release of held breath.

"I planned a trip for our one-year anniversary next month. Let's talk about what we want during our time together now. Then in a few weeks, we can be in a better place. Okay?" Lachlan responds as he clasps my hands between his.

"Okay," I say, knowing it's a pivotal time in our relationship.

Lachlan offers a small smile and kisses my lips.

"No matter what, I have always and will always love you, Haley Steele," he murmurs.

My breath catches, and I swallow back more tears.

Too overwhelmed to respond verbally, I nod and bury my face in his neck. Once again, I inhale the scent of his cologne deeply to imprint it on my mind forever.

LACHLAN

"Thank you again for rescheduling our meeting. My legal team will await the contracts. Enjoy the rest of your stay in London."

I shake hands with my latest distributor for Jackson Liquor brands as we part ways in front of the restaurant. Theodore opens the back door of my sedan, and I slide onto the plush leather seat, my mobile already in my hand.

The call rings to voicemail. I disconnect and try to reach My Little Temptress again, with the same result.

"Well, Naughty Girl, I presume you are still asleep after our initial tryst. However, when I arrive, we will get you into position," I state in a voicemail.

Minutes later—but not fast enough—Theodore stops in front of STEELE Mayfair. I hop out and damn near jog through the lobby to the elevator for the President's Suite. The ride up passes with me shrugging out of my suit jacket and removing my cufflinks and tie to stuff them into my trousers pockets. I roll up my sleeves and unbutton the top of my shirt. By the time the elevator doors ping open, I'm ready for My Little Temptress.

A grin spreads across my face as I unlock the suite's door. I'd really like to cuddle My Baby Girl for a while to lose myself in her warm embrace. But I have to follow through with her punishment. My grin widens, knowing how aroused she'll be afterwards and what that'll mean for our lovemaking. Yeah, baby!

But first…

"You did not answer your mobile, Naughty G—"

My words die in my throat, and my heart skips a beat.

She stands before me, disheveled, with a tear-stained face and red eyes swollen behind her glasses. What stops my heart completely is the sight of her luggage.

I open my mouth to speak, but words fail me. I gape like a fish.

What the absolute fuck?!

My brain reengages when Haley moves forward.

I reach out and grasp her shoulders to stop her.

"Whoa, Haley! What's wrong?" I ask.

My heart that no longer beats shatters when she yanks away from me and cries aloud.

When she refuses to answer, and instead storms into the bedroom. I follow.

"Tell me, *Lachlan*, what happened?" She throws my words back at me, along with a magazine.

Fiona and I stare back.

Fuck. Me.

"Haley, it's not what you think. The photos don't tell the entire story and they're out of context. I visited her art gallery to get my father off of my back. It was nothing more than an obligation."

I stop speaking when she runs from the room suddenly. Enough!

I chase after Haley and throw her over my shoulder before I straddle her on the bed. She will not get away without listening to me.

"Haley, you will hear me out and not leave here until I finish. If I let you leave at all," I growl as I sit back and grasp her wrists in my hands. I hold them on her lower belly to pin her in place.

"No, nothing happened between Fiona and me. Yes, I went to the art gallery. Yes, I double kissed her cheek in greeting. Yes, she linked arms with me, and I allowed it. No, it meant nothing to me. Yes, we left together but only because a client of Jackson Liquor who purchased paintings invited us to a menu tasting at his restaurant. No, Fiona and I did not fuck afterwards. Yes, I went home. Alone. Business only."

I stop, chest heaving.

No response…

I take a deep breath and ask, "Haley, do you have anything to say?"

When she claps back by insinuating the dinner she had with Venturi—the multibillionaire playboy—was more than business, my brain explodes.

"What. The. Fuck. Haley?" I snarl.

"What. The. Fuck. Lachlan?" She growls.

I growl as I gnash my teeth.

She continues, "Oh, doesn't sit well with you, does it, Lachlan? Well, guess what? It hurts me too."

When she reveals her pain, the remnants of my heart flutter away in the wind.

I take another deep breath to stop my world from spinning out of control.

"H-Haley," I start. "Haley, I'm so sorry. I promised to never hurt you, and I did. Please forgive me and don't give up on us. Don't leave me."

Her platinum gray eyes fill with tears as my vision blurs.

"Where do we go from here, Lachlan?" Haley asks sadly.

The breath I was holding comes out in a shudder. Think, Lachlan. Make it better. You cannot lose the woman you've loved for so long. No.

I look down at her lap, where she twists her hands and pick them up. We need this connection. We need to ground one another before we follow my heart and float apart.

"I planned a trip for our one-year anniversary next month. Let's talk about what we want during our time together now. Then in a few weeks, we can be in a better place. Okay?" I ask, then hold my breath again, hoping she'll agree.

"Okay," Haley responds.

With a wan smile, I slant my mouth over hers for a tender kiss.

"No matter what, I have always and will always love you, Haley Steele," I vow.

Her breath catches before she nods and buries her face in my neck.

I stand from the bed to toe my shoes off and strip out of my clothes. But I keep my black boxer briefs on.

A few sniffles don't prevent Haley from watching me intently. Or for her face to flush, not from sorrow. No, her body reacts to mine with carnal need.

I crawl on to the bed and kneel before her. The blue sweater gets tossed to the floor and the orange silk pants drift after it. The flush extends to the tops of her tits as her chest rises and falls eagerly.

Our eyes lock.

But instead of ravishing her body in passionate makeup sex, I turn down the bedding and slip her beneath it. I follow and wrap her in my arms, forehead to forehead. Our breath mingles as I close my eyes and give a silent prayer of thanks My Baby Girl won't leave me.

She shifts as her hands skim down my chest to the waistband of my boxer briefs. Fingers slip behind the elastic, causing me to shudder.

I shake my head and bring her hands to my lips.

"It's time for the cuddle you wanted earlier, Baby Girl," I tell her.

She tilts her head to the side to consider my words, while her heated gaze bores into my eyes. When I don't give in, she sighs and lays her head on my shoulder.

"Fine, meanie," My Baby Girl pouts.

I chuckle and kiss the side of her head.

"I love you," I murmur against her hair.

She presses her body closer to mine to meld us as one.

"I love you, too," she whispers.

My world rights itself again.

* * *

"I'M TIRED OF HIDING, Lachlan. I know it may seem childish, but I want the fairytale romance and the happily ever after with my prince charming. It's always been your face in my dreams, Lachlan. We're so close to it in reality. That's what I want."

Haley studies my face after she sits back.

We used the last two days to move past the photos fiasco. Instead, we spent time making love and going to out-of-the-way cafés or ordering room service.

Now I ask Haley what she wants.

I remember when she was little, I found her playing with paper dolls dressed in gowns and formal wear. So intent on her play, she didn't notice me watching from the door. She had them attend an elaborate wedding of a princess and her prince.

When Baz called out to me, Haley jumped and whipped her head around. Her face turned crimson, and she gathered her paper dolls and the set before she rushed out of the library's side door.

I thought it was sweet. Had I known she was thinking of me, I don't know what I would have thought at that time. She was so much younger than me then—twelve to my sixteen. She was my best friend's kid sister and my cousin, so no thoughts of attraction existed.

But that was then, and this is now.

I can be her fairytale prince—no longer a dream only—in reality. We merely have to get past the guardians of her virtue, one of whom is still my best mate.

Fuck.

My Baby Girl waits for my response. Her beautiful expressive face reveals the myriad emotions going through her: fear, anxiety, hope. She pushes her glasses up her nose and glances away.

"Baby Girl," I say as I cup her face to return her gaze to mine. "It's not childish. At. All."

I tell her about the paper dolls, and she smiles at the memory.

"I want your dreams to become our reality, too. Just give me some time to work things through with Baz. Okay?" I ask.

She bites the corner of her mouth as she considers my request. Then she nods.

"Words, Baby Girl. I will have your words," I demand, taking control of the situation.

She blinks behind her glasses and starts to nod before she corrects herself.

"Yes, Sir," she responds firmly.

"Good. Our first step is dinner. I'll make reservations at your favorite restaurant, Sketch's Lecture Room and

Library. Wear your prettiest outfit. I want to show of my girlfriend," I tell her with a wink.

My Baby Girl claps and shimmies before she leans over to peek my lips and jump from the sofa.

I watch, mesmerized by the sway of her shapely ass and hips as she hurries to the bedroom. The only downside to coming out of hiding is less alone time to plunder my personal playground.

Ah well. Keep Baby happy…

"I LOVE THIS RESTAURANT! It's so whimsical and has the most scrumptious food!"

My Baby Girl all but bounces on her red velvet armchair in the Lecture Room and Library. Her gaze just as animated as her body flits from the golden walls to the elaborate floral designs, hanging lanterns, and bright pink, fuchsia, and gold patterned carpet.

"I'm glad you love the restaurant. But what about your boyfriend?" I ask with a cocked eyebrow and a smirk.

She reaches for my hand.

"If my boyfriend tasted as delectable as their Perfumes de Terre, he might rank a close second," she deadpans, then giggles when I scowl. "Only joshing you, My Lord. Kindly forgive my boldness, Sir."

I smirk and brush my thumb over her knuckles.

"Good thing I love you, Baby Girl," I respond.

The server takes our drink orders, and we opt for the

Tasting Menu with its Wine Pairing. As expected, the three Michelin star restaurant delivers. Our meal comprises tasty dishes including Shellfish From the British Coast and Pork Loin Marinated With Sage and Cumin and Petits Fours.

It pleases me to find a couple of Jackson Wines matched for the pairings. I ask the server to give the chef my regards. In return, she exits her domain to greet us at our table. I promise to send a case of wines for her to sample for the next rendition of her Tasting Menu. She thanks me and leaves us with special digestifs.

"That was incredible!" My Baby Girl exclaims as we walk arm-in-arm along the street. We forewent a ride back to STEELE Mayfair to take advantage of the lovely London evening. Theodore rides alongside us in the street.

I smile down at her.

"It really was a treat. I'll have to tell Lucien he has competition for Michelin stars!" I chuckle.

We come across an art gallery bustling with activity. Haley insists we go inside since she sees a sculpture that intrigues her.

I snag glasses of wine from a server's tray as we stroll through the space holding hands. We reach the statue and pause to study it. As I lift the wineglass to my mouth, a familiar voice calls my name.

"Lachlan?"

Fiona.

Fuck. Me.

My Baby Girl stiffens beside me.

Not good. At. All.

Slowly, I turn as I try to figure how to handle this turn of events.

Fiona stands with another woman. Her violet eyes dart from my face to Haley's, then to our entwined fingers. Fiona blinks her gaze back to me.

Deftly, I loosen my hold on Haley and extend my hand to the unfamiliar woman as I greet Fiona. I refuse to turn to Haley when she glances up at me.

"Hello, Fiona," I say, then turn to the woman. "Hello, Lachlan Jackson. This is Haley Steele, my best friend's sister."

A slight frown crosses Fiona's face as she glances between Haley and me. I still refuse to look at her. Instead, I listen raptly to the woman as she chatters on.

Then Fiona speaks to Haley.

"I remember meeting you at Thanksgiving. Your mother and the marchioness are best friends," Fiona states. "What brings you to London?"

"Business," Haley responds. "And you?"

Fiona flicks her eyes to me again then responds, "This is my friend's gallery. I introduced Lachlan to her earlier this month. Do you remember, Lachlan?"

She turns to me and flashes a dazzling smile.

I can feel the heat emanating from Haley's body as she must remember the photos. This has to end now before she blows.

"Yes," I respond, then glance at the woman. "It was nice to meet you. Kindly excuse Haley and me. Good evening."

I nod and place my hand at the base of Haley's spine to

guide her away from them. Once we round a corner, she jerks away and storms for the gallery's front door without a backwards glance.

Fuck. Me.

I keep up with her easily and follow her to my sedan. Theodore rushes from the driver's seat. But I wave him off and open the back door. Haley jumps inside and presses herself against the opposite door, head turned to the window.

"Haley—"

She raises her hand—palm out—to shut me up.

I bite my tongue, knowing it's best to let her be.

Once the door to our suite closes behind us, she whirls on me. Eyes narrowed, nostrils flared, face flushed crimson. She stands akimbo, ready for battle.

Fuck.

"Haley—"

"*This is Haley Steele, my best friend's sister*!!!! Are you fucking kidding me, Lachlan! You just threw everything we discussed right out of the damned window, you fucker!" She explodes.

And that's only the start. Haley reams me out. If I were a lesser man, I would curl into a fetal position and bawl my eyes out. However, I let her run out of steam before I clarify what happened.

"Haley, if I were to introduce you to Fiona as my girl-friend, she would call her mother immediately and tell her. She in turn would tell Fiona's father, who would then tell my father. He would react in one of two ways: call me to ask what the hell is going on or call your father and announce my engagement to you. The latter would cause Sebastian and the rest of your brothers to hunt me down and relieve me of my family jewels. Thereby ending any possibility of a Jackson heir and your fairytale wedding."

I stop and let my words penetrate Haley's haze of anger.

She narrows her eyes as she digests my words.

"How convenient," she snaps.

I shake my head and respond, "I know you get it, Haley, and I don't want to argue with you. I said I want what you want but need to get shit in order first. You agreed. So I tell you what: meet me at the at the top of the lighthouse in Punta del Este if you still want your fairytale."

With that, I stride into the bedroom and undress for bed.

Minutes pass before Haley turns out the light on her nightstand and slides under the covers. She keeps her back to me.

It's the first time I've not held her in my arms as we fell asleep.

LACHLAN

*O*nce again, I find myself waiting for My Baby Girl to meet me. This time the view depicts the vast Atlantic Ocean as it stretches endlessly three-quarters of the way around the Punta del Este Lighthouse with the capital Montevideo to the west.

I chose the resort town in Uruguay—known as the *Monaco of the South* and *St. Tropez of South America*—since it's known internationally as a spot for the jet set. Most members of our social circle frequent Punta del Este during high season.

Hopefully, this will prove to My Baby Girl I no longer want to keep our relationship secret either.

A few tourists mill about to snap photos, but the lighthouse isn't as crowded as the Eiffel Tower. I can see the door to the spiral staircase clearly. Each time a shadow appears, my heartbeat increases. When My Baby Girl hasn't arrived ten minutes after our planned time, I begin to doubt she'll come.

I glance once more at my mobile. No text message. No missed call.

With a sigh, I slip it back into my jeans pocket and push off from the wall. My hands run through my hair as I wonder what the hell to do next.

Should I call her or give her the space she wants, obviously?

Fly to New York, and demand she speak to me?

Call Aunt Shelley for advice?

"Fuck!" I grumble.

A couple trying to collect their two little kids who scamper about blocks my path at the exit. The girl glances up at me and waves shyly. I can't help but smile and wave back. The lightness in her breaks my dismal mood. The distraction allows her father to scoop her up. He nods at me and leads his family into the lighthouse.

I watch after them for a moment, wondering what it would be like to have children with Haley. What type of father I'd be; how many children she'd want; which of our family traits they'd get. I tug at my hair again. That's not in the plans for us since she's a no-show.

Without looking, I pivot and bump into a smaller figure.

"Oomph!"

"Pardon me! I didn't see—"

The woman lifts her face.

Haley!

I grab her to my chest and bury my face in her silky ebony hair. The elegant and intense blend of Acqua di Parma - Gelsomino Nobile's jasmine, orange flower, and musk fills my nose. She slips her arms around my waist and flattens her body against mine perfectly.

The world fades as we embrace.

"I'm so glad I caught you—"

I capture her mouth with mine and kiss her deeply. No words necessary.

My Baby Girl moans as my tongue slips between her lips to twine with hers. She melts in my arms, and I carry her to the Range Rover I hired.

Her driver places the luggage into the trunk of my Rover while my driver opens the back door. I clutch My Baby Girl closer to my chest. I refuse to let her go even as I sit on the back seat.

She settles on my lap and puts her arms around my neck.

"I missed you," she whispers.

I brush my lips against hers and murmur, "I missed you too, Baby Girl. You gave me a scare when you didn't show up after ten minutes. Everything okay?"

She nods.

"A traffic jam delayed me. I tried to call, but it went to voicemail. You didn't get my message or text?" She asks with a slight frown.

I shake my head and pull out my mobile. When I unlock it, the screen lights up with dozens of missed phone calls, text messages, and emails. Now I frown.

"The lighthouse must have had interference. Thank goodness you waited," My Baby Girl says relieved.

I nuzzle her neck with my lips, planting open-mouthed kisses on the sensitive skin. Her soft moans and the tugs to my hair make me hard as granite. The pads of my fingers dig into her ass and one hip.

"I need you, My Lord," she groans as she strokes my burgeoning erection wedged between her upper thigh and my crotch. When she tweaks the tip, I damn near cum in my jeans.

"Hold on, lass, or we won't make it to the hotel," I warn.

She giggles and tilts her head to give me better access to her fragrant neck. Then squeaks when I mark her. I growl in male satisfaction.

Once we arrive at the beachfront resort and spa, we hop into a golf cart for the ride to our villa nestled amongst the verdant foliage. I grab her luggage, and we hustle down the stone path to the front door.

My Baby Girl gasps at the spectacular sight of the infinity pool and the southern Atlantic's turquoise waters as the waves lap at our private beach.

"It's so beautiful," she breathes as she walks towards the wall of glass and sliding doors.

"Ah, no… I have plans for you, Baby Girl," I say, using the luggage to herd her towards the primary bedroom suite.

She giggles and loops her arm around mine.

"I'm sure you do, My Lord," she laughs.

Inside the bedroom, I give her no time to appreciate the

decor of light wood furniture and floors with a soft palette of sand, cream, and pale blue accents. Another wall of glass faces the ocean with sliding doors to access the deck. A spa-like, quartz bathroom nearly the size of the bedroom has a shower large enough for four people, a sizable sunken tub, two vanities, and a water closet. An outdoor rain shower set amongst the flowers adds to the bathroom's allure.

My Baby Girl can revel in the villa's sumptuousness when I bathe her after hours of lovemaking.

Which starts now…

I step back into the bedroom from the walk-in closet to find her staring out of the open sliding doors. Wisps of ebony tresses slip out of the topknot to tickle her neck. A light breeze blows the backless linen dress around her ankles and bare feet.

As I stalk towards My Baby Girl, I disrobe. From behind, I slide my hands along her narrow waist to rest on her lower belly and press the angles of my body to the curves of hers. Again, I inhale her fragrance mixed with her natural scent and her pheromones heightened by her proximity to me.

I trail my lips along the side of her head to the shell of her ear.

"Tell me, Baby Girl, when I slip my fingers inside of your pussy, will they come away dripping with your sweet juices?" I rumble.

She rubs her thighs together and mewls.

A nip to her bare shoulder makes her squeak an affirmative verbal response.

I chuckle wickedly.

My hands skim her hips, outer thighs, and calves as I crouch to gather the hem of her dress. It rises over her head as I stand kissing every inch of exposed skin before I toss the dress to the couch behind us.

She shivers not from her nakedness, rather in anticipation when I align our bodies with my erect cock at the crack of her ass and her back to my front.

"Lachlan," she breathes in a husky voice laced with need.

"I've got you, Baby Girl," I rasp as I scoop her up and stride through the doors to the nest of oversized pillows on the deck.

I kneel amongst them and lower her onto her back with my knees between her spread thighs. The sight of her glistening pink pussy confirms my suspicions: My Baby Girl is aroused as fuck. I close my eyes and inhale her musky scent deeply.

Her fingers grasp at my hair when I lower to my belly and eat her pussy like a starved animal. Amorous sighs fall from her parted lips like music from a well-played violin. She strums in time with my tongue, teeth, and fingers.

Succulent juices coat my nose and chin as she comes undone for me in rhythmic succession. I lap at the well of her pussy to swallow every single drop.

My fingers scissor inside—relishing in the tightness of

her inner muscles—to prepare her to take my girth after weeks of being apart.

My Baby Girl's hips lift from our nest as her fingers claw at the soft silks of the pillows.

"Lachlan… Please… I need you," she pleads, tossing her head side to side.

In response, I suck on her clit. Hard.

Once again, she explodes with a garbled cry.

Immediately I cover her with my body and drive my hungry cock inside of her pussy with one thrust, eager to experience the sensation of her walls clenching from her climax.

"Oh, fuck, Haley…" I groan, head thrown back with my eyes closed tightly. "Feel… so… good."

She pulsates around my dick, and I almost cum like a randy first-time teenager.

I remain still to regain control. A nudge from below and a whine bring me back. My mouth covers hers and I swallow her complaint with a growl as my hips swivel and draw back to slam forward.

Her full tits bounce as I jostle her. Beaded nipples drag along my chest. I groan from the sensation of my cock thickening in response. My Baby Girl gobbles up the sound and adds a moan of her own.

I alternate long, slow strokes with circling my hips to touch each area of her pussy. The brush of my bulbous tip against the rough texture of her G-spot draws another chord from her parted lips.

More sweet music fills the air surrounding us. It mingles with the sound of the waves along the shore and the calls of birds as they fly from the palm trees around the deck.

I murmur words of love and forever as I bring her to climax until she begs for no more as she clings to my shoulders with legs locked around my hips. Then I chase my release with rapid pistoning strokes. My heavy balls draw up as my cock swells impossibly hard. Ropes of my seed shoot out as my tip hits her cervix.

My mind goes back to the little kids at the lighthouse.

If only my seed can take root in My Baby Girl's womb. The thought makes me pump harder to spill every drop within her source of life. I roar through the last stage of my release as though I can command her womb to grow my seed for a baby of our own. Mine!

She cries out in wild abandon as she meets each of my powerful thrusts.

Spent, I collapse on top of her with my face buried in her neck. Hot breath blows across her sweat-dampened skin, and she trembles. I wrap my arms under her shoulders and roll to my back. She lays her head on my wet chest and sighs.

I caress her back as I stare up at the white gauzy canopy. The sun filters through to dapple our skin with shadows. My fingers wander to her arm to trace the patterns. She entwines our fingers and brings them to her lips.

"Happy Anniversary, Lachlan Jackson. I love you, My

Lord," My Baby Girl whispers as she brushes her lips across my knuckles.

"Happy Anniversary, Haley Steele," I murmur, staring into the depths of her platinum gray eyes filled with joy. "I love you more, Baby Girl."

As we drift off to sleep wrapped in each other's arms, I smile to myself.

My Baby Girl came back, and she loves me. All is good in our world.

HALEY

"You know, Baz nor Malcolm or Roger have said anything to me. Not even my Dad or Harris. What did Baz say to you after you spoke with him about us?"

Over the last couple of days, we've been so busy: making love, watching the Punta del Este ePrix electric car race, dining at the gourmet restaurants and the local eateries, swimming naked in the moonlight. It's been incredible, even more so when Lachlan told me he chose the resort town to prove he's more than ready to come out of hiding with our relationship.

Which reminds me there's been radio silence from my family about Lachlan and me dating. Of course, my mother knows and asks how things are going. But the others have been mum.

Not that I mind! Trust me when I say I'd rather my

brothers focus on their love lives and stay out of mine, permanently.

Lachlan and I returned from dancing at the most popular nightclub moments ago. I'm in the bathroom getting ready for a refreshing shower and call out to him while I wash the makeup from my face.

When he doesn't answer, I walk over to the bathroom door and lean against the jamb smoothing cream on my clean skin.

"Hey, did you hear me? What did Baz say when you guys spoke about us?" I repeat.

Lachlan runs his hand through his hair and averts his gaze from mine. He doesn't answer.

My stomach churns.

"Lachlan, you did speak to Baz like you said you would, didn't you?" I ask as I stand upright, then continue when he fails to answer. "You didn't speak to him."

The flat tone of my voice brings Lachlan's eyes back to me. He shakes his head and holds out his hands.

Is he serious with me right now?! After all we said in London about what we wanted and how he'd make things right with Sebastian, Lachlan hasn't even spoken to him.

I'm so over this shit.

With a low growl, I spin on my heel and stomp into the bathroom. My mind in turmoil. Every time I think we're making progress, we fall again. Am I crazy to keep putting myself through this with Lachlan or what?

I step beneath the multiple shower heads and tilt my face upwards for water to cascade from my hair to my toes.

As I reach for the shampoo, I laugh out loud mirthlessly when the song about a woman washing a man out of her hair pops into my mind. How did it work out for her, I wonder.

The scent of lavender cannot calm me. So I take deep breaths, like Starr taught me to center my mind. It doesn't work well. I'll need to call her for a new remedy…

After I dry off, I wrap my hair in a towel and don a fluffy white robe. Perhaps some time on the deck with fresh air and the soothing sounds of the waves will ease my troubled soul.

I stride past Lachlan—who knew better than to come into the shower with me—and head for the sliding doors.

The underwater lights of the pool and the torches along the perimeter give the deck an ethereal feeling. A warm breeze carries the scent of the flowers mixed with the salty water.

I sit on a sunbed with my back against pillows. My eyes close as I focus on my breathing.

"Haley, I haven't spoken to Baz yet only because our business schedules have been too busy. I don't want to just call him up and tell him you and I are a couple. That's a conversation best made in person. We have some available dates, so I'll see him soon," Lachlan says.

I open my eyes to stare up at him.

Resigned, I shake my head.

"Lachlan, I don't know what else to do anymore. Perhaps it's best if we—"

"Marry me."

My mouth falls open when he drops to one knee and clasps my hands between his sizable ones. He stares at me; I stare at him.

What the hell?

I'm absolutely flabbergasted.

In fairytale land, my heart races with excitement: Lachlan asked me to marry him! Yes!!! Woohoo!!

Then there's the reality: Lachlan asked me to marry him, not because he means it. But because I was about to break up with him. Whomp, whomp…

Tears prick the backs of my eyes. Once again, I shake my head in dismay.

"No," I respond.

I extricate my hands from his and slide to the edge of the sunbed. Standing, I stare down at him, still on one knee. Of their own will, my fingers run through his sable brown hair and tug gently.

He tips his head towards my palm and kisses it.

"Haley, I mean it. I want you to be my wife and to have my babies. Marry me," Lachlan says, taking my hands in his again. "I love you more than anything, Baby Girl."

"No," I repeat. "I don't want you to marry me to stop me from leaving. I want you to come willingly into a forever relationship with me, not because you feel I forced your hand—"

"Haley—"

"You can't get past telling Sebastian for fear of upsetting him and your friendship. It outranks you and me—us. I don't want to be with a man whose arm I have to twist to give me what I want in my life. I'm going tomorrow morning," I say.

Lachlan attempts to hold on to my hand. But I pull away and walk back to the bedroom, where I slip out of the robe and towel before I climb into the bed.

"—FINE, MATE! LET ME GO ALREADY!"

The sound of Lachlan's shouts wakes me.

I jump from the bed and grab my robe, tying it as I rush to the living room. Then stop short.

Lachlan hangs between two burly men—even taller than his six feet, four inches—dressed in dark suits with communication pieces in their ears. His hair is a mess, and his clothes disheveled. He glares from one man to the other.

One notices me and nods.

"Pardon us, *señorita*. Your boyfriend disrupted the other patrons at the bar, so we had to remove him. Are you fine to take care of him?" The security guard asks as Lachlan struggles and calls out to me.

"Haley! I love you, Baby Girl!" He shouts. "Don't leave me, lass!"

I push my glasses up the bridge of my nose as I assess the situation.

"We can keep him at the security office, if you're afraid—"

"Fuck you, wanker! I'd never hurt the love of my life!"

Lachlan shouts and yanks free of the guards—or rather they let him go—and falls to his knees.

He glares up at them and staggers to his feet.

"Baby Girl, please…" he says as he makes his way towards me with his arms outstretched.

I glance from him to the guards and back. With a sigh, I wrap my arms around his waist as he leans on me. His breath reeks of alcohol.

"*Señorita?*" The first guard asks, eyeing Lachlan warily.

"We're fine. But if you'd be so kind as to help me get him to the bed, I'd appreciate it greatly," I respond with a wan smile.

They nod and take a complaining, drunk Lachlan by the arms and carry him between them to the bedroom. Once he's settled on the bed, I see the guards out, then rush back to his side.

"Baby Girl! You didn't leave me. Thank fuck," he says as he falls back onto the bed. "Fuck, why is the room spinning? It's too bloody bright!"

He groans and throws his arm over his eyes.

I take a deep breath and walk over to him. He already kicked his loafers off, so I reach to unbuckle his belt to pull his pants down.

"Oh, Baby Girl, I want you too. Fuck… I always want you. I've never wanted another woman as much as I want you…" Lachlan rambles on. He sits up on one elbow and covers my hand with his. He drags it to his crotch. "See how much you turn me on, Baby Girl? All for you…"

I slip my hand from his erection as I roll my eyes.

This man right here is an absolute mess. Drunk and horny. Ugh!

"Okay, Casanova, let's get you undressed," I respond.

"Yes!" He whoops and grabs his shirt by the neck and rips it over his head. "You too, Baby Girl. Let me see those luscious tits. Yum, yum!"

He licks his lips and reaches for me.

I swat his hands away and yank his pants down. But damn if my eyes don't stray to the massive bulge inside his boxer briefs. For a moment, I consider dropping my robe to straddle him and sink my throbbing pussy onto his long, fat dick.

Down, girl, I admonish myself.

"Marry me, Haley Steele. Be mine forever."

In a moment of clarity, Lachlan cups my face to bring our eyes on the level. His blaze with emerald fire. Then they dim and close before he passes out. He falls back on to the bed with a grunt. Lachlan is out cold.

I check his pulse, then roll him to his side to pull the bedding back enough to slip the sheets and cover over his sleeping form.

He mumbles a few more words of love and forever sporadically. After a while he quiets down. His chest rises and falls steadily as soft snores come through his parted lips. A lock of hair falls across his forehead.

I reach over and smooth it back. My fingertips trail over the side of his face to the three-day stubble on his cheeks and chin. I stroke his cleft and cup his face.

Even in sleep, Lachlan leans into my palm like a moth

to a flame. It reminds me of Janet Jackson's song "That's the Way Love Goes."

I sigh and go to the walk-in closet to pack. I won't lose my resolve to let Lachlan go and to move on with my life. No matter how much my love is blind to him not standing up for our relationship to his best friend, my big brother. None of us are kids anymore. We have the right to love who we love.

Baz has Lola. Why can't Lachlan have me?

The situation is too unfair for words.

My heart aches with each piece of clothing I fold in my luggage. When the closet is empty save for Lachlan's things, I move on to the bathroom. I gather my cosmetics and toiletries into their cases, then stow them in my luggage. Last, I pack my tech gadgets but leave my mobile out.

I take it back to the bedroom and sit at the foot of the bed with my arms wrapped around my legs held to my chest. My eyes stay glued to Lachlan as I watch him sleep soundly. I won't leave until I'm certain he won't get sick.

As the sky over the Atlantic Ocean changes from inky black to brilliant streaks of purple, gold, and orange. Birds chirp to welcome the morning sun as they flit beyond the open sliding doors. Through them the gentle laps of the waves meet the sand.

I stand and stretch.

Lachlan doesn't stir.

When I return from the bathroom fully dressed, I stop by the side of the bed. My eyes scan Lachlan for any sign of distress. He rests peacefully. I lean over and press my lips to his mouth. When I stand, I wipe a tear from my cheek and place my pain on his lips.

"I will always love you, Lachlan Jackson. But you are not my fairytale prince. I wish you well, My Lord. Goodbye."

* * *

Lachlan & Haley's Story Continues: *Tease My Desires*

**Turn the page for the Steele & Jackson Family Trees, Author's Note,
and Previews of *Tease My Desires* and of The STEELE International, Inc. Series Book 1 *Fulfill My Desires* Sebastian & Lola Part I**

THE STEELE FAMILY

STEELE INTERNATIONAL, INC

Multigenerational, multibillion-dollar business luxury real estate development and management corporation

Headquarters & Family's Primary Residences:

The STEELE Tower, New York City

A modern, gray-tinted glass fifty-seven story mixed-use skyscraper on southwest corner of Fifty-Seventh Street and Fifth Avenue within Billionaires' Row

Global Offices:

- The United States of America (New York City, New Jersey, Chicago, California, Miami, Las Vegas)
- The Caribbean (St. Maarten, St. Barth's, St. Lucia)
- The French & Italian Rivieras (Nice, Cannes, Positano, Capri)
- Monaco (Monte Carlo)
- The United Arab Emirates (Abu Dhabi, Dubai)

STEELE FOUNDATION: A STRONG AND SUPPORTIVE HOUSE

Builds and manages attractive, affordable housing for urban, lower-income families

Available for download at **bit.ly/STEELEFamily**

THE JACKSON FAMILY

JACKSON CORPORATION

Multigenerational, multibillion-dollar business fine dining,
distilleries, and vineyards corporation

Headquarters:

Jackson Town House, Aberdeen, Scotland

A landmark property built by the founders of Aberdeen granite
on Union Street; the second largest granite building in the world.

Global Offices:

- The United Kingdom (Aberdeen, Scotland; London, England)
- The United States of America (New York City, New Orleans, Miami, Chicago, Los Angeles, Napa)
- The Caribbean (Puerto Rico)
- France (Paris, Cannes)
- Monaco (Monte Carlo)
- Australia (Sydney)
- The United Arab Emirates (Abu Dhabi, Dubai)

JACKSON FOUNDATION: ENJOY LIFE RESPONSIBLY

Operates alcohol treatment centers for lower-income individuals and support for their family members

Available for download at **bit.ly/JacksonFamilyTree**

Author's Note

Thank you for reading Part I of Lachlan and Haley's sexy, sizzling romance! I hope you enjoyed the start of their forbidden love affair. If so, I'd love to hear your thoughts, please share a review at **bit.ly/CLBooksSI-JC1Review** and tell your friends.

Click below for what's up next for this darling duo:

Tease My Desires Lachlan & Haley Part II Click Here

Also, did you catch on to the dynamism of Sebastian and Lola? Well, you'll have your answers!
Visit books2read.com/u/3RLy0D

Fulfill My Desires Sebastian & Lola Part I Preview

At **CharmaineLouise.com** take the *Four types of lovers. Which are you?* **Quiz** to match your Sexy Fantasy: sub, Voyeur, Dominatrix, or Dominatrix sub Switch.

Follow me on social media including my CLBooks Coterie Fan Club below or on your favorite channels below and subscribe to my newsletter at **bit.ly/ CLBooksNewsletter** for a **Free Book**.

Fulfill Your Desires.

xoxo

Charmaine Louise

BB bookbub.com/authors/charmaine-louise-shelton
f facebook.com/CharmaineLouiseBooks
instagram.com/charmainelouisebooks
g goodreads.com/charmainelouisebooks

**STEELE International, Inc. - Jackson Corporation
A Billionaires Romance Series Crossover Book 2**

Tease My Desires Lachlan & Haley Part II

Click on the link below or visit books2read.com/u/
4DPzve to get your copy.

Tease My Desires Lachlan & Haley Part II

Books in the Series:

Tempt My Desires Lachlan & Haley Part I

Tease My Desires Lachlan & Haley Part II

Grant My Desires Lachlan & Haley Part III

Intrigue My Desires Harris & Kat Part I

Decode My Desires Harris & Kat Part II

Honor My Desires Harris & Kat Patt III

A Trilogy of Desires Lachlan & Haley Parts I-III

A Trilogy of Desires Harris & Kat Parts I-III

Series Extras

Series Playlist

Visit CharmaineLouiseBooks.com for the complete list.

COMING NEXT: TEASE MY
DESIRES LACHLAN & HALEY PART
II STEELE INTERNATIONAL, INC. -
JACKSON CORPORATION A
BILLIONAIRES ROMANCE SERIES
CROSSOVER BOOK 2

"*Oh*, come on, bro! I *cannot* believe you've been moping around for the past two months like your favorite puppy ran away. What the bloody hell is wrong with you, Lachlan? And do not give me any more of your bullshit excuses either."

My youngest brother Laurent throws his hands up in the air, then slaps them on top of my desk as he leans over to scowl at me. His bottle green eyes—so like my emerald ones, a Jackson family trait—blaze.

When I don't answer, Laurent growls as he stands to his full height of six feet, three inches and runs his hands through his collar-length sable brown hair. Frustrated, he paces my office in Aberdeen, Scotland at Jackson Town House, the headquarters for Jackson Corporation—our family's multigenerational, multibillion-dollar company.

Its repertoire comprises fine dining, distilleries, and vineyards worldwide. Our Irish and Scottish family created the finest single malt Scotch Whiskey and became billionaires years ago in the Granite City. King James VI titled the Jackson family as Marquess of Huntly with our family seat—Jackson Castle—in Banff, Aberdeenshire. Our father Connor and mother Lucinda—aka Lucie—use their titles. Even though I'm the heir apparent, my siblings—Lydie, a year older at thirty-five, Lucien thirty-two, and Laurent thirty—and I prefer less formality and use our titles rarely.

Each sibling works at Jackson Corporation: Lydie, Overall Vice President and Vice President of the Board; me, President of Liquor and Second Vice President of the Board; Lucien, *The Sexy Chef*, President of Restaurants/Bars/Lounges and Third Vice President of the Board; Laurent, Director of Jackson Corporation Cigars Division and member of the Board.

Our mother runs the Jackson Foundation. It operates alcohol treatment centers for lower-income individuals and support for their family members. The annual fundraising gala is the highlight of Aberdeen's social calendar. Patrons from across the United Kingdom and the world attend.

Connor holds the head position as CEO and Chairman of the Board and expects to retire in a year. Our father also expects me—as the eldest son—to take over despite Lydie being the firstborn and busting her ass for years. Lydie's sole goal to prove herself worthy to follow in the steps of our forefathers to lead Jackson Corporation. Unfortunately, her gender proves the problem for Connor...

If I don't use my title of Earl of Aboyne as the heir, I really avoid the role of CEO to the vexation of our father. My allegiance is to my sister. I will do nothing to hurt her. It would crush her very soul to lose the position she's compelled to get since our father gave us a tour of Jackson's first distillery at eight and seven, respectively. Lydie deserves CEO, and I won't stand in her way. For anyone.

To my vexation, my father's insistence on me bearing the next Jackson heir has increased over the last year and a half. Especially since my best friend Sebastian Steele—who's two years older than me—finally tied the knot. Like me, Baz is the eldest son and an Alpha Dom whose time focused on STEELE International, Inc. as recently promoted CEO and president of the Retail Properties Division.

STEELE is his family's luxury real estate development and management corporation based in New York City. One-night trysts to satisfy his sexual and Dom needs supplemented his work. Marriage? Yeah, to STEELE until he met Lola Lewis, and the rest, as they say, is history.

Thanks to the Matriarchs, the Jacksons and Steeles are as close as cousins. My mother and her best friend Michelle *Shelley* Steele spent most of their adult lives together in New York City after my mother ran away from her home in New Orleans. The duo formed a closer bond than they have with their blood siblings and relatives.

As fate would have it, our mothers met our fathers while working as a bartender in one of the Jackson pubs and as a shopgirl in a STEELE retail space. Both families became close even without sharing DNA. Hence our cousin relationship and Aunt Shelley and Uncle Morgan.

Aside from Baz, the rest of the Steele clan includes Malcolm *The Enforcer* thirty-four, Roger *The Responsible* thirty-three, and fraternal twins Harris and Haley the Dynamic Duo thirty. Like Baz, they work at STEELE: Malcolm president of the Entertainment Properties Division; Roger, president of the Residential Properties Division; Harris and Haley, co-founders of the subsidiary STEELE Technology and Cyber Security.

Although the Steeles call New York City home and the Jacksons have Aberdeen, our families spend a lot of time together. Summers at our Southampton Village beachfront compound in New York near to theirs. Our mother insisted we not loll around the pool, so my siblings and I interned at Jackson's New York City offices. We alternate Thanksgiving between Jackson Castle and The STEELE Tower and Christmas at a STEELE resort. Lucien and Malcolm, Laurent and Harris are best friends, like Baz and me.

Everything was great growing up with our American cousins. Until that summer fourteen years ago, when I was on break from Pembroke College at the University of Oxford. Little Haley—who tagged behind Baz and me as we went about our escapades as kids and teens—at sixteen no longer reminded me of a little sister.

The night Haley fell and hurt herself as she followed us through their darkened beachfront mansion and looked up at me with soulful platinum gray eyes that shimmered with tears behind her glasses, my heart stuttered. As I tucked a long lock of silky ebony waves behind her ear, then stroked tears from her heart-shaped face, a tingle passed throughout my body.

It was at that moment, I realized Little Haley was no longer just my cousin I regarded as a little sister. She was more. Her behavior towards me changed that summer, too. She was more shy; averted her eyes when our gazes met; lingered near me with a faraway look on her face. It made me wonder if Haley felt the same connection.

But the enormous problem? The obstacle that could keep us apart forever?

Haley was Baz's little sister—*my best friend's* little sister. Completely off-limits to me. Taboo.

Despite the deep part of me she ignited unexpectedly. What I sensed from her didn't matter one bit. Not to mention, she was only a sixteen-year-old girl, and I was a twenty-year-old man. Not happening. Or so I thought...

Thirteen years later and countless trysts with nameless women I fucked who were the direct opposite of Haley with their blonde hair, slim figures, and not stellar brains, I have no choice but to come to terms with my desire for her. My Baby Girl was a fully grown, curvy, brainiac of a woman who came to me to express her desire for more. A desire born from a teenage crush that simmered with a slow burn, despite being held back for years.

We began a forbidden love affair secret from her brothers—The Big Four—and from our families, except for our mothers who gave their absolute approval. I made

Haley Steele mine when she gave me the greatest gifts—her innocence and her innate submission. For a beautiful year of unimaginable bliss, our relationship flourished; our love grew.

Sure, we had bumps along the way. Fiona Ridel the twenty-nine-year-old Scottish heiress my father wants me to marry to seal a merger with her family's oil business. Harris figuring My Baby Girl and me out; Lydie the same situation. And, of course, the ever-present shadow of Baz hanging about the periphery. The tolls of keeping our relationship secret, along with the long distance between Haley in New York City and me in Aberdeen.

We reached the edge more than once—not only the erotic one.

But it was during our one-year anniversary trip to Punta del Este where My Baby Girl realized I hadn't spoken to Baz about our relationship that drove her from my arms. To make it up to her, I asked her to marry me. However, it was too late and not the fairy-tale ending she wanted.

My Baby Girl left me.

No matter the amount of pleas or requests for her to come to my flat one floor below hers at The STEELE Tower, Haley refuses to see me, let alone rekindle our love. Two fucking months of sheer hell. My head and heart ache —not to mention my cock and fist.

So excuse the *fuck* out of me, little brother, if I've *been moping around for the past two months like your favorite puppy ran away.* In a way, she did.

I sigh aloud and roll my eyes inwardly as I rise to my full height of six feet, four inches. The muscles of my sizable frame—honed from decades of Scottish martial arts just like Laurent's body—tighten from stress. One of my hands runs through my slicked-back, sable brown hair while the other swipes over my three-day stubble. Who cares to shave?

Thank fuck it's after working hours.

I stride to the bar on the side wall and pour two fingers of Jackson Special Blend Scotch into Waterford Crystal snifters.

"Shit, Lach, you look a mess, bro," Laurent says as he takes the proffered glass. "What happened to the movie star Cary Grant lookalike all the women adore?"

Now, I roll my eyes blatantly as I grunt into my snifter. What a way to drive in the last nail, little brother, I muse to myself.

"Earth to Lachlan. Have you lost your tongue, *dhuine?*" Laurent asks.

"No, but if you keep bugging the shit out of me, you'll wish I had," I threaten with a cocked eyebrow as I drop onto the tufted leather sofa.

He lowers himself into a club chair across from me and places his snifter on the coffee table.

"No, seriously, Lach. Is everything okay with you? Lydie called me concerned, too," he adds.

I haven't told Lydie. Only our mother knows about the breakup. The advice I received was to give Haley some time. Even Aunt Shelley voiced the same opinion. So a month ago, I flew back to Aberdeen. But how much more can a man take?

And I know Haley can't feel any better.

I miss My Baby Girl. My urge to care for her grows stronger every day. But what the fuck more can I do?

"Fine, don't tell me," Laurent says exasperated. "However, your ass will be on my jet in the morning. Even if I have to spend the night in your penthouse to get you to the airport, bro."

I stare at him blankly.

"Oh, for fuck's sake, Lach!" He says once again throwing his hands into the air. "The Young 3's 3-0 Birthday Party?! Hello… my thirtieth birthday celebration with Harris and Haley. How could you forget, bro?!"

I blink. Then a slow smile spreads across my face.

The answer I've been seeking. Thank fuck!

My Baby Girl won't be able to avoid me at their party. And it won't appear odd for us to be together.

So hell yeah, I'll be on Laurent's GulfStream G650, ready to get my woman back in my arms. Where she belongs. Forever.

"HAPPY BIRTHDAY, BABY GIRL."

She startles, then spins around to gaze up at me. Her wide platinum gray eyes peek out from behind an elaborate mask made of pearls against a cream silk backing with strands that twine up into her hair piled high atop her head.

The length of her swan-like neck emphasized by the turtleneck of her cream-colored stretch-PVC mini dress. The tight fit of the long-sleeves and bodice that flares out to a pleated skater skirt shows off her full tits. It would be demure except for the cut-out back. Her mile-long toned legs end in clear PVC mules. As always, the contrast of My Baby Girl's sinfulness and sweetness tantalizes me. The sexy look fits in with their party's masquerade theme and venue they closed to members for their private birthday celebration.

LEVELS New York the flagship location of the global, luxury, members-only BDSM/dance clubs in Manhattan's Meatpacking District. It caters to the crème de la crème of society and the über-wealthy—politicians, titans of industry, celebrities, and royalty—who prefer to keep their consensual sexual proclivities private with rigorous background checks and nondisclosure agreements. They choose between Global All Access or Dine/Dance memberships.

Lucien and Malcolm selected the historic location as a play on the area's name. Put a club where men pack their meat into willing women and willing men allow women to pack them with their toys. The theme is minimal and industrial. The fixtures and furniture that appear well worn are high-end, modern replicas used to add authenticity without the grime of old pieces.

All Access members can choose from any of the seven

levels. While the Dine/Dance members only have access to the party levels—Sky Lounge, Dance Club, and Level 4 Restaurant. For consistency and members' comfort, locations share the same layout with varying views:

Seven levels: 7th Sky Lounge that offers for the Meatpacking location a stunning, 360-degree view of Manhattan and across the Hudson River to New Jersey's shoreline, a bar, restaurant by day dance club by night, a coverable pool that's open during the warmer months, and a glass-retractable roof; 6th and 5th multilevel dance club with two bars and a lounge for food and drinks; 4th Level 4 Restaurant and bar open for breakfast, lunch, and dinner; 3rd has twelve private suites for members to continue their pleasure apart from the BDSM levels; 2nd Peepshow for BDSM with seating alcoves, primary stage, mini-stages, performance rooms, and a bar that serves non-alcoholic mocktails; below ground the Cellar, a BDSM dungeon with mocktails bar.

The wild ones of our families cooked up the idea while Lucien finished his hospitality and culinary training at Le Cordon Bleu in Paris.

When they came to Baz and Lydie with the idea, I agreed with them when they questioned: who the hell goes through that prestigious training to come up with a titty bar? Well, years later Lucien's idea proves it's bigger than that and has a high profit margin with more locations in Paris and London.

The LEVELS clubs are one of many business partner-ships that STEELE has with Jackson Corporation. Our products pair well within STEELE's casinos, hotels, resorts, and residential and retail properties.

Right now, the partnership that's my top priority stands before me.

My hands itch to run over her lush curves; my fingers want to trail along her inner thigh before they slip beneath the flirty hemline of her mini dress; my arms flex to pull her to my chest tight.

It takes all of my will to not cover her mouth O-shaped in surprise with mine and kiss her breathless until she melts against me. Then carry her to a private suite to make up for all the days we've been apart.

But most of all, I want My Baby Girl to tell me she still loves me and wants to marry like I asked weeks ago. I send up a silent prayer for a positive reaction from her.

"Lachlan? Wh—what are you doing here?" She asks as her eyes skitter everywhere around the room except my face.

Not quite the response I hoped for. My heart slams in my chest. This won't be as easy as I thought. Damn.

"Baby Gir—"

"Don't! Do *not* call me that, Lachlan," she whisper yells, platinum grays flash like lightning. "I *cannot* believe you're here and calling me what I am not to you anymore! Please… Please leave me be. What we had ended when you failed to uphold your promise to me. I will *not* get back on that merry-go-round with you again, Lachlan Jackson. Move on. I did."

With a shattered heart, I stare after the love of my life as she stalks away without a backwards glance.

***

Click the Link Below or Visit books2read.com/u/bp8d7X For Your Copy

Tease My Desires Lachlan & Haley Part II

PREVIEW STEELE SERIES BOOK 1: FULFILL MY DESIRES SEBASTIAN & LOLA PART I

Sebastian

"Good evening, Mr. Steele," one of the two stunning greeters purrs as I step into the lobby for LEVELS New York.

This is the flagship location of the global, luxury, members-only BDSM/dance clubs in Manhattan's Meatpacking District. They chose the historic location as a play on the area's name. Put a club where men pack their meat into willing women and willing men allow women to pack them with their toys. The theme for the lobby is minimal and industrial. The fixtures and furniture that appear well worn are high-end, modern replicas used to add authenticity without the grime of old pieces. The two sides have coordinating greeter stations that allow access to the separate Dine & Dance levels and the BDSM levels. The other greeter turns her head in my direction and briefly smiles at me before she returns her attention to a couple entering the BDSM side.

My cousin Lucien Jackson cooked up the idea and roped my younger brother Malcolm into it. Lucien literally cooked it up since he thought of it as he finished his hospitality and culinary training at Le Cordon Bleu in Paris.

Who the hell goes through that prestigious training to come up with a titty bar? Well, five years later his idea proves it's bigger than that and has a high profit margin with more locations in Paris and London. That's all that concerns me: will it add to STEELE International's bottom line? Yes, well, it's a go. No, then no go.

LEVELS is one of many business partnerships that STEELE has with Jackson Corporation. World-renown for their award-winning eateries, choice cigars, and distinguished liquors and wines, their products pair well within STEELE's casinos, hotels, resorts, and residential and retail properties.

On the personal side, my mother is best friends with the Jackson matriarch. They spent most of their adult lives together forming a closer bond than they have with their blood siblings and relatives. Not sharing DNA doesn't keep our families from being a close-knit group.

"Good evening," I respond as I make my way to the D&D elevator.

Once inside, I place my keycard against the panel to select the third floor for the Level 4 Restaurant. I'm a Global All Access member. I can choose from any of the seven levels: 7th Sky Lounge that offers a stunning, 360-

degree view of Manhattan and across the Hudson River to New Jersey's shoreline, a bar, restaurant by day dance club by night, a coverable pool that's open during the warmer months, and a glass-retractable roof; 6th and 5th multilevel dance club with two bars and a lounge for food and drinks; 4th Level 4 Restaurant and bar open for breakfast, lunch, and dinner; 3rd has twelve private suites for members to continue their pleasure apart from the BDSM levels; 2nd Peepshow for BDSM with seating alcoves, primary stage, mini-stages, performance rooms, and a bar that serves non-alcoholic mocktails; below ground the Cellar a BDSM dungeon with mocktails bar. The Dine/Dance members only have access to the party levels—Sky Lounge, Dance Club, and Level 4 Restaurant.

Tonight, I need to eat and fuck hard in that order. I'm bound to find a female at the restaurant or bar who's willing to be my pet for the evening. One night only, maybe two if she's not clingy or a gold digger, but two fucks is my maximum. I'm not looking for a relationship and damn sure not marriage, just enough time to satisfy my Dom needs and my physical release for the moment. A short-term encounter to balance out my business-focused life.

As president of the Retail Properties Division of STEELE, I bust my ass fourteen hours a day to make it super profitable and to prove that I deserve my future role as CEO of the entire luxury real estate development and management company when my father retires next year. It's not just my last name getting me into the head position.

I'm damn capable since I've worked my way up the ranks to learn our multigenerational, multibillion dollar business combined with my Harvard undergrad and MBA degrees.

My father, Morgan, trusts me to carry the legacy into the future and my younger brothers and sister respect me and accept my leadership. Each sibling works at STEELE: Malcolm president of the Entertainment Properties Division; Roger, president of the Residential Properties Division; Harris and Haley, fraternal twins, co-founders of the subsidiary STEELE Technology and Cyber Security. At 35, I take my role as the eldest seriously, so I don't have time for nor care to get involved in a relationship. Thanks to Lucien and Malcolm, LEVELS provides exactly what I need.

As I step off of the elevator, I take in my surroundings. The bar is bustling as usual with the crème de la crème of society. They hobnob with top-shelf drinks. Seating ranges from the leather and black metal stools at the long, reclaimed-wood covered bar to the dozen high-top tables styled to match. The bar along the right wall features a floor-to-ceiling mirrored wall of shelves of only the best spirits and wines—most are from the Jackson labels. The bartenders serve signature cocktails. Tables on the left complete the layout of the open-plan room. A path between the two areas leads to the LEVEL 4 Restaurant's maître d' station. There, the patrons eat delicious meals prepared by chefs trained by Lucien. My destination awaits.

As I stride towards the maître d', my gaze alights on

several recognizable faces enjoying nightcaps at the bar area's high-top tables. Tonight, the U.S. Attorney for the Southern District of New York, the former governor of California, and a high-powered female CFO of a Wall Street investment bank are present. The club caters to the most wealthy and influential in society. They prefer the relative safety that one can expect from the ironclad nondisclosure agreement that LEVELS requires every member and their guests to sign.

I smile and nod in greeting—every Steele is instantly recognizable—but keep it moving as I'm not here tonight for small talk. As I approach the hostess at the dining area's maître d' podium, I also notice several pairs of lust-filled eyes including those of a few men track my movement as I walk past them. Sadly for the men, I'm strictly a female to a male individual. As I approach the station, the maître d' on duty tonight looks up with an alluring smile on her pretty face.

"Good evening, Mr. Steele," says Susan, as her name tag denotes. She angles her chin down to allow her to peek up at me from beneath her long eyelashes without direct eye contact.

"Your usual table, Sir?"

I don't miss her emphasis on Sir as a sub innuendo. Susan is one of many LEVELS employees who want to have my marks on them and my dick in every one of their holes. Disappointingly for the staff though, I don't mix business with pleasure. That can only end in a messy situation and unnecessarily complicate matters—doesn't fit with my trajectory.

"Good evening, Susan. That's good, thank you," I reply.

Susan's full lips curl up into a dazzling smile as she visibly preens. Her reaction as though I petted her head for a job well done after I fucked her throat and she didn't spill a single drop of my copious amount of cum. Susan seductively sways her hips, long legs stressed by stilettos and her form-fitted, black mini dress molded to her curvy body. She leads me to my table in the center of the room with an unobstructed view of the large dining area and of the bar. A spot from which I can easily observe all the patrons to cherry-pick my companion for tonight. However, the sight before me has me second-guessing my no business/pleasure rule. Susan deliberately bends over the table to straighten the napkin, giving me a visual of her cuffed to my pommel horse and a cane in my hand. Damn if my cock didn't just twitch from looking at her plump bottom and grip-worthy hips. Fortunately, I hadn't unbuttoned my suit jacket, or my piqued dick would be on full display.

I give the heads, on my neck and at my groin, firm, shakes to clear the vision. Then, without making eye contact, I thank Susan, take my seat, and pick up the menu discouraging further attention.

With an audible sigh, Susan bids me, "Enjoy your dinner, Mr. Steele," and walks away. Then on second thought she turns and offers, "Should you need anything at all, please let me know."

Keeping my gaze on the menu, I nod, and Susan dejectedly walks away with less sway to her hips, albeit still an eye-catching vision. Sorry, sweetheart.

If I'm not entertaining business associates or attending social gatherings like charity functions, I frequently dine at Level 4. I prefer that then eating takeout at home or hiring a personal chef to cook for only one person. Both are extravagances that I can afford, but why waste resources with my mutable schedule that changes as often as I change boxers.

Dinner out at whatever time is convenient in a city with thousands of excellent restaurants suits my lifestyle. Level 4 is one of them with a menu that offers the expected fare typical of Continental cuisine of pastas, meat, and steaks with favorable sauces. Lucien complements the usual dishes with appealing specials that change daily to keep the choices fresh and habitual guests like me from getting bored.

The client care is impeccable. So, I don't flinch when the server quietly appears at my side and places a napkin-covered basket with an assortment of warm, fresh-baked breads on the table. I glance up to see a youthful man who is model-perfect and well-groomed with a clean-shaven jaw, slicked-back ebony hair, and intelligent brown eyes. His all-black uniform of a long-sleeved shirt, pants, butcher apron, and shiny Oxford shoes is spotless—the de rigueur fashion for LEVELS employees.

"Welcome to Level 4, sir. My name is Andrew and I'll be your server this evening. May I take your drink order?"

"Thank you, Andrew. I'll have a bottle of Pellegrino," I respond with a pleasant smile.

"Very good, sir. We have some lovely specials tonight. May I share them with you?"

Since I plan to play tonight, I select a light meal comprising the tossed salad to start and the grilled langoustines with white wine sauce entrée. A clear head is best for my evening plan of play.

As Andrew heads to the kitchen to submit my order, my gaze wanders around the room admiring the décor. Just as with the lobby and the bar, Lucien and Malcolm stayed true to the original use of the warehouse. Clean lines and antique pieces for the decor: floor-to-ceiling mullion windows allow natural light to filter through to the room during the day, now dimly lit for dinner; light fixtures hang from the ceiling where the dark metal duct work and copper pipes are visible; exposed brick walls; the floor poured concrete; the well-heeled patrons sit on antique leather chairs at wooden tables. The guys really did a hell of a job with their enterprise. Few can pull off and maintain a high-end, respectable establishment, especially one that's a combo BDSM/dance club with a restaurant.

Perfectly situated for visibility by those at the bar and within the dining room, sit two lovely beauties laughing and tossing their long, glossy hair over their shoulders. Their eyes roam the vicinity hoping to connect with potential partners. The duo is more focused on attracting company for the evening, then on eating the salads that they absentmindedly move around on their plates.

The blonde spots me watching them, and a grin appears on her face lighting up her baby blues. As she nods her head to show her friend she's spotted a potential hookup, her little pink tongue pokes out to dampen her glossy, lush lips.

I wonder if her pussy is as shiny and wet as that mouth.

Her friend shifts slightly in her seat to adjust her position casually. As she runs her red-manicured hand through her sable-colored, shoulder-length hair, she spies me. The green darkens with lust when I wink at her. With a smirk, I turn my attention to Andrew as he places my salad in front of me. Now that I have the attention of both women, I nod and eat. I know they're interested, so no need to rush my meal. They'll be a double order of tonight's dessert special.

I spend the next thirty-five minutes purposely ignoring them. I only allow my gaze to shift occasionally in their direction, never direct eye contact. That dominant behavior—and who I am—will keep them intrigued. As they cross and uncross their legs, the movement affords me a better view higher up their toned thighs. Green Eyes has on a clingy, silk wrap dress that showcases her ample cleavage, the red color complementing her bronze skin. The blue of Luscious' eyes, enhanced by the cobalt color of her strapless, stretch-jersey dress, make them as prominent as her pebbled nipples. Delightful.

First item on tonight's agenda is complete—dinner eaten, now it's time to fuck.

They automatically place the bill on my membership account, so no need to waste time signing the check. I stand and take my time to button my suit jacket, drawing the attention of my pets. Once our eyes lock, I walk past their table to head to one of the high-tops at the bar.

Susan gives me a wistful stare and bids me, "Good night, Mr. Steele. We look forward to seeing you again soon."

"It was a pleasure as always, Susan. Good night," I offer her in consolation.

Moments after I settle at the closest available table, I feel one hand caress my back and another hand lands on my forearm.

I glance to my left and am greeted with a sultry, "Hello." Green eyes glitter in the candlelight like vivid emeralds.

A squeeze to my forearm draws my attention to my right to see freshly glossed lips beaming, "Hello. There aren't any other tables available, would you mind it if my friend and I share with you?"

"Would your friend and you mind sharing me for a fuck?"

Without missing a beat, Green Eyes responds breathlessly, "Absolutely."

***

Click the Link Below or Visit books2read.com/u/ 3RLy0D For Your Copy

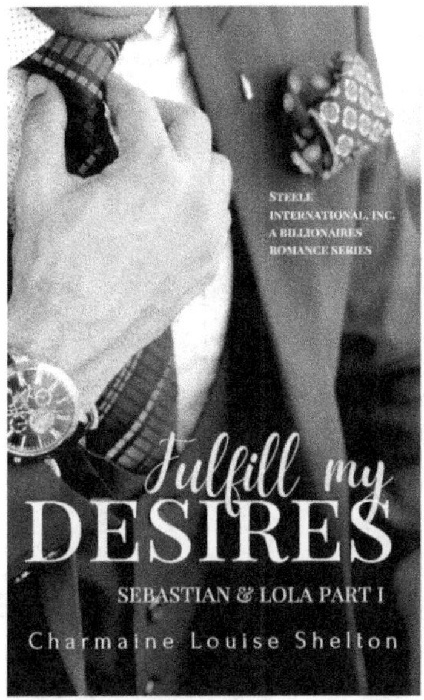

Fulfill My Desires Sebastian & Lola Part I

I dedicate this novel to lovers who face obstacles to their Happily Ever After. Go for who you love.

Fulfill Your Desires.

xoxo
Charmaine Louise

WELCOME TO CHARMAINELOUISE — THE SENSUAL LIFESTYLE

GLITZY. GLAMOROUS. STEAMY.

CharmaineLouise New York, Inc. invites you to indulge in *The Sensual Lifestyle* through **CharmaineLouise Books** and **CharmaineLouise Intimates**. CLBrands immerse you in *Sexy Fantasies* with CLBooks contemporary romance novels and give you *Sexy Under Things & Loungewear* with CLIntimates.

Charmaine Louise Shelton the Founder, CEO & Author of CLNY loves all things classic, elegant, feminine, and of course with an erotic edge! Favorite outfit of choice is a cashmere cardigan, leather pencil skirt, and seamed silk stockings with stiletto heels. Sexy Fantasy Type: sub with a dash of Voyeur. When not writing and designing, Charmaine Louise travels and spends time with her Maltese buddies, ZIGGY and Jynger.

CharmaineLouise — *The Sensual Lifestyle*

~ Visit online at **CharmaineLouise.com**

~ Subscribe to **CharmaineLouise Newsletter**

~ Find us on Facebook **@CharmaineLouiseNewYork**

~ Instagram **@CharLouNY**

CharmaineLouise Books *Sexy Fantasies* launched summer 2020. Sizzling, contemporary romance with your soon-to-be favorite Alpha Doms, Powerful Billionaires, and the women they lust after and love for second chances, insta-love, enemies-to-lovers, and more.

Want to chat it up and share your thoughts with other CLBooks Lovers? Read our blog, join our Charmaine-Louise Books Coterie Fan Club and follow us on my author pages and social media to be in the know about the book release dates, exclusive content, giveaways, contests, and more!

~ **Purchase your eBook and paperback novels from my Author Page by clicking here!**

~ Read and subscribe to our blog *The World of Sex*

~ Connect on **Amazon Author Page**

~ Goodreads Author Profile

~ <u>BookBub Author Profile</u>

CharmaineLouise Intimates *Sexy Under Things &* *Loungewear* debuted in 2003. Inspired by the sensuous sirens and sylph swans of the past and present, the hand crochet cashmere and silk collections are for the sexy: hence, the line names Ginger — Bombshell; Diana — Showstopper; Jackie — Timeless; Lena — Classic. Also known as The Movie-Star from Gilligan's Island; Ms. Ross The Boss; Mrs. Kennedy Onassis; Ms. Horne.

Do you thrive on seduction and being sexy lounging at home? Read our blog and follow us on social media to receive the tips, the latest additions to the collections, private sales, and more!

~ Read and subscribe to our blog *The Art of Seduction*

~ Find us on Facebook **@CharmaineLousieIntimates**

~ Instagram **@CharmaineLouiseIntimates**

Fulfill Your Desires.